Santé, société et politique en Afrique

Auteur

Cheikh Ibrahima Niang est enseignant chercheur à l'Université Cheikh An Diop de Dakar, Sénégal. Il est spécialisé en Anthropologie Sociale et en Scienc de l'Environnement. Il a réalisé plusieurs travaux sur les aspects sociaux d VIH/SIDA et des problèmes de santé publique au Sénégal, en Côte d'Ivoire, a Rwanda, au Burkina Faso, en Gambie et en Guinée. Il a effectué plusieu publications sur la sexualité, les impacts sociaux et politiques du VIH et l approches culturelles en matière de prévention des épidémies. Il a servi comm conseiller technique dans plusieurs organes des Nations Unies (ONUSID OMS, Banque mondiale, PNUD, BIT, etc.). Il coordonne actuellement le Rése SAHARA (Social Aspects of HIV/AIDS Research Alliance) pour l'Afrique l'Ouest.

The Widow's Cross

Ikechukwu Umejesi

SPEARS MEDIA PRESS

Spears Media Press
7830 W. Alameda Ave, Suite 103 Denver, CO 80226

Spears Media Press publishes under the auspices of the Spears Media Association.

The Press furthers the Association's mission by advancing knowledge in education, learning, entertainment and research.

First Published 2016 by Spears Media Press
www.spearsmedia.com
info@spearsmedia.com

Information on this title: www.spearsmedia.com/thewidowscross

Ordering Information:
Special discounts are available on bulk purchases by corporations, associations, and others. For details, contact the publisher at any of the addresses above.

ISBN: 978-1-942876-13-7 [Paperback]

To the memory of my dearest mother, the late ***Mrs. Julia Ojiugo Umejesi,*** a social crusader who spent her lifetime fighting for the rights of women and other marginalised groups in her community.

CONTENTS

Preface xi

Chapter One 1
Chapter Two 13
Chapter Three 27
Chapter Four 41
Chapter Five 65
Chapter Six 100
Chapter Seven 126
Chapter Eight 141
Chapter Nine 157
Chapter Ten 167
Chapter Eleven 180

Glossary of Igbo Phrases & words 203
Select Igbo Proverbs 208

About The Author 213

PREFACE

This is a work of fiction, set in the patriarchal Igbo society of Eastern Nigeria. As a child, I had observed with the utmost dismay two cultural practices that helped shape my adult life. Firstly, the attention, respect and reverence of certain animals (totems), and the punishments often meted out to those who, either deliberately or mistakenly, harmed or killed them. Secondly, the manner in which the society treated some of the most vulnerable groups, such as widows and orphans.

In different communities of Eastern Nigeria, widows and orphans are often on the lowest rung of the social strata. They have no visible protection from their communities, local or national governments. As a child, I empathised with these people whenever I encountered any injustices meted out to them by their society or relations. I have hoped to contribute to the understanding of the nature of these practices in traditional Igbo communities of Eastern Nigeria.

Hence, *The Widow's Cross* is an answer to many years of empathy toward this class of ordinary people. Using fictional characters and places, *The Widow's Cross* portrays real and likely events. Angelina, a well-educated, evangelical Christian widow, will not complete her society-imposed post-bereavement rites for her late husband, Polycarp. She is convinced that she has an inner call to use the gospel of Jesus Christ to liberate her community, Umuocha, from the clutches of evil cultural practices, which she thinks have made the Umuocha community lag behind her neighbours where these practices have long given way to Western/Christian civilisation. With this belief, Angelina heads on a collision course with a group of very formidable cultural protagonists led by *Mazi* Ikenga, the traditional prime minister of Umuocha community.

This book describes the socio-cultural transformation that have revolutionised traditional beliefs and practices in Igbo communities of Eastern Nigeria, and perhaps in different post-colonial societies in Africa. It is also a classic examination of Western/ Christian cultural 'triumphalism' in Igbo society, the ruptured indigenous identity of communities and the start of a 'post-tradition' era.

My expectation is that this book will educate its readers about certain gender-sensitive practices in various parts of Africa and inspire changes where necessary. I also wish that readers might find strength to stand up for the rights of the less privileged in our societies. For clarity, all the scripture quoted in this book are taken from the New International Version (NIV) bible. The relative meanings of the Igbo proverbs and expressions used in this book have also been included for a clearer understanding of the messages they convey. In addition, Igbo words and phrases are italicised and explained in a glossary for clarity.

Ikechukwu Umejesi
2nd February 2016, East London, South Africa.

CHAPTER ONE

The Morning Cry

"Mom, it is very early in the morning. What are you doing?" Ifeoma asked her mother, Angelina. Angelina did not respond to her daughter's question, but busied herself with her preparations. Ifeoma slept for a while but this wasn't deep enough as the occasional disturbances from her mother woke her up a few minutes later. This time Ifeoma, who always enjoyed her early morning sleep, woke up, sat on the edge of her bed and covered her body properly with her mother's wrapper.

It was harmattan season, dreaded by most children because of its accompanying chilly dry winds. Other children of Ifeoma's age would think it atrocious to be woken up so early under any circumstances.

Ifeoma was quite an obedient child in her mid-teens. She loved her mother dearly and shared a lot in common with her, including her bedroom since the death of her father, Polycarp.

Looking at her mother, she wondered what was wrong with her. She picked up her worn out wrist watch, went close to their rusty kerosene lantern, yawned, wiped her eyes, cleared her throat, and in a surprised voice said, "Mommy, it is quarter after 1 o'clock in the morning." This time, the busy Angelina replied, "Ify, I think a good way to start your day would be to first say, 'Good morning' to your mommy. Not with a barrage of questions."

Ifeoma shook her head remorsefully, and then said: "I am sorry mom, good morning!" "That is my good daughter, the beloved daughter of my beloved Polycarp who has gone to be with our Lord and he's there, waiting to receive us," Angelina said with a sense of pride as she smiled at her daughter.

The mention of her father's name did not go well with Ifeoma, who had lost her darling father and friend only three weeks ago. She kept silent, looking injured. Realising her daughter's feelings, Angelina burst into Ifeoma's favourite song:

When peace like a river,
Attendeth my way,
When sorrows like sea billows roll,
Whatever might be,
Thou hast taught me to say,
It is well; it is well, with my soul...

Ifeoma, sitting motionless on her bed, with her head bent down as if she was praying, sobbed quietly as her mother continued singing her favourite song. When Angelina sang the last stanza, she thought Ifeoma would join in as she used to, but not this early morning. Ifeoma was hurt in her spirit as the mention of her father's name brought back old memories of the most loving man she had ever known. To her, Polycarp was a father, friend, provider, guardian and protector whose death made her family vulnerable to undue persecution from her relatives and community.

When Angelina looked at her daughter, she realized she was sobbing and her eyes were heavy with tears. She knew why her daughter was hurt, yet she feigned ignorance. Angelina sat on the bed close to Ifeoma, reached for her right hand, cuddled it and said to her "*Adannaya* (the pet name her father used to call her which means, father's daughter), how have I offended you this early morning?"

Ifeoma at this moment was beginning to recollect herself and would not want to hurt her mother. She raised her head, looked into her mother's face, gave her a faint smile and embraced her mother. At this time, Angelina almost shed some tears as her emotion was beginning to build up as well. Ifeoma cleared her voice and in a bid to encourage her mother said, "It is well with our souls."

That was all the assurance that Angelina needed as she pulled herself together and continued her preparations, preferring not to reveal her mission to her daughter. After a while Ifeoma, who could not go back to sleep and who was beginning to wonder why her mother chose to hide her mission from her, then went close to her mother, touched her back, and asked, "When did you start hiding your plans from your *ada*?"

Still not wanting to reveal her mission to Ifeoma, Angelina laughed and asked her jokingly, "Ifeoma, are you my new husband?" "I can't be both a daughter and a husband at the same time. More so, women do not become husbands," Ifeoma replied with a sense of seriousness. Noticing her curiosity, Angelina pleaded with Ifeoma to lower her voice in order not to wake up Obinna and Amaka, her siblings who were asleep in their bedrooms.

Noticing her mother's fear, Ifeoma decided to exploit it. She threatened to wake up her siblings. This threat broke her mother's resistance. "Now I will tell you what my mission is and where I want to go, if that will calm your nerves this early morning," her mother told her in a hushed voice. "I am all ears," Ifeoma said to her mother.

Angelina took Ifeoma down memory lane, "You remember what my daily programme used to be before the unfortunate incident that happened to us three weeks ago?" "You mean daddy's death?" Ifeoma interrupted. "Yes," Angelina replied. "I remember," Ifeoma said with a sense of recollection. Now their discussion was beginning to be more relaxed but not in the friendly manner it used to be. "Ifeoma, can you help me recollect what I used to do every morning before your father died three weeks ago?" Angelina asked her.

Ifeoma was reluctant to say anything to her mom. Rather she

looked up to the ceiling with a feeling of pain, and remembered some socio-cultural restrictions for widows as applicable to her mother. She became uneasy, giggled, and bent down her head as though she would cry. She looked her mother straight in the eyes and said to her, "Mother, I respect your zeal for the Lord's work. I respect your calling as a local evangelist, I respect your passion for the perishing souls in this community and your efforts to salvage them, yet I want you to tread cautiously for the sake of our lives and future among our people". She paused. "Go on, my wise daughter," Angelina teased Ifeoma with a note of disappointment in her daughter with whom she had shared her passion for early morning evangelism. Ifeoma continued, "Mommy, I am not implying that the 'Morning Cry' be scrapped". "May I know what you are implying, Ifeoma?" her mother replied sharply. "Mommy, this should not develop into a quarrel. You are a daughter of this community, although from a different village, yet there is no issue that relates to widowhood you are not aware of. You are much more knowledgeable on these issues than I am. After all, I am only fifteen years old," Ifeoma said, looking the other way.

Ifeoma continued, "Our culture and the position of the *Igwe*, *Nze-na-ozo*, *Umuada* and *Alutaradi* regarding mourning is that a widow, like you, must remain at home for at least three months. During this period, she must wear black clothes with her hair completely shaven. She must bathe only once in four days, must not go to the market or to the farm, and if she works in the civil service, as you do, she should apply for leave from the government to enable her to perform all these rites. She also must not shout at the top of her voice no matter the level of provocation, must not eat quality foods because she is mourning, must not join in the celebration of the New Yam festival, Christmas and Easter celebrations…mommy, please remind me of other ones."

Angelina laughed and teased Ifeoma: "I am enjoying your lecture on *Culture 101* and *Widowhood 201*. Please go on and lecture me some more. I wonder where you learnt all these do's and don'ts of our people and at what age you have become so knowledgeable in these anti-Christian practices." Having calmed Ifeoma with these words, Angelina told her that everything that she had mentioned was a revised version of post-bereavement rites that widows were subjected to. She said, "In the olden days, when a woman lost her husband in this community she was treated like a murderer". "In what ways, mommy?" Ifeoma asked enthusiastically. "Let me tell you that so many young girls who witnessed the treatments meted out to their widowed mothers refused to marry for fear of being treated like their mothers," Angelina told Ifeoma.

After a moment of silence, Ifeoma, now gripped by fear, asked her mother to mention some of those acts meted out to widows in the olden days. "For instance," her mother said, "widows were kept indoors for up to three years with unkempt dreadlocks! Where a woman was suspected of having had a hand in the death of her husband, she was forced to bathe her husband's corpse and drink the bath water. In such situations, the widow was usually stripped naked or covered with only *Jigida* and *Omu*. She was given a basketful of rubbish, then paraded round the Eke Market Square on a market day!" "That's too evil, mom", Ifeoma said with loathing. "Wait, the Americans would say, 'you ain't seen nothing yet'", Angelina replied. "In some cases, one of the widow's left fingers was chopped off and buried with the husband."

At this moment, Ifeoma closed her ears and pleaded with her mother to stop mentioning these horrific old practices. "Mommy, if I were born in those evil days I would not marry any man," Ifeoma declared seriously.

Hearing this, Angelina laughed and said, "Who knows who would have died first, you or your husband?" "Now in the situation where a wife died before her husband, what were the husband's post-bereavement rites?" asked an inquisitive Ifeoma.

Angelina responded, "My daughter, you should understand

that this is a male-dominated society. It is a 'winner takes all' situation for the men. The man is as free as the birds in the air in such circumstance. After a few days, he goes about his normal business with or without wearing black clothes. In certain situations, some men remarry about three months after their wife's death." "Mommy, that era is gone for good," Ifeoma said. "Now listen to me, my daughter," Angelina advised Ifeoma, "that era would not have gone if not for the liberating gospel of Jesus Christ which was brought to us by the European Christian missionaries. They did a lot of good work with the bible. They preached salvation in the name of Jesus and had converts who continued to shed the light of the gospel of Jesus Christ in Africa long after their departure. The evil widowhood practices were only a fraction of what was repudiated by the gospel of Jesus Christ." "Mommy, could you tell me about some of the other practices?" Ifeoma requested. "Yes, if you want," Angelina responded. "Go on, mom," Ifeoma said. "Have you not heard about the killing of innocent twins?" "Mommy, that means it was the missionaries that saved you and aunty Nkiru, your twin sister?" Ifeoma asked. "Yes, God used them to save us. We would have been dead the first day we were born through a very cruel process I will not bother you with. Our mother too would have been banished for some weeks as if she had committed some heinous crime. This cruelty was meted to women who had twins and to their innocent children. Have you heard about slavery and slave trade?" the mother asked her. "Yes, I have heard, Ifeoma answered. "What do you know about that?" Angelina asked. Ifeoma replied, "Our history teacher said it was an ugly era in African history when her productive and reproductive population was carted away in a period of over four centuries to the far away newly discovered Americas where they worked the farms. Their produce was then taken to Europe where they fed the upcoming industries as a result of the industrial revolution in that continent." "Have you exhausted your knowledge of history?"

Angelina asked Ifeoma.

"No", Ifeoma answered. "These raw materials, such as sugar, cotton, tobacco, etc., were then used to manufacture some goods, which were exported to Africa and other parts of the world. Our teacher called it, 'The Triangular Trade', co*nne*cting Africa, the Americas and Europe. He also said that so many Africans died in the process of capturing these slaves in Africa, and that the trade also recorded many fatalities during shipment to the Americas. Our teacher called this journey, 'the middle passage'. And he said that a lot more also died in the farms where the white slave masters dehumanized them," Ifeoma concluded.

"I guess your teacher is knowledgeable enough in his subject, what is his name?" Angelina asked. "Our history teacher is Mr. Chima Okeke," Ifeoma replied. "I know him; he was a good student at Suka University. He was a year my junior in the university. You know that graduates of Suka University are the best in the country," Angelina boasted with a sense of pride in her alma mater. "Mom! You always extol your alma mater, is it because you graduated with a first class degree in that school?" Ifeoma asked humorously. "Think about it, most important people in this country passed through Suka University, and mind you the greatest man I have ever met in my life passed through Suka University". Angelina said, smiling. "Do you mean daddy?" Ifeoma enquired. "Yes, of course," said her mother.

Ifeoma sighed and, not wanting more mention of her dad, requested that they should go back to what brought about this discussion of history. "Please remind me where we stopped on the main topic of our discussion this morning, Ifeoma?" Angelina asked pretentiously.

"It was about your renewed interest in early morning evangelism, I mean, the morning cry," Ifeoma answered. Angelina paused and resumed in a deep voice, "Having gone through memory lane on the loathsome practices of our society, some of which still hold our people captive, despite their profession of Christianity, should we, the redeemed of the Lord, keep silent? No, we should continue to preach repentance from dead customs. There is a move to revive the old and forgotten practices in this community and that would not augur well with the word of God in this land.

"That is why I go out early in the morning every day, not minding the unseen dangers of evil forces and powers in this community, and the snakes and other reptiles that pose dangers to my life. I also cry out for purity in the land, for repentance from dead customs, for more interest in the word of God, and against immorality, stealing and other forms of corruption in the land.

"My husband, your dad, supported me in this project, he even bought the electronic speaker I use. He also accompanied me on this mission on several occasions. On his deathbed, he held my hand, prayed that the Almighty God would strengthen me to continue to speak out every morning in our community. He commissioned me and encouraged me. He was part of this vision and I do not want to let him down, even in death.

"Remember, your dad was your best friend, so you must support me as he supported me."

"Mom you have spoken well and I share your vision for our community. However, I fear for your life," Ifeoma interjected.

"In what sense?" Angelina asked.

"My father's relations may not tolerate your leaving the house so soon after his death to do this every morning, I mean to preach in our community as you used to do. They will prefer that you complete the mourning rites for their departed brother, that is, stay indoors for three months among other rites," Ifeoma advised.
"Ifeoma, my daughter, I am older and more experienced than you are. Before I decided to go out this morning, I counted the cost and weighed it on a scale. The Lord counselled that before you start building a house, you should first estimate the cost to know if you can carry the burden of the project. This I have done, my

daughter. I know that your uncles, aunts and the community would frown at me, but I have chosen to do the will of God rather than to obey the ordinances of men," Angelina submitted.

"Mommy for being so resolute in your convictions about obeying and doing the will of our God, I will support you and go with you just as daddy supported you," Ifeoma promised.

Angelina was so elated that she embraced her daughter and both of them held hands and sang Ifeoma's favourite song: *When peace like a river attendeth my way...*

* * *

While they were singing, Obinna, Ifeoma's older brother and the only son of Angelina and Polycarp woke up from his sleep. He said to himself, "When did this start, we are used to having our family prayers together, why have mom and Ifeoma decided to exclude Amaka and I?"

He knocked on her mother's bedroom door, interrupted their song and requested to know why he and his younger sister Amaka were excluded from the family's Morning Prayer. After listening to Obinna, Angelina and Ifeoma, looking at one another, laughed, but did not offer Obinna any explanations. Obinna stood, looking pitiable and expecting to hear from his mother or Ifeoma. Their silence did not go well with him, but he quickly realised he had not greeted his mother that morning. He hurriedly greeted, "Mommy, good morning, but why are we excluded from this morning's family altar?" He asked, looking bewildered.

Angelina responded to the greeting and asked him to tell her what the time is.

He looked at Ifeoma's wristwatch and replied, "It is a few minutes to 4 AM." "We have been awake since 1 o'clock," his mother replied.

A baffled Obinna asked, "Awake, doing what...?"

Ifeoma interrupted him: "Truly we've been awake since 1 am thrashing out some issues."

"Some issues like what?" Obinna demanded to know.

Ifeoma was reluctant to tell him of their mother's resolve to resume her early morning evangelism. At this point, Angelina feared another bout of opposition and explanations.

After a period of suspense, Angelina then explained to him the reason for being awake for so long and all the issues she had tackled with Ifeoma. After listening to his mother, Obinna did not say anything. However, after a thoughtful moment of silence, he reached out to his mother's hand and, in what seemed a surprise move to Angelina, gave his full support to her. He also pledged to make himself available to go even as far as the Eke Market Square, dreaded as the dwelling place of some bad spirits, to preach the gospel early in the morning to those living close to the market square.

Angelina was so elated that her shout of "Praise the Lord!" and the response of "Hallelujah!" from her two children woke her last child Amaka, who, on hearing their voices, ran out of her room, wondering what was wrong with the household.

Angelina calmed her. Amaka, a nine-year-old girl did not really have an independent view on the raging argument about 'morning cry'. She sat quietly near her mom, properly covered with a wrapper to prevent the chilly air filtering through the wooden window blinds.

The family prayer session did not take the usual format that morning as Angelina asked Obinna to pray for her and Ifeoma and commission them to go and preach righteousness to the community that morning and for the grace of God to continue to do this, always.

* * *

Obinna was a well-built and good-natured seventeen-year-old boy. He was in his final year in the secondary school and had a deep passion for evangelism. He was also the president of the Scripture Union Fellowship in his school. Obinna was knowledgeable in biblical issues. He started by requesting his mother and Ifeoma to kneel down and raise their hands to the Almighty God in total submission. As they knelt down, a bemused Amaka, still recovering from hours of sleep in the cold night, also knelt down with the duo. Obinna asked Amaka, "Do you really understand what we are doing this morning?" Amaka did not respond to her brother's question. She did not want to miss the remaining part of the event she had not been part of since it started several hours ago.

Obinna then took the old New International Version bible his father had given him a few minutes before he died. He opened to the book of Isaiah chapter 54:16-17 and read the promises of God to her mother and sisters as they knelt down before him. He read out the verses as loud as if he was standing before a congregation in a large auditorium: *"See, it is I who created the blacksmith who fans coals into flame and forges a weapon fit for its work. And it is I who have created the destroyer to work havoc; no weapon forged against you will prevail, and you will refute every tongue that accuses you. This is the heritage of the servants of the Lord."* Obinna was not yet done with his commissioning as he flipped the pages of his old bible back to Psalm 91:1-16. This time he enjoined them to echo "Amen!" at the end of each verse. This, they did with rapturous shout. Amaka's tender knees were beginning to hurt and she sat on the floor close to her older sister, Ifeoma.

At the end of the reading, Obinna lifted his hands over them and prayed against opposition to his mother's vision for their community, opposition to the preaching of the gospel of Jesus Christ, evil customs, the deities and immorality among the youths. The prayer took longer than Ifeoma had expected. Ifeoma and Angelina echoed a loud 'Amen' at the end, but Amaka had fallen asleep midway into Obinna's long prayers.

Ifeoma, who a few months ago had nicknamed Obinna "Pastor" when he won The Sunday School Award as the best student to memorise bible passages, jumped on her feet, shook Obinna's hand and said, "Mommy, your son will be better as a Pastor than this doctor thing he is dreaming of." Angelina, who was in love with both professions, smiled and said, "If Obinna should combine both it will make him a better soul winner and a member of Jesus army". "Mommy, I feel humbled by all of these titles, just pray that I make my dream grades in the GCE exams," Obinna said. "Excellence is your portion my child," his mother assured him.

At this juncture, Ifeoma took her wristwatch and informed them that it was exactly 5 AM. She wore her sandals and head tie, picked up her new Revised Standard Version of the Bible she used for Christian Religious Knowledge at school and told her mom, "I am set for this battle for the soul of our community with you, let's go!"

An elated Angelina asked her, "Ify, where is your weapon of warfare?" She brandished her bible as if it were a real sword.

"You are in the spirit," Obinna told Ifeoma jokingly.

As they opened the door, the chilly wind oozed in and their mother admonished Obinna to take adequate care of Amaka who was still fast asleep. Obinna assured his mother that he would not fail to take care of Amaka. Angelina and Ifeoma had a torchlight with which they illuminated the thick darkness of the harmattan season in this tropical community.

CHAPTER TWO

Drawing The Battle Line, Killing The Python

As they stepped out of the gate of their compound, about a hundred metres from their home, it began to drizzle. Angelina tuned a song in Igbo, "*Mmiri na anwu maaram ebe m na eso Jesu, anwu maaram ebe m na eso Jesu*" (I was drenched by rain and beaten by the sun in my pilgrimage with Jesus). Ifeoma complained they could be wet before they reach their location and suggested going back home to pick her umbrella.

"My daughter, the Lord will seal up the heavens for our sakes," her mother assured her in faith. "Amen", Ifeoma agreed.

Remarkably, the rain stopped a few minutes after Angelina gave that assurance. "Mommy, indeed, the Lord heard your declaration", Ifeoma told her mother. "That is our first miracle and if we can believe the Lord in this mission, he will give us this community for Jesus to reign supreme in it," Angelina said. Ifeoma nodded in agreement.

After about ten minutes' walk, they reached the community's playground from where they intended to evangelise the neighbourhood. Ifeoma reminded her mother that they had forgotten to test their electronic speaker, which had been unused for the past three weeks. "Fear not, my daughter, even if it is dead, the Lord will cause life to come upon it as He did to the dry bones in the book of Ezekiel chapter 37," Angelina assured her daughter. Ifeoma laughed and said, "Amen".

* * *

The community's playground was where the children used to gather to play hide and seek games, and the boys played soccer while girls played *ogaa*. The playground was about fifty square metres and was roughly grassed. The villagers called it *Ukwu Udara*.

Among various Igbo communities, the *Udara* tree has a lot of mystical significance. For instance, it is taboo for anyone to pluck the *Udara* fruit from the tree. The *Udara* tree is allowed to drop its fruits when they are ripe. It is believed that the *Udara* is a very 'generous' tree and whenever anyone who is kind-hearted, or little children come near it, it drops some of its fruits for them. It is also thought to withhold its fruit from evil people. Hence, it is *aru* for anyone to pluck *udara* fruit wilfully. Plucking the *udara* fruit is like extorting its fruits.

There are other myths about the *Udara* tree going back to the olden days. It is famed as the dwelling place or meeting place of ancestral spirits of the departed progenitors of the clan. Children were told that some of their ancestors climbed the *Udara* tree and dropped some fruit when they came around as their contribution to their upkeep. This aspect of the *Udara* mystique as the dwelling place of the spirits often scared children away from the *Udara* tree. Hence, they preferred to go to the *Udara* tree at the playground in groups rather than as individuals.

Ifeoma, who was born in the village, was aware of these myths and as a young person, was frightened by the presence of these spirits around the *Udara* tree. She had struggled with this fear, which conflicted with her Christian faith. Her mother always assured her that these were empty legends popularised by idol worshippers to glorify the devil. She agreed, but never really believed her mother.

* * *

It was still dark when they arrived at the playground. Ifeoma was gripped by fear and her voice began to crack. She could hardly sing aloud despite the urgings from her mother. Ifeoma saw a shrub about four feet tall and, thinking it was a spirit, she screamed in fear, "Jesus!!" and suddenly stopped singing. Angelina noticed Ifeoma's panting. She held her and started binding any demons that may have "come around to interfere with the purpose of God for the community". Angelina asked, "Ify, what is the problem?" She pointed at the shrub with her torchlight and behold it was an *Ahaba* shrub, a very delicious fodder for local goats.

Angelina could hardly contain herself as she laughed and urged her daughter to back her verbal profession of Christianity with due faith. Ifeoma was troubled and asked her mother, "Are there no other places where we can spread the word of God apart from this place?" Her mother responded, "And why not this place, Ify? I chose this ground because I am not a coward; if truly the demons in this community gather here at night, then they should be dislodged and sent to where they belong so that our community is free from their influences". Ifeoma did not ask any further questions.

Angelina switched on the electronic speaker. As it came on, she became excited. She greeted the neighbourhood and apologised for this early morning disturbance with the gospel of Jesus. She quoted Romans chapter 1:16, "I am not ashamed of the gospel, because it is the power of God for the salvation of everyone who believes". Thereafter, she commenced her sermon.

About two hundred metres away was the house of a man named Ikenga, who was known for his opposition to Evangelical Christianity and the born-again Christians in his community. He is an *Ozo* titleholder, an educated man with a university degree and a core traditionalist, although he was a nominal member of the Roman Catholic Church.

As Angelina read out the bible passage and started her sermon, Ikenga called his wife, Martha, from her sleep and asked her,

"Whose voice am I hearing this early morning?" Initially, Martha could not decipher whose voice among the born-again people in the community, it was. However, after a period of rapt attention she shouted at the top of her voice and jumped from her bed exclaiming "*Aru! Aru!!*" and "*Tufiakwa*". "Martha, tell me who is that woman whom the gods have sent to deny me sleep this early morning?" Ikenga asked, with characteristic fury.

Martha remained silent, as she leaned on the wall wondering if Angelina, Polycarp's widow, has become insane. "Martha, if at the count of five you did not tell me whose voice that is, I will pour hot water on you since the weather is too cold for you to talk to me!" Ikenga threatened.

Knowing her husband's short temper, Martha replied, "This community, Umuocha, has seen evil in the late Polycarp's wife! She is that shameless idiot disturbing the whole village with her sermons this morning. Imagine, a woman who lost her husband three weeks ago, has left her house for a morning cry". Ikenga remained speechless. He had never seen such brazen contravention of customs in the past. He could hardly bear it. He jumped up from where he sat, took his machete and headed out to go and kill the widow, Angelina. Seeing this, his wife rushed and snatched the machete from him.

Ikenga stood for some time, looked up and said, "When it is time for a dog to die, it does not perceive the odour of faeces. Maybe this is the time to rid this village of the likes of Angelina". Martha replied, "Our people said, 'He whose house is on fire does not pursue rats'. Angelina with all her education is in a burning house, and rather than save herself from a raging fire, she is busy pursuing frivolities. A widow such as Angelina should at least remain at home within her courtyard for three months. Did she mistake three weeks for three months? Why has she decided to attract the wrath of the gods upon herself?" Martha asked rhetorically. "I cannot answer those questions," Ikenga said in anger. He continued, "That is the character of all women. Maybe she killed Polycarp". "Do not generalise, how many widows in this community have behaved like this before?" Martha asked.

Ikenga bent his head, as if in sorrow, and muttered, "I warned the late *Igwe* not to allow this new church a foothold in this community in order to avert the wrath of our ancestors on us. Now it is happening, but I will fight them with my blood."

As Ikenga and his wife were fuming in his house, Angelina and her daughter, Ifeoma were rending the air with the message of salvation from sin, Satanism and all forms of anti-Christian practices. She spoke eloquently against practices such as the *Osu* caste system.

The *Osu* caste is common among the Igbo, whose traditional society is highly stratified. They are a group of people whose lineages are said to have been offered to the deities as a result of the taboos committed by their forefathers. They are discriminated against in several ways. For instance, they are not allowed to marry the freeborn and also are not admitted into the privileged and exclusive noble class of *Nze-na-ozo* and age grade associations of the freeborn.

In most instances, *Osu* are maltreated and denied justice. During the emergence of the Christian faith in Igboland, the *Osu* ran to the church missionaries, became converts, were educated and emerged as civil right campaigners fighting for the eradication of social discrimination. However, despite the efforts of the missionaries to integrate them with the larger society, the so-called freeborn have built a brick wall against them, choosing rather to maintain the status quo by indoctrinating their children early to avoid the *Osu*. For example, one common instruction a non-*Osu* parent gives his or her child in Umuocha community is "no matter how beautiful or intelligent and well behaved an *Osu* might be, he or she is not qualified to be your spouse".

With the advent of firebrand evangelical Christianity, the

born-again Christians threw the doors wide open to the *Osu* and have tried to pull down this wall of social discrimination. This fraternity with the *Osu*, among other cultural issues, has angered the traditionalists and other cultural protagonists in the more orthodox churches.

Hence, as Angelina read the book of Revelation 22:14-15, part of which reads "Outside are dogs", to buttress her stand against the *Osu* caste, she insisted that, "those outside Jesus Christ are the true *Osu*, no matter their position in the society".

Immediately Ikenga heard those words, he closed his ears with his hands, entered his lounge, took a piece of paper and pen and wrote, "*Aru*! Angelina, wife of the late Polycarp, called all of us in this village *Osu*, including the *Igwe*, all *Nze-na-ozo*." He gave it to his wife and she read it. Martha said to her husband, "No, no, Angelina did not go to that extent; she was only reinforcing the point that the *Osu* caste system is evil".

Ikenga shouted at his wife, "Shut up, you ordinary woman, if you have your way you would treat me like Angelina is treating Polycarp." "I am not in support of Angelina, but let us put issues right, she did not insult the *Igwe* ... or *Nze-na-ozo*," Martha insisted, but she was interrupted by her husband. "You are a wicked Angelina supporter. If you treat me like that when I die, I will rise up from the grave, inflict you with insanity and then kill you after a torturous five months. Our people have a proverb that, 'When truth is guilty, look around and you will see bribery lurking in the corner.'" "God forbid that proverb, Angelina did not bribe me to support her. I have not supported an evil act like hers, all I have said is that she did not insult the *Igwe* or the *Nze-na-ozo*," Martha insisted.

An enraged Ikenga was beginning to transfer his annoyance to his wife. He asked Martha, "Tell me the truth, will you not leave the house one or two weeks after my death?" "Do you know who will die first, Ikenga?" Martha asked her husband, and continued:

"Now tell me if you will stay at home for more than a day or two if I, your wife, should die today? Nobody talks about that. All we hear is that women should be under 'house arrest' for three whole months after their husband's death. Nobody asks how long a man should remain at home for post-bereavement mourning when he loses his wife. That kind of custom should be re-examined. It is too lopsided."

Ikenga could not believe the effrontery of his wife as he stood, gazing up as the day was brightening up. He soliloquized, "I knew before now that this woman will not mourn my death, just as Angelina is not mourning Polycarp. It is possible she has a boy-friend outside." "I am hearing all you are murmuring to yourself," Martha interrupted his soliloquy. "Answer my question, will you stay longer than one or two days at home if I, your wife should drop dead now?"

Ikenga looked up and said to her, "Why should I mourn your death longer than two days? How long did your father mourn your mother when she died? Are you not a common woman? I used my hard-earned money to pay for your bride price, bought all the wines and sundry articles that my in-laws, your people, requested from me. How dare you ask me to mourn your death longer than two days when I bought you with my money? Two days is even too much for you! "I bought with my money just like I bought you that she-goat from Eke market two days ago". "Oh Ikenga, you are comparing me with the goat you bought from Eke market, *aru*!" Martha fumed.

"Shut up and listen, Martha!" Ikenga continued, "My mother mourned my father for three years between 1956 and 1959. She never left our courtyard during this period, she did not cut or wash her hair, she had lice all over her hair, had her bath only once every Eke market day. When she finally completed the three-year mourning period for my father, she could hardly recognize the world outside our courtyard.

"It was this stupid late Polycarp and a crop of young university graduates that fought for women's rights in this community in the years after the Nigerian/Biafran civil war, in the 1970s. They fought that widows should be allowed to perform post-bereavement rites for one month. After thoughtful deliberation, the *Igwe* and his council of *Nze-na-ozo* allowed three months. They came up with this argument that there were so many widows in the community because of the civil war, and that if they were kept at home for three years, then their children would all die of hunger and kwashiorkor. We consented on the ground of pity.

"Now look at the way Polycarp is being rewarded by Angelina. He got three months for widows, and now that bitch, Angelina, has on her own reduced it to three weeks for Polycarp without the approval of the *Igwe* and *Nze-na-ozo*. She shall not go free. I will give her the fight of her life and all of you who are her allies should get ready for this epic battle." "I am not anybody's ally. As educated people we should try and uphold the equality of all persons, not minding sex, creed or status," Martha pleaded.

"Just shut up your smelly mouth," Ikenga replied. "It is as if you got intoxicated in your dream with palm wine from your maternal home. Have you forgotten this proverb which says that 'All heads are equal is only in words' or Orwell's Animal Farm, 'All animals are equal but some are more equal than others'.

"Listen, Martha! I am not equal with you! You are an ordinary woman! Did the bible not record that Eve was created from only one of Adam's ribs? So how can you compare the intelligence and physical strength of one rib to all of Adam? Even St. Paul admonished the Corinthian women to shut up and learn from men when they go to church. Today, Angelina and Martha want to stand and teach a man like me, the word of God. How can you contravene the word of God and claim to be teaching the word of God, impossible!"

"Ikenga, I did not know that you are so knowledgeable in

biblical precepts, yet you do not live according to them," Martha charged.

"Yes, that is your judgment! Very soon you will either call me an *Osu* or a dog just as your ally called the whole freeborn of Umuocha today. In your own frail judgment, I do not live out the word of God because I do not go to Mass every day or receive the Holy Communion as you do. That is your yardstick for judgment. I say congratulations to you, St. Martha. You got up this morning to insult your husband, a titled chief, educated at Suka University, a District Counsellor during the British colonial era, a recipient of the Officer of the Federal Republic (OFR), a Divisional governor in the former Republic of Biafra. God have mercy on you. A prophet is without honour, not just in his village, but before his silly and a goat wife," Ikenga said frowning angrily.

"Do you mean that I am silly just because I did not accept your misrepresentation of the widow's statement?" Martha interrupted.

"You are not only silly, you are foolish multiplied by stupidity. It is only a woman suffering from your kind of problems that wakes up to confront her honourable husband the way you have done this morning. No woman has ever done this to me. My mother did not do that to my father. I knew your parents and I married you because I thought you would behave like your mother. You were spoiled by your education. Your father sent you to school against the advice of his uncle. You were trained at the Polytechnic in Enugu to be responsible, but I wonder if you are. You came back with certificates and skills, but you dropped reasoning at the motor park where you boarded the vehicle that brought you back to this community," Ikenga said.

As he was fuming in anger against his wife Martha, his daughter Chioma, a fifteen-year-old girl, came out of her room, hid in a corner and eavesdropped. The raging words of her dad did not please her and in her bid to stop the quarrel between her parents, she showed herself as she shouted, "Daddy and mommy, good morning!"

A pretentious Ikenga, who normally did not want any of his children to see or hear him shout at their mother, jumped from the chair he was sitting on, motioned to his wife to end their hassles. He quietly turned to Chioma and lied that he had been praying the Holy Rosary with her mother for the past forty minutes. As he faced Chioma, his wife sneered at him and muttered, "You hypocrite, Rosary prayer warrior."

* * *

It was now a few minutes after six AM and the day was fast brightening. Angelina and her daughter Ifeoma had completed their set assignment that morning and were heading home under the fast fading darkness of that chilly, windy harmattan morning.

About forty metres from their gate, they observed that their neighbour's dog was barking, not at them, but at a large python, over ten feet long, that was crossing the narrow road leading to their house. Initially they could not comprehend what it was that crossed the road leading to their home. At a closer look, Angelina jumped up and screamed, "Jesus! Jesus Christ! No weapon of the enemy formed against us shall prosper." On sighting the long snake, Ifeoma broke down in tears, shouting, "Daddy! Daddy!! I am dying!" She ran away leaving her mother alone to her fate. Angelina's reaction and Ifeoma's action exemplified the opposing perceptions of totemic ritual in the land of Umuocha. While Angelina saw the python as a symbol of satanism, which must be destroyed by God's children, to Ifeoma, a neophyte Christian girl, the python represented a dreaded mystical symbolism that could spell disaster for anyone in her community.

It was taboo in the land of Umuocha for anyone to kill a python for any reason. The python was treated as a totem and revered by the traditionalists, who sometimes carried it in their hands and caress it as if it was a child. It could enter anyone's house in Umuocha, hunt for rats and other rodents and leave after some days. It was harmless in Umuocha so long as nobody killed it.

However, the coming of the missionaries with their new converts threatened the python population. Christian zealots in the early 20th century killed and even ate pythons in defiance of what they saw as unpleasant cultural practices. They considered these practices inconsistent with their newfound religion.

During the de-colonisation era in Nigeria, that is, from the 1940s to 1960s, there was a wave of cultural renaissance and a tendency towards reviving some fast-dying cultural practices. Hence, the few remaining pythons received protection from the communities who argued that the white man had no right to destroy their cultures in the name of religion. This movement towards cultural revival created a rift between practising Christians and mere churchgoers in different communities of Eastern Nigeria. It is important to note that, while almost all the people of Umuocha identified with one of the established churches or another, not all actually gave up their traditional beliefs, especially totemic ritual.

Hence, people like Ikenga, who belonged to the Catholic faith, opposed most of the Christian teachings that did not agree with their traditional practices. These were the protectors of the totems. They also outlawed fishing at the two major streams in the community, *Oka* and *Iyioma*. These streams are natural spring waters with very large populations of fishes that have not been harvested since time immemorial. These fish have become numerous and are quite used to humans. They often come very close to humans, rubbing the bodies of those who go to the streams to fetch water. The fishes in these streams are regarded as sacred, in fact, they are seen as members of the human community in fish form. Practically, these totems, such as fishes and pythons, are revered beyond imagination, and those who kill them mistakenly or on purpose are made to undergo harsh punishments. Offenders must hold funerals for them, and these funerals must be held with full formalities like those of *Nze-na-ozo*. Their killers also attract the collective wrath of the *Igwe* and his council, the *Umuada*, indeed the entire community. They believe that the killer has directly confronted the ancestors who made these laws, and that if the society tolerates such effrontery, it might suffer ancestral wrath.

After the end of the Nigerian civil war in 1970, there was general despair in the former Biafra (Eastern Nigeria) and a deep hunger for spiritual reawakening in some people. This awakening gave rise to the emergence of Evangelical or Pentecostal Christianity, which to some adherents, provided a solace for hope and salvation.

This new set of Christians, who came mostly from the Anglican, Roman Catholic, Methodist and Presbyterian churches, became non-conformists to some cultural tenets they considered unbiblical. This stance led to a direct confrontation between the cultural antagonists and cultural protagonists. While the latter tended to protect certain practices, such as totemic ritual, the former sought to eradicate them and cleanse the land of such evil practices, which they saw as worshipping the created instead of the creator.

Angelina, belonged to this minority puritan group. She hated the python, and with her husband had killed many. Pythons irritated her and her husband, and whenever one strayed near their home, they crushed its head, and disposed of it at night to avert the wrath of their community.

On this fateful day, Angelina faced a great challenge. She was fresh from The Morning Cry, where she had contended with what she regarded as the satanic practices of her community. Now she faced what she considered a brazen physical challenge by the devil. The die was cast for a historic decision by this Christian and enlightened widow who wanted to save her community from the wrath of God as a result of their deep commitment to unchristian practices.

So many thoughts ran across Angelina's mind that morning. As a born-again Christian widow, she and her children had little support within the larger Ibe family. Her late husband and her relations would not protect her, as many of them were nominal Christians who would fall back on traditional practices in the face of persecution. Her local church was not strong enough to stand up to community pressure, as they are few in number and faced serious persecution.

Having struggled with these thoughts and the big python still motionless in the last five minutes, a passage of the bible, Isaiah 6:8, ran across her mind. She muttered this passage to herself: "Then I heard the voice of the Lord saying, 'whom shall I send? And who will go for us?' And I said, 'here am I. Send me!'" The last sentence of the passage re-echoed several times in her ears. Then she felt a compulsion in her spirit, telling her, "Go, the Lord is with you." She stepped forward towards the python, looked to her right and behold, a log of wood four feet long was there as though it had been provided by an angel of God. "Yea, this must be the rod of Moses," Angelina thought.

She picked it up and felt its weight and it was strong enough to kill the python. Ifeoma watched her mother's solo drama from a distance and as her mother made for the head of the python, Ifeoma cried from a distance, "Mommy, don't kill it! If you kill it, we could be killed!" Angelina staggered backward, as though pulled by Ifeoma's cry. "No, this could be another Peter telling Jesus, do not die on the cross to save the world," she said to herself. "I will do it, even if it means that I die so that this community may be saved, I choose it, it is the pathway to greatness and eternal honour," she thought. She regained those lost steps forward and as she lifted her hand with the club, Ifeoma shouted, "Mommy, don't kill it!" "Get behind me Satan!" was Angelina's response to her daughter's fearful shout. As her spirit gave her the final push, she struck the head of the mighty python with a shout of "Jesus!"

The python wriggled violently towards Angelina. It was writhing in pain and blood oozed out from its head. Angelina did not run away from the approaching python, rather she struck the snake two more times, with the last strike finally incapacitating the snake. The enormous python was dead. Angelina fixed her eyes on it with a sense of accomplishment over her. She said, "Three strikes, one each for the Father, the Son and the Holy Spirit."

"Obinna! Obinna!!" shouted Ifeoma as she ran to their courtyard looking for her older brother to report the killing of the python. She fell to the ground crying and rolling on the sandy patio, "Mother has brought us woes, she killed a python on the road," Ifeoma screamed. A bewildered Obinna ran out of their house without even getting dressed to get better understanding of Ifeoma's behaviour. He tried in vain to comfort Ifeoma and pull her to her feet, but she would not be consoled.

Frustrated by Ifeoma's refusal to be comforted, Obinna left her. He went into the house and put on his shirt. He looked up to the ceiling as if someone above called his attention. After about a minute of gazing at the ceiling of his room, he bent his head down as a few teardrops rolled across his cheek. He knew, just as Ifeoma knew, that their mother's action had indeed drawn a battle line and brought untold woes to the entire family of Polycarp Ibe. According to the Igbo, Obinna had become the head of this family as the first and only son of Polycarp.

Obinna's thought ran back and forth. He thought of his extended family; his uncle, aunts, and their community. He could not find any support. He remembered the land case, which his uncle, Titus, initiated against him and his mother after his father's death. Obinna, still with his dewy-eyes, muttered in a buried voice, "Mother, you have killed a python, you have drawn the battle line."

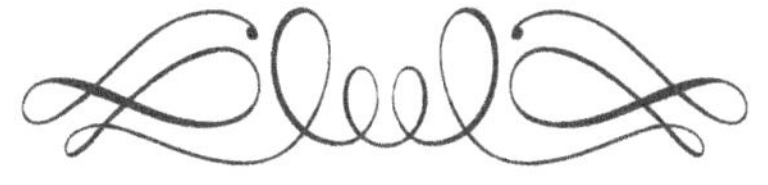

CHAPTER THREE

The Crafty and The Clumsy: Two Friends, Two Evils

One week after Polycarp's death, his younger brother, Mazi Titus, who had never liked Polycarp's deep religious commitment, looked for a way to foment trouble with Polycarp's widow, Angelina. Titus, a feeble character, had the crafty and arrogant Ikenga as his best friend and adviser, and consulted Ikenga on what to do to hurt Angelina.

Ikenga asked Titus, "What is Angelina's crime?"

Titus did not want to reveal the reason for his ill feelings toward his late brother's wife. He merely told Ikenga that he wanted a portion of the land that Polycarp had left for his son, Obinna. Although Titus did not reveal the major reason behind his action, a more elderly Ikenga read in between the lines: he knew that jealousy and lust were behind his friend's move.

Ikenga smiled and soliloquized, "He desires to inherit Angelina, his brother's wife, but this practice was common in the days of our forefathers."

Titus did not hear his friend.

Titus also complained to Ikenga, "Since my older brother married Angelina, she has become very proud and disrespectful of her in-laws." When Ikenga asked him to substantiate his allegation, Titus said, "As a woman married into our family, I expect Angelina to always prostrate herself any time she sees me as a mark of respect to me, an in-law." Ikenga laughed at Titus, pointed his finger at him, and reminded him, "While you refused to go to school and preferred wine tapping and farming in this village, Angelina burnt the midnight oil studying and winning accolades at Suka University where she graduated with a first class degree in Agricultural Science. Do you think that a woman of her calibre will bow to an ordinary village person like you?"

Ikenga's opinion did not go well with Titus. With his usual bluntness, Ikenga emphasised his statement, "It is really difficult for such a person with her intellectual endowments and exposure to prostrate herself for a nonentity like you." Titus stood up from his chair in anger and walked out on Ikenga. Ikenga smiled, saying, "My friend, truth is often bitter to the ear."

As Titus was leaving Ikenga's house, he told Ikenga, "I did not visit you this morning to receive insults, but to get counsel on how to deal with Angelina." After much persuasion from Ikenga, Titus came back and sat close to his friend, Mazi Ikenga. They both drank from a keg of palm wine, which Titus had brought.

After about twenty minutes of drinking and jesting, the liquor was beginning to control a better part of Titus and his words became uncoordinated. Noticing that Titus was intoxicated, Ikenga felt very sad and murmured, "Why would an educated lady like Angelina respect a village drunk like Titus?"

Titus had fallen asleep and did not hear Ikenga's remark. Ikenga sneered at him and went into his house to chat with his daughter, Chioma, who complained about Titus's snore. This angered Ikenga. He took a cup of water and poured it on Titus who was now slumbering. He jumped up, staggered and shouted, "Blessed Virgin Mary, I love you for a wonderful rain." Ikenga's daughter laughed him to scorn. "I know you will only thank Virgin Mary, what of Joseph? An idiot like you," Ikenga raged.

Titus was beginning to recover from his drunkenness. He remained silent for few minutes and did not utter a word. "Ikenga, if you are a good friend why did you watch me drink away my senses?" Titus asked Ikenga.

"It is because the holy book says we should give drinks to those who are perishing, like you." Ikenga answered him.

"Oh, you are now Pastor Ikenga and no more Mazi Ikenga," Titus replied sarcastically. He continued, "So you understand the holy bible so well, Pastor Ikenga, and you have not allowed the will of God to be done in the case of my brother Polycarp and his wife."

Ikenga stood up and told Titus, "You are the biggest fool in this village."

Titus reminded Ikenga that, "The Old Testament book of the bible says, when a man dies and does not have a son to maintain his name, a close relation should have children for him."

Ikenga replied, "You are a dreamer; and I guess that you are suffering from malaria for thinking that a first class graduate like Angelina, with all her religious convictions would stoop so low for you, a village urchin." This did not go well with Titus, who for a second time responded sarcastically, "Pastor Ikenga, you are breaking the law of God".

Ikenga called him names such as "Lusty he-goat", and suggested other methods of dealing with a born-again Angelina. He told Titus that the Old Testament did not include Polycarp in that group because he had a son, Obinna.

Titus replied, "Obinna will grow to be a loner. You know that a loner is like nobody in Umuocha." Now, growing impatient with Titus, Ikenga told him, "come back on an Nkwo Market day with a cup of tobacco snuff in order to hear wise counsel on how to deal with Angelina and her children, rather than dreaming like a lusty he-goat."

Titus thanked Ikenga and left for his house with his empty palm wine keg.

* * *

On the appointed Nkwo Market Day, Titus arrived with a cup of European-made tobacco snuff as demanded by Mazi Ikenga. On seeing Titus, Martha, Ikenga's wife, became angry. She was returning from the farm that hot afternoon with her daughter Chioma, and said to her daughter, "Look at this good-for-nothing drunk", referring to Titus. "He could even drink urine in the name of wine. He has come to waste his time with your father, an accomplished man who is old enough to be his father," Martha said.

Chioma replied, "No, daddy is the guilty one. He has failed to give the right counsel to a good-for-nothing young man." "I do not completely agree with you, my daughter," Martha said to Chioma. Continuing, Martha asked Chioma, "What do you say about a young man who is not challenged by the progress of his age mates in this village? He had every opportunity to go to school like his late older brother, Polycarp. He threw that opportunity away; rather, he chooses to become an eyesore in this village. After all, their father was a great yam farmer whose barn was second to none in the whole of Umuocha community and beyond." "Mother, are you being protective?" Chioma asked in protest. "In what way?" her mother asked.

"I had expected you to lay some blame on my dad. He is a friend of a good-for-nothing young man and has failed to rebuke him and direct him to the right path. Rather, he encourages him by keeping silent and hosting these ungodly meetings, where they drink and talk rubbish," Chioma said, frowning. "You are free to complain but be careful that you do not insult your father. How could you say your father is talking rubbish?" Martha said, staring Chioma in the face.

"I am sorry if that offends you, mom, but the best thing to do to save the situation is to walk Titus out of our house one of these days before the curse upon his head is extended to us," Chioma suggested. "I do not know if there is any curse upon him. I have heard your views, but according to our customs I do not have the authority to walk a man out of our house. The man of the house is the only one permitted to take such an action. If I should do it, it may be another Angelina jumping the mourning rites for a morning cry," a cautious Martha replied.

They entered their gate and Titus and Ikenga were chatting and laughing, exchanging proverbs, sniffing tobacco and drinking from a jar of raffia palm wine. Titus, who loved idioms and proverbs, wanted the proverb contest he was having with his host to continue.

It is often an interesting experience when friends discuss proverbs. They can spend hours churning out proverbs and idioms until one of them exhausts his catalogue of idioms and proverbs. No one asks for the interpretation of any proverb or idiom as that would imply that the bride price his father paid for his mother was a waste and that his mother gave birth to a fool and ignorant fellow.

Titus said, "The forest where thorns pricked the sole of a fowl would not be entered by a human being." Ikenga wondered who taught Titus these proverbs, and replied, "Whatever the fowl chases after, under rain and under sun is very important to it."

On hearing this, Titus laughed and reminded Ikenga that his mission to his house that hot afternoon was as important to him as that thing the fowl chases relentlessly under sun and under rain. Ikenga pretended not to know why Titus came. He asked, "Why are you here, Mazi Titus?"

Titus smiled, then frowned and said, "Our forefathers said, 'an old man who does not know how to dig a hole is only a pretender'. Mazi Ikenga, when will you stop pretending?"

"I am not a pretender; it is only that old age has taken a toll on my memory," Ikenga said.

"Are you now suffering from amresia?" Titus asked Ikenga (he meant to say Amnesia).

Ikenga shouted at him, "Shut your dirty mouth; are we now mates? You are an illiterate man. You cannot even pronounce that word properly. It is not amresia, it is amnesia, and if that is my problem, you are suffering from its older brother called Alzheimer's disease."

Titus tried several times to pronounce "Alzheimer's" but could not. He laughed and told Ikenga he was proud to have an educated man as his friend. Ikenga replied him, "I am ashamed to have an illiterate man as my friend, a man who bites his tongue attempting to pronounce Alzheimer's."

Ikenga pointed at him and said," "Enough of these proverbs before you insult me again. Our fathers said, 'He who competes with his father in proverbs should endeavour to pay his father's debt." Having been subdued by his furious host, Titus murmured silently, "Are you my father?" He did not speak aloud for fear of being walked out of the house. "Okay, I am sorry, Mazi Ikenga, what must I do to my late brother's wife that will increase her pain as a widow?" Titus asked. Ikenga did not answer immediately as he turned his face away.

After some minutes, Ikenga turned to Titus and said, "Now you have to take this advice seriously or behave like the fool you have made yourself. You know the importance of land in our community, now you have to wrest that big land at *Ukpaka*nyi from your brother's wife and her children. I envied your brother, Polycarp, because of the size of that land which he inherited from your late father as the first male child. That land is worth several million naira, and if you allow that widow and her children to own that land, then they will be greater than you and your descendants for ever. Our forefathers said: 'It is only a foolish son that buys yam seedlings from his father's barn'. That land is also yours."

Titus became nervous, because the land was duly the right of Polycarp or his son, Obinna, to inherit. After a period of thoughtfulness, Titus responded, "How can I engage in this battle with this woman, the *Igwe* and the *Umuada* will probably support her?" He continued, "Surely, even the gods of the land and the spirit of

Polycarp will drive me mad," he feared.

"That is why I have always called you a woman or a coward! May I ask, did your parents castrate you? I wonder if God did not make a mistake the day he created you. He gave you the body of a man to house the spirit of these weaklings called women. Take my advice, or leave it!" Ikenga thundered.

"Now advise me how to go about realising this great task," a fidgeting Titus requested. "Now you are showing signs of a real man," Ikenga said, nodding his head. He adjusted his seat and continued, "Listen attentively. I am the traditional Prime Minister of Umuocha, next only to the *Igwe* in importance. I can use my office to help you. You have to raise some money, get some kegs of palm wine and come to the *Obi* on our meeting day, which is on Eke Market day when the *Igwe* meets with *Nze-na-ozo*. You should dress properly as a reasonable fellow. I will be there, but I shall pretend ignorance of your intent. Tell the council that you do not agree with the Will your late father, Ibe, wrote before he died apportioning that big expanse of land to only one of his sons, Polycarp. Tell the council that our ancestors said that, 'if a dead man did not write his Will properly, the living rewrite it'. When you have exhausted your grouse, I shall take up from there. Our forefathers said that, the dog told its owner, throw the bone at me and leave the fight with the spirit for me. So do not be afraid, just throw the matter open and leave the rest for me. I will handle it with the rest of the council members."

Titus felt some relief after this assurance. He thanked Ikenga and said, "There is one other issue I want to clarify with you, Mazi Ikenga."

"What is that issue?" Ikenga asked.

"It is the issue of money with which you will bribe the other council members to favour me in their judgment," Titus said. Ikenga looked at him and said, "I have always said that you irritate me most times. In modern times, we do not use that word 'bribe'. It is anachronistic. We call it P.R. and not that word. Do you want *Amadioha* to kill me! *Nze-na-ozo* does not take bribes, it is forbidden by the gods of this land and by the God of heaven."

"I am very sorry, Mazi Ikenga," Titus apologised.

Seeming assuaged by Titus's apology, Ikenga's voice mellowed and he said, "Listen, you do not have many problems on the issue of money. I will lend you the amount of money you need for this PR"

On hearing this promise, Titus jumped to his feet and danced *Iyololo* around the room, bowed himself before Mazi Ikenga and sat down without uttering a word.

After some minutes, Titus asked Ikenga, "How much will you lend me?" and Ikenga told him, "Twenty-five thousand naira."

Titus then asked, "What are the terms for this loan, or is the loan in the name of helping a friend realise his objective?"

Ikenga laughed and said to Titus, "You will pay no interest on the loan." Titus nodded in agreement.

"However, there is one thing which you must do", Ikenga added.

"What is that one thing I must do?" a curious Titus asked.

"Go and think of what you must do to reward this kind gesture," Ikenga advised him.

"Please, Mazi Ikenga, do not keep me in suspense," Titus pleaded with his host.

"If you wish to know, then I will not fail to let you know. I will not request to have any of your children as a slave to me, or your wife to be my concubine; after all, I go to Church, which believes in one man, one wife. You must just do one thing," Ikenga stopped suddenly, fixing his gaze on Titus. This heightened Titus's curiosity as he looked away from the intimidating eyes of Ikenga, and he wondered "What is this one thing that I must do to get this loan?"

Ikenga excused himself to ease off, and promised to re-join him later. He was just piling up pressure on Titus. The longer Ikenga waited before revealing his demand, the more pressure he put on a curious Titus, who was restless as he sat thinking about the puzzle Ikenga had in mind. His friend Ikenga was quite a mis*chi*evous character; he knew the temperament of Titus. He was simply exploiting his weakness to the fullest.

Ikenga did not re-join Titus as promised; rather he went to the backyard of his house, where the kitchen and goat pens were situated, and chatted to his wife and daughter, and leaving Titus consumed with curiosity.

* * *

After about an hour Chioma entered the sitting room where Titus was sitting to pick up a machete with which to gather pasture for their goats. As she entered, Titus, thinking it was Ikenga, stood up to welcome his host back. Realising that it was Chioma, he quickly sat down and pretended he was exercising his legs by repeating some movements several times.

Chioma ran back to the kitchen and reminded her father that Titus was in the sitting room. Ikenga shouted, "Oh the God of Umuocha oo! I forgot that my friend was still waiting for me." He dashed back to the parlour where Titus welcomed him with a feigned sense of humour. Titus said, "I thought you were cooking in the kitchen with your wife and I decided to wait and taste your food for the first time." He said this intentionally to hurt Ikenga's feelings because it was an insult to think or say that an *Ozo* titleholder of the calibre of Ikenga was cooking with his wife in the kitchen.

Although Ikenga felt insulted by this statement, he did not react in his characteristic manner. Rather, he told Titus, "I will beat you and your wife in any cooking competition whether it is African or European dishes." They laughed, and Ikenga continued: "You are a true son of your father, but you disobeyed his wise advice to get educated." Titus did not reply as his attention went back to their initial discussion. His mind ran back to that thought, "What is this one thing that I must do to get this loan from Ikenga?" and he voiced it to Ikenga.

Ikenga reclined on his seat, took his snuffbox, cleared his voice and uttered a proverb, "It is the animal that climbs trees with its teeth that can tell a bitter tree." He glanced around, stared Titus in the face and continued, "Titus, it is the lender of money whose purse is assailed, not the borrower's. That is the meaning of that proverb. Titus, initially, did not really understand the relevance of this proverb to the issue before them, but he did not dare ask for an explanation or Ikenga would tell him that his mother's bride price was a waste. He nodded in agreement while waiting for another surprise from Ikenga.

"Let me cut this meeting short so you can go and meet with your family," Ikenga pretended to care for Titus and his family. "What you must do is this: you must mortgage your land to me in order to receive the financial help which we shall use as P.R. to get you a much bigger expanse of land." Titus looked dazed at Ikenga's loan condition.

After a brief moment, Titus cleared his voice and said, "The toad does not run in vain at noontime; there must be something pursuing it. Something pursued me from my house to your house. I must get that thing, no matter the price, even if it costs me the whole of my inheritance in order to reach my goal. However, Mazi Ikenga, if that land were to be mortgaged, it will not be less than a hundred thousand naira." "Have you ever seen the colour of a hundred thousand naira or known its weight before? Can you even count it correctly?" Ikenga asked Titus. "Does a bundle of a hundred thousand naira have a different colour?" Titus asked Ikenga. Ikenga, who was beginning to be irritated by Titus, replied with another proverb, "A visitor should not weary his host so that when he is leaving he will not develop a hunch back." He looked straight at Titus, pointed his finger at him and said, "Do not weary me in my house with your stupidity, Titus."

"I understand and I am not here to weary you, but reason with me that that your twenty-five thousand naira is too little for the size of my land," Titus appealed. "Take it or leave it," Ikenga replied. "I accept because I have no alternative," Titus surrendered. Titus's acceptance gladdened Ikenga. He stood up and eulogized Titus, calling him *Ekwueme, Obata-osu, Dike-na-dimkpa, Nwan-naya* and so on. These names did not appeal to Titus. This was the only land from which he derived his living. Knowing he had won a big price, he sought to reassure Titus of his unflin*chi*ng support. Ikenga told Titus: "Listen, my young friend, our fathers said that, 'He who accompanies a lion eats what the lion eats, and that is meat; but he who accompanies a goat also eats what a goat eats, and that is grass'. You have accompanied me over the last three years; you will always eat meat, not grass". Noticing that Titus was not so interested in his lecture, Ikenga went close to him, and in low voice, whispered: "My late mother used to tell me a proverb: 'My son, it is with patience that the earthworm burrows the ground'. Just be patient and we shall accomplish this task. The land will become yours". Titus did not respond to this proverb.

* * *

On the appointed Eke Market day, the *Nze*-na-*ozo* members were seated waiting for the majestic arrival of the *Igwe* and his train of courtiers. It was not long before he arrived amidst the shout of "*Igweee! Igweee!!*" by the *Nze-na-ozo* who stood with their hands raised in solidarity to the *Igwe*. As soon as he sat down on his throne, his three armour bearers went behind him with their swords while Ndi *Otimkpu* and the multitude in the train went outside the *Obi*.

All those present were silent until the musketeers shot seven ground-quaking muskets heralding the *Igwe*'s arrival at his court and the commencement of the sitting. All the judges, *Nze-na-ozo*, stood at attention while the *Igwe* took his seat, and then indicated them to take their seats and they echoed, "*Igwe*ee, may you live forever!" symbolising solidarity with the *Igwe*. As these formalities were taking place, Titus was sandwiched in the crowd of onlookers, highly disturbed and confused about whether he had any chance of winning such a case in which almost everyone would likely support the widow. His only confidence was in the assurance of Ikenga. He shook his head in admiration of the pomp and majesty that accompanied the *Igwe*'s arrival. He muttered this proverb to the man on his right, "A king's wealth and might are expressed in the multitude that follows him." The man nodded in support and said, "Yes, our people say that, "The pride and prestige of the king is in his entourage."

When these formalities were over Ikenga, the traditional Prime Minister, stood up and took a wooden plate containing kola nuts from one of the palace attendants. He took the plate to the *Igwe* who lifted it up and said, "God in heaven, here are kola nuts," and the council echoed, "come and be with us." The *Igwe* broke one of the kola nuts and threw the pieces on the floor. He also took a cup of palm wine, poured libations and said, "Our ancestors, here are kola nuts and drinks, come and be with us in today's proceedings." The council again shouted, "come and be with us."

This concluded the prayer rituals and the council was now set for the day's business. The palace secretary called out those with complaints. They lined up and the case of Mr. Titus Ibe was read first. This was the handiwork of Mazi Ikenga. He had influenced the position of the case file by offering a bribe to the palace secretary. He wanted to test the views of the council members and observe the reaction of the spectators.

The suit was brief, well crafted by Ikenga but hand-copied by Nnamdi Ibe, the first son of Titus, because Ikenga did not want his handwriting to be noticed. It read, "My Father, Mazi Ibe Nnadi of Akpu Village in Umuocha community, who died on December

27, 1977 did not portray equity in the distribution of his lands among his children, especially with regard to the large expanse of land at *Ukpaka*nyi. He favoured my late brother, Polycarp. I pray this distinguished council to redress this injustice. Our ancestors said that, 'When a dead man writes a will improperly; the living rewrites it.' Please let this council rewrite this injustice."

Having read the suit, the whole council fell into confusion, with many raising their hands in opposition. Ikenga remained silent and did not utter any words. The crowd became noisy and was almost turning restive as one man from Angelina's village, Ngali, Mazi Nduka, wanted to beat up Titus but some palace guards prevented him. The chaos almost degenerated to an Akpu village versus Ngali village showdown. Angelina was born in Ngali village, but she married an Akpu man. Both Ngali and Akpu are villages in the community of Umuocha consisting of a total of seven villages.

The *Igwe* finally got up from his throne and threatened to call in the *mmanwu* (masquerades) to deal with any recalcitrant person trying to disrupt the peace. This finally brought the noisy crowd under control. Masquerades in Igboland are masked men. In Umuocha, masquerades are used as police to enforce law and order. They perform other functions, such as entertainment during New Yam festival, Christmas celebration, Easter and funeral ceremony for an *Ozo*. Beyond these social roles in Umuocha, masquerades are believed to come from the spirit world. Although they are human beings, in order to endow them with mystical significance, they are viewed more as spirits and are dreaded by non-members of the masquerade cult.

The *Igwe* directed that Angelina and Obinna should be summoned to their next sitting. Written summons were prepared and sent to Angelina and Obinna while the other cases were read out. After deliberations on two of these cases, the *Igwe* gave his verdict in consultation with the *Nze-na-ozo*.

The *Igwe* stood up, thanked the Almighty God and the

forefathers of Umuocha and adjourned the court session to the next month to enable him attend some urgent meetings with the state security panel in the state capital, Owerri. He was a member of this august body, a highly privileged group of first class traditional rulers and state officials.

Obinna had received the court summons from the court messenger about ten minutes before he heard Ifeoma's cry that their mother had killed the python on the road. He had barely read through his summons before the news of her mother's action got to him. It became a double tragedy for him as he almost collapsed on the floor on a day he had commissioned his mother and sister to go boldly and preach the gospel of Jesus in the community to deliver it from evil.

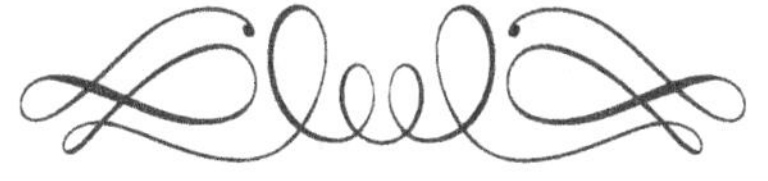

CHAPTER FOUR

The Widow's Cross and Its Pangs

"My children, stop crying. Why are you wetting the house with your precious tears? Is that the strength of your faith, or are you mourning the python on the road like those ungodly fellows would do when they see its carcass?" Angelina asked her children as she entered the courtyard through the gate. She continued, "Revolutions that bring profound changes do not smell like roses or taste like honey. They are usually bitter as gall, rougher than the roughest edges of Mount Kilimanjaro and hotter than the centre of Sahara Desert. I weighed my action and its likely outcomes. I was not scared because I saw victory in the end and the "well done" we would receive from our God if we stand out against what is evil in this community."

There was dead silence in the house. Her words did not really convince Ifeoma who was quite sceptical of the situation ahead. Obinna got up, wiped the tears on his face. "Mother did you really count the cost of your actions?" he queried with a shaky voice. Angelina answered Obinna, "Yes my son. Be a man, your dad Polycarp was a real man who never feared death. His ideals and convictions meant much more to him than death. Fear according to the bible has torment and it does not work with faith; they are miles apart. I need your support at this time; let us create a chapter in the history book for our community for ourselves, and a page for our names in the annals of God's faithful children. Are you okay with my explanation?" Angelina asked.

Obinna did not say a word but nodded in agreement. Ifeoma called Amaka, who was still enjoying her sleep undisturbed, to go and take her bath and prepare for school. She had resolved not to go to school that day in order to witness what would befall her mother from the community.

"Mother, if I may ask, is the python's carcass still there?" Obinna asked.

"Yes, of course."

"I will go and bury it with a shovel or throw it into the pit latrine," he suggested.

Angelina smiled and said, "None of this shall happen. It is war booty and you do not hide your war booty. You let the world see it. They should know that we are against those practices that amount to animal worship. Leave it there. I made that mistake with your father. During his lifetime, we killed many pythons and quietly disposed of them. Now, this practice must stop! Any python I kill must be exposed for the whole world to see," she opposed Obinna.

"Mother, I support Obinna's view, please I do not want any troubles from anyone in this village or the entire Umuocha community," Ifeoma said fearfully.

"Ify, I know your little strength. Make it up with a mustard seed faith and you will grow to be the mighty woman of faith the Lord wants you to be. Persecution is a mark of the Christian pilgrimage; when it comes, it establishes your faith properly. If Jesus never wanted troubles, he would not have left the comfort of heaven to come to earth where he was mistreated, sentenced and killed so that you and I would enjoy eternal life," her mother exhorted her. Ifeoma's mind was not prepared for any sermon on faith this morning as fear had taken the greater part of her.

As Angelina was reasoning with her children, they heard a shout from Mazi Okoli, a prominent palm wine tapper, who was on his way to tap a palm tree close to Angelina's house.

Umuocha, gather here oo!
Umuocha, the morning has turned into night oo!
Umuocha, our mother is dead oo!
Umuocha, let every family assemble here oo!
Umuocha, come oo, young and old!

Okoli alerted the entire community from the top of his palm tree.

He had quickly climbed the palm tree on sighting the dead python so that his voice could go further. He was so awestruck that he almost fell from the top of the palm tree. He was not able to tap his wine as he hurried down and ran straight to the *Igwe*'s palace.

As he was running to the palace of the *Igwe*, the entire village was beginning to assemble around the dead python beside Angelina's house. Some villagers, especially the aged women, wept uncontrollably, bemoaning and cursing whoever killed it. They cursed the killer in the name of some very deadly deities in Igboland, such as *Urashi, Ogwugwu, Amadioha, Ibini-Ukpabi* and *Agbala*. Some men ran back to their homes, took black bands, and tied them on their heads shouting, "*Tufiakwa*! *Obu aru*!". Within an hour of Mazi Okoli raising this alarm, about a thousand people both young and old gathered, most of them rolling on the ground, crying and cursing the killer of the python.

* * *

On arrival at the *Igwe*'s palace, the guards stopped Okoli who was running straight into the palace's inner chambers without observing any protocol. "Who is that bush animal running into the *Obi* in that manner? Don't you have respect for the palace?" shouted one of the guards at Mazi Okoli.

"My son, I am not a bush animal. I have come to report an abomination that I saw this morning near the house of the late

Polycarp, the school principal in Akpu village who died about three weeks ago," Okoli said panting as he tried to gather his breath, exhausted from his exertions.

"Did you see a pregnant man or a woman with a horn that made you defy the sanctity of the palace this beautiful morning?" the enraged palace guard questioned a fainting Okoli.

Okoli answered, "Something worse than the abominations you just mentioned has happened this morning."

"What?" the guard queried with surprise. Their conversation was beginning to attract the attention of other guards. As this encounter was taking place, the *Igwe* was coming out of the palace grove where he had gone to pour early morning libation to his ancestors. He heard shouts from the Akpu village playground and initially ignored it as a minor issue. The sound of the shouts became louder, and as he listened, the noise sounded like shouts of abhorrence of evil and this made him agitated.

Having been told that a python was found killed close to the house of the late Polycarp Ibe, the guard broke down in tears. He ran straight through the inner gate of the palace to the *Igwe*'s secretary and personal assistant, whom he told, "The world is tumbling down in Umuocha community, do you not you hear the wailing?" The secretary demanded to know what that meant, but the guard insisted on meeting with the *Igwe*.

The secretary ran to the *Ufo* (the *Igwe*'s personal residence in the massive palace). "What is the problem this early morning?" The *Igwe* asked his confused secretary; himself, also agitated. "I do not know why this guard is crying. He refused to let me know and insisted on meeting you," the secretary told the *Igwe*.

The *Igwe* was known for his poise and calculated reasoning. A well-educated man, he attended one of the best universities in England. His belief in modernity sometimes clashed with his highly conservative council, the *Nze-na-ozo*. The *Igwe* described many of the customs of his community as "anachronistic customs begging to be scrapped." He reluctantly accepted the stool (position) after the death of his father, the former *Igwe*. It had taken the Umuocha community about three years to convince him to abandon his flourishing legal practice in England to come back and occupy what was his birth right since the position of the *Igwe* is hereditary and passes on automatically to the first son of a sitting *Igwe*, on his death or abdication.

"What is the matter, my friend?" The *Igwe* asked the guard.

The guard could not hold his composure as he wailed at the top of his voice, "We are finished in Umuocha!"

"Finished for what? You are not fit for this job of guarding the palace! So if there is a threat of bomb upon our heads, you cannot hold your composure and face the situation as a uniformed man?" the *Igwe* yelled at him.

"A Python was killed oo!" He finally revealed.

"Ala Umuocha oo!" shouted the secretary.

"Come on, stop that, Mr. Secretary! Let me get the details right," the *Igwe* said looking at the guard.

"*Igwe*, let me call Mazi Okoli from Akpu village who brought this abominable message to you," the guard said and ran to where the other guards were gathered, discussing the incident with Mazi Okoli.

He motioned to Okoli who ran towards him. He led Okoli to the *Igwe* and the secretary. On sighting the *Igwe*, Okoli broke down and cried, "*Igwe* oo, your people are finished, an untold abomination has happened in your land and the whole land is demanding purification. *Tufiakwa, aru, aru*! As I was on my way to tap the palm tree near the house of the late teacher, Polycarp Ibe, I noticed an ugly sight. A very mighty python curled on the road. I thought it was alive and wanted to do obeisance, but I found it in the pool of its own blood. I discovered its head was smashed and it is dead oo!"

"Ok, I have heard you, Mr. Okoli, you can go. I will be there in a few minutes to see things for myself," the *Igwe* said. The guard and Okoli went out, leaving the *Igwe* and the secretary.

"Tell me, what is wrong with killing that irritating snake, for God's sake? Is that the reason why the entire community is being disturbed this morning?" the *Igwe* asked the secretary.

"What are you saying, *Igwe*? It is time you forgo this European behaviour and face your business in Africa as the custodian of the customs and traditions of our people. In this case you have to act fast in order not to attract the wrath of the gods," the secretary said with a heavy sigh.

The *Igwe* looked the other way and muttered, "My God, this is why I resisted this kingship thing for three years and this community continued sending emissaries to England to persuade me to come home for this kind of life where humans are placed under a system that is supposed to have been discarded with the passage of time." The secretary did not say a word. He feared the *Igwe* might sack him and he would lose all his benefits.

"Now, Mr. Secretary, advise me on what to do, you are older than I and more experienced in the culture of our land," *Igwe* said. The secretary was a seventy-five-year-old retired headmaster of St. Patrick's Primary School in Umuocha, an experienced historian who had worked with the British colonial officials in Owerri, the provincial headquarters during the colonial era.

He said, "*Igwe*, according to our records, the last time a python was brazenly murdered..."

"Did I hear you say 'murdered?'" *Igwe* interrupted him. "Is it now a human being?" He asked the aged secretary.

"Sorry if that offends you," the secretary pleaded and then continued. "In 1940 a British military officer, who came for a recruitment drive to take some young men for enlistment into the WAFF (West African Frontier Force), to help them in their military campaign in Burma, South East Asia, killed and ate a python near the Iyioma Stream. As soon as the community got wind of it the whole Umuocha community went rioting, and but for the timely intervention of the army detachment that came with this officer, he would have been lynched by our people. In the end, the recruitment exercise was thwarted, some houses were burnt and about seven of the rioters were killed by the soldiers."

"How many British soldiers did the rioters kill?" the *Igwe* interrupted the secretary. "None, they had higher fire power, while our people had fought with only bows and arrows. It is only a madman that challenges a gun-toting fellow," the secretary reasoned.

"Now can you see why I am not comfortable with some of your... no, our customs," the *Igwe* corrected himself. "Listen to me, secretary, one python was killed and eaten by a hungry Brit, several houses belonging to local people were burnt and as many as seven African lives were lost in that brutal fight you simply called a 'riot,'" the *Igwe* said, shaking his head in disappointment.

The secretary said, "Yes, our people were happy that this python was one of our forefathers who came to prevent the mass enlistment which was turning into conscription. Now, do you know how many of our young men would have been killed if they were taken to Burma? Perhaps, over fifty of them would have died."

"So the seven sacrificed themselves for others to live?" the *Igwe* said humorously.

"Maybe, yes," the secretary replied.

"Now what do I do in this matter?" the *Igwe* asked the secretary.

"Firstly, the *Mgbadi* has to be sounded to alert the living and the dead that an evil incident has happened in the land," the secretary advised.

The *Mgbadi* is a very large round wooden musical instrument kept at the *Eke* market near the *Urashi* shrine. It is sounded occasionally whenever any evil happened or was about to happen. For instance, it was sounded when British forces conquered Umuocha in 1898 and exiled its *Igwe*, the great grandfather of the present *Igwe*, to far away Accra, Ghana. It was also sounded in 1937 when a British soldier killed a python. The *Mgbadi* sounded last when the former *Igwe* died. Whenever it is sounded, neighbouring communities prepare for condolence visits to Umuocha because it is believed that a great calamity such as the death of their *Igwe* has occurred. The *Mgbadi* is over one hundred and fifty years old and was made from a large Iroko trunk.

"So you mean that over seventy years after the *Mgbadi* sounded for a python, it has to be sounded again for the same animal?" *Igwe* asked with a tone of surprise. "Please, stop calling it an animal. It is more than an animal. It is a god!" the secretary pleaded.

"Shame on you, Mr. Secretary, I thought you are a communicant in your church and your name is Godwin; yet you refer to a python as a god," *Igwe* said in utter disregard for Godwin's old age.

Godwin, the secretary, bent his head low as if hiding his face from the blazing eyes of the *Igwe*. After a while he raised his head, looked at the *Igwe* and said, "The community needs your leadership in the face of this abomination. Let us go to the scene of the incident. They are waiting for you there and wasting more time will not serve your interest well."

"I have heard you, Mr Secretary. Call the drivers to get the cars ready and let us go to the scene of incident to see things by ourselves," the *Igwe* told him.

"One more thing," the secretary said, "If you do not have any serious thing to tell the people when we get there, behave as though you are mourning with them and keep silent."

"I have heard, and make sure that the masquerades are sent there to maintain peace and order among the people," the *Igwe* commanded.

* * *

At the scene of the incident, the throng from across Umuocha and beyond already numbered over three thousand. There were masquerades already there, singing and dancing and controlling the crowd, while the noise of wailing and cries prevented any reasonable discussion.

There were various groups such as the youth organised according to their age grades, *Umuada*, *Alutaradi*, *Otu Umuagbogho* and so on, singing funeral songs and raining curses on whoever killed the python. They were waiting for the *Igwe* to come and address them, after which the chief priest of *Urashi* goddess would bury the python with the accolade due an *Ozo* titled man and then purify the land. The formal ceremonies for the burial of the python could take as many as seven days.

The *Igwe* and the secretary with about fifteen of his palace guards set out for the scene of the incident. He was driven in his Toyota Land Cruiser 4x4 vehicle with the signage "The *Igwe* of Umuocha." He was in his full regalia and as they drew near the throng, the *Igwe* shouted at the top of his voice to the amazement of Godwin and his personal driver, "Oh men, what am I seeing? Why have these people gathered here, leaving their businesses to be here? This is terrible, ignorance and poverty have destroyed my people."

Godwin countered, "It is not ignorance and poverty, it is love for their customs, their identity. I tell you anyone that hears and refuses to come risks calamity on his head."

"It is a bloody lie, Mr. Secretary," the *Igwe* responded.

On arrival, the entire convoy of the *Igwe* was swallowed up by the throng of mourners, especially the old women, so that the *Igwe* could not easily alight from his vehicle. He was later advised by the lead masquerade to remain seated in his vehicle while the crowd was cleared away from his convoy. After much verbal appeal, and no compliance from the crowd, the masquerades used whips to push back the crowd from the *Igwe*'s convoy in order to allow him come out of his vehicle. It took another twenty minutes of appeal by the *Nze-na-ozo*, the *Igwe*, his secretary and the masquerades to get the crowd's attention to listen to the *Igwe*.

When he mounted the rostrum provided by the Akpu village youths, the *Igwe* was laden with emotion. He looked at the people with pity and much pain in his heart. He thought their major problem was pervading ignorance. Inwardly, he blamed the state officials for this ignorance. The *Igwe* believed that if the people had meaningful jobs and good education, they would not be here mourning one unfortunate snake that had been killed.

He waved at the crowd with his royal fan, cleared his voice and said, "My dear people of our great land of Umuocha, the land of light where darkness has no room, I greet you all in the name of our ancestors who I represent today as your leader. Indeed, I have seen the grief that has befallen our land and people with the killing of the python by a yet to be known evil person. May the python fight for itself."

"*Iseee*!!!" the crowd echoed.

The *Igwe* continued, "I have never witnessed this kind of abomination since my ascension to the throne of my forefathers and may this be the end of such."

"*Iseeeee!!!*" the crowd shouted with greater fervour.

"Now listen to me. The perpetrator of this dastardly act must not go unpunished. The gods of this land will find him or her out. However, let me warn you, do not, I repeat, do not, act on hearsay or take laws into your own hands. Our ancestors said that, 'If the dog enters the bush with a bag in anger, then all the faeces in the bush will be eaten.' If anyone is suspected, let him or her be reported to the masquerade cult or to the state police who will formally arrest him or her and keep such a person in protective custody, from where he would be charged to court. Even in the court, he will be assumed innocent until proven guilty in a competent law court. Once again, I greet you all and hereby mandate Ezekwunna, the High Priest of Umuocha and *Urashi*, to carry the carcass of the python with his assistants and bury it, as the custom requires. May this evil never happen again ooo!!"

"*Iseee*!" the crowd echoed.

The *Igwe* stepped down, exchanged pleasantries with the *Nze-na-ozos* and headed home with his convoy of retinues. As he entered his vehicle, the secretary, Mr. Godwin, said, "You are the true son of your father."

"Keep quiet Godwin, and leave me alone! This is nothing other than a celebration of ignorance and a dance of shame. I said those words to them because of what cultural protagonists like you would say and to disperse the throng of hungry folks. I did not go there with the whole of my heart and did not say what I said from my heart. I am not part of this nonsense."

Godwin never said a word but was satisfied with the *Igwe*'s appearance, after all.

At the scene, the crowd was beginning to disperse as Ezekwunna and his fellow priests wrapped the body of the large python in white linen and lace materials and put it in a human coffin. They made some sacrifices, killed seven he-goats, seven sheep, one cow and fourteen cocks. They took the coffin containing the carcass of the python to *Ohia Udonshi*, where they gave it the full honour of a human burial and promised to do everything possible to discover the heinous killer of the python.

* * *

Angelina and her children, in whose vicinity the throng had gathered, did not come out of their house during the time the crowd had gathered. They were inside their house praying against the curses that were rained on the killer. They heard all that was said, including the *Igwe*'s address. They prayed for the *Igwe* to receive the gospel of Jesus in his heart so that the truth of the knowledge of God might set him free from the mistakes of his ancestors.

Amaka had gone to school that morning. She was the only person from Angelina's household who had gone out that morning as the others stayed with their mother to witness any events that might unfold.

Amaka was a very playful girl, barely nine years old. She took everything in fun and was talkative, especially when she was playing with other children. Angelina had once warned Obinna and Ifeoma not to discuss any secret in the presence of Amaka for fear of revealing such to outsiders.

On many occasions, Ifeoma had lashed Amaka mercilessly for what she described as "Amaka's loose tongue". One such occasion was when Ifeoma, in confidence, revealed to her mother that her classmate Chioma, Ikenga's daughter, told her that she had an abortion twice in one year with the help of her mother. Ifeoma had pleaded with her mother not to reveal it to anyone. Angelina had heeded Ifeoma's instruction and kept the secret.

One day, Chioma's younger sister, Chika, aged ten, called Chioma "an abortionist" because of a misunderstanding they had over domestic chores. Chioma, infuriated by that tag, demanded to know who told her that she had had an abortion. Chika refused to tell Chioma and when the matter was reported to her mother, Martha, Chika was thoroughly beaten and forced to reveal how she came about that information. She revealed it was Amaka Ibe, Polycarp Ibe's youngest daughter, who told her on their way to the Iyioma Stream to fetch water and do laundry. Chioma wept uncontrollably and felt betrayed by her close friend, Ifeoma.

Early the next morning, Chioma pretended that all was well, even though she was ready for a fight with Ifeoma on their way to school. Chioma and Ifeoma had always gone to school together in the company of other girls. When they were midway to school, Chioma's emotions overcame her and she held Ifeoma's uniform and tore it, revealing Ifeoma's bare body. While Ifeoma was trying to cover her bare body, Chioma took a handful of sand and poured it into Ifeoma's eyes before they were separated.

Ifeoma fell on the ground, crying "Chioma, why me, what did I do to merit this treatment, may my God forgive you your sins." Chioma left her reeling in pain and continued to school. She did not tell anyone why she treated her best friend in this way. Ifeoma continued lamenting her ordeal as one of her friends led her back to her home.

When Angelina was told of this assault, she prayed silently and went to Chioma's classroom, called her to the staffroom and asked what led to the assault on her friend, Ifeoma. Chioma could not say a word because the other teachers were listening. When Angelina persisted, Chioma, now beginning to cry, told her, "I prefer a private chat with you, Madam Angie", which was the name students called their Agricultural Science teacher, Angelina.

Angelina obliged, and when they got out of the staffroom and into a private corner, Chioma broke down and cried aloud. Angelina was baffled and asked why she was crying. Chioma said "My best friend, your daughter, betrayed me when I told her a secret concerning my abortion." Angelina pretended not to understand and asked what she meant by that. Chioma revealed what Amaka had told Chika.

At this, Angelina comforted Chioma, preached the word of God to her and also revealed to her the dangers of abortion at her age. She promised a thorough investigation at home. Angelina was very disappointed in Amaka and when she got home she whipped Amaka thoroughly. She had eavesdropped the day Ifeoma revealed this secret to her mother.

* * *

Amaka, who pretended not to know what was rumbling in her home between her mother, Obinna and Ifeoma about the killing of the python, went to school with this news and told her classmates and her teacher.

Amaka boasted to Chima, a naughty boy in her class, that her mother, Angelina was stronger than Chima's mother. Chima insisted his own mother was stronger than Amaka's mother. Amaka said, "To prove my mother's strength, this morning, she killed a mighty python on the road." Their class teacher, a lady, who pretended no interest in the pupils' conversation, exclaimed, "*Tufiakwa, nkea bu aru*".

She asked Amaka to repeat what she just said in the presence of a male teacher, who ran to her class when he heard the exclamation of rejection and abomination. Amaka again boasted that her mother was stronger than both her class teacher and the male teacher put together. The male teacher teased Amaka, "Your mother must be a superwoman, young girl." Amaka was elated and then smiled.

The male teacher then asked her, "How do you know that your mother is stronger than all of us put together?"

Amaka asked both teachers, "Have anyone of you killed a python before?"

The teachers chorused, "No, no!"

Amaka replied with a sense of fulfilment, "But my mommy killed one this morning."

"Who is your mommy, young girl?" The male teacher asked Amaka.

"My mommy is Madam Angie, the Agric teacher at Umuocha Secondary Technical School," Amaka answered with a sense of pride.

"That's okay, my brilliant girl," he teased Amaka and left the classroom with the gait of a spy who has just obtained the most important secret information he sought for.

The teacher headed to the *Urashi* Shrine to meet Ezekwunna, the High Priest, to report Angelina as the killer of the python. On reaching the grove, he removed his shoes and shouted the nickname of Ezekwunna, "*Okara mmadu, okara mmuo!*" (Half human, half spirit!). Ezekwunna had been in mourning since the incident, hence, did not respond with his usual suave. He looked miserable. It was his primary responsibility to find the perpetrator of this dastardly act according to the tradition of Umuocha.

He was received by Ezekwunna, who asked him to sit down and explain his mission. The teacher did obeisance to the chief priest of Umuocha and *Urashi* grove, and then explained his mission. Ezekwunna was happy that the puzzle about who killed the snake had been solved. Ezekwunna led the teacher out of the grove, thanking him and calling him great names that suggested he was a patriot among patriots in the land of Umuocha. He bade him farewell and re-entered the gate backwards. The chief priest does not enter the grove facing forwards, because it is believed that if he enters facing forwards, he will see deadly spirits, and that could lead to his death. Once inside the grove, he mutters some incantation, clap his hands seven times and nods in agreement seven times, then sits on his chair.

The position of the chief priest of Umuocha is a hereditary one. The right to produce the Priest of Umuocha was vested in the family of Ezekwunna for very many years. It is the duty of the last male child of his lineage to become the chief priest. The chief priest remains celibate in his lifetime. He keeps a dreadlock of very long hair, behaves in a weird manner, and lives a vegetarian lifestyle, among other peculiar pious practices. The chief priest does not shake anyone's hand including the *Igwe* of Umuocha.

Ezekwunna then called the trainee priests (seminarians) by sounding the *oja* and they came out of their huts, entered the groove, bowed their heads before Ezekwunna and sat on the floor. Ezekwunna danced around his *chi*, sat in their midst and informed them that *Urashi* deity had caught up with the killer of the python. They were all excited as they jumped up and bowed down to the grove. However, he did not tell them who it was. He called off the meeting and they left but were very anxious to know who it was that had committed that heinous crime. Ezekwunna called his most trusted student, Ekene, and instructed him to run like a gazelle to the house of Agodi, the masquerade cult leader, and summon him to the grove. Ezekwunna emphasised the urgency of the message to Ekene: "Our ancestors said that, 'Any message sent through the smoke has reached heaven'. Run and do not look back."

On seeing Ekene running towards his house, Agodi, who was getting ready for his farm work, dropped the machete and the hoe he was holding. He was apprehensive because it could be a bad omen for anyone to receive any message from Ezekwunna, the dreaded high priest of *Urashi* Deity and Umuocha community.

Agodi shouted, "Ekene, am I safe or have the gods condemned me to die?"

"I do not know, Agodi, if you are safe or not, but remember our forefathers said that, 'the toad does not run in the afternoon in vain,' you are needed at the grove immediately by *Nna anyi* Ezekwunna." Ekene did not answer any other questions from the agitated Agodi.

Agodi called on Alice, his wife, and told her to take the children to the farm while he went to answer the call of the gods, which might mean death or life for him. He ran after Ekene and got to the grove five minutes after Ekene had arrived. As he entered the grove, Ezekwunna made incantations and spoke in an unfamiliar language. Agodi called him, "Half man, half spirit."

Ezekwunna looked at Agodi straight in the face, pointing his hand towards him and said: "The drum sounds twice for the warrior, either in life or in death; when the head disturbs the wasp it suffers sting; the snake that bites the tortoise is only injuring its teeth; finally, the rat should not dare eat the native doctor's bag, the native doctor should not dare beat up the rat."

All these proverbs brought more confusion and suspense to Agodi who thought it was time for the gods to take his life: maybe he had offended in one way or another, he did not know. He did not understand that Ezekwunna was talking about the killer of the python.

As Agodi stood startled, Ezekwunna continued, "Now listen, Agodi, the gods of Umuocha have answered our prayers by revealing who our number one enemy in this land is."

Agodi still did not understand what was going on as his host stopped talking, took some concoctions, danced around, and made some signs in the air with the eagle feathers in his hand. He asked in awe, "*Nna anyi*, am I the enemy? Tell me if I am the one."

Ezekwunna interrupted him and said, "The defiled feet do not tread on holy ground. If you are the one you would have died immediately you stepped into this grove."

This assurance then brought Agodi great relief and he gathered his composure. He danced the dance of the gods and shouted, "Who is that wicked heart that has annoyed the gods of Umuocha? *Nna anyi,* tell me."

Ezekwunna stopped his dance and said, "Not even a man like us, but a common woman killed the python! I mean an ordinary being that squats to urinate! My forefathers said that, 'When it is the time for a dog to die, it does not perceive the odour of faeces'. I can see that the gods are about to kill her, but she does not see the handwriting on the wall."

Agodi lamented and cursed her by the name of *Ibini-Ukpabi,* the great deity of *Arochukwu*. "What is her name and who is her coward husband?" an enraged Agodi asked.

"She is Angelina, the late Polycarp's wife from Akpu village."

Agodi was struck at the mention of that name. His first son, Okwudili, never stopped giving compliments to Angelina's great teaching skill, especially in Practical Agriculture. He once told his father that she was his mentor at school and that he was probably going to study Agricultural Science at the university if he passed the matriculation examination. Agodi had once sent some mango fruits to Angelina through Okwudili to thank her for the great skills she had imparted to his son. Agodi believed that his son's knowledge of agricultural science had greatly contributed to his farm's improved yield, and this was all thanks to Angelina, his son's teacher.

Quietly, Agodi soliloquized, "May nothing happen to you wonderful daughter of Umuocha." He could not say it aloud for fear of Ezekwunna and the entire community. He just pretended to hate Angelina before Ezekwunna.

Ezekwunna went into his hut, brought a jar of raffia palm wine and two calabash cups. He cleared his voice, filled a cup and poured it in libation to the *Urashi* Deity and said, "May you avenge the death of the python on Angelina."

Agodi mumbled but did not say "*Iseee*" as tradition requires, and Ezekwunna did not notice Agodi's silence. He gave Agodi a cup of the wine, which he guzzled while still worrying about the incident and the killer. When Ezekwunna had finished drinking, he told Agodi that he should mobilize at least thirty masquerades: ten *Mgbadike*, ten *Oku Ekwe* and ten *Achikwu*.

Agodi was instructed to lead these masquerades to Angelina's house very early the next morning and to have her and her children arrested. Ezekwunna warned Agodi, "Do not create a scene: be gentle on her because she is a widow, or else her dead husband will strike you dead! Do not talk to her in any foul language, she is a widow, do not force her children to follow you, they are fatherless; if you break any of these rules, their father could kill you. Take them gently to the police station and report the matter to the superintendent in charge on behalf of the *Igwe* of Umuocha. I am heading towards the palace to brief the *Igwe*. They should be locked up pending the completion of investigation by the combined team of the *Nze-na-ozo*, and perhaps the state police officers. The masquerades should not enter Angelina's gate with whips or they may go blind, remember she is a widow and her children, fatherless. I will instruct Ekene to go to Titus, her brother-in-law, and inform him officially of this criminal action of Angelina, his late brother's wife. You know that Titus is a next of kin of the late Polycarp. We have to follow every cultural prescription in treating this matter.

"Our hands are tied because she is a widow and we are operating under the more powerful laws of the country that may not have much regard to our customs. Remember, the *Igwe* is a notable lawyer both in this country and in England, a Senior Advocate and a Queen's Counsel in England. He told the throng that gathered at the scene where the python was killed that the offender is presumed innocent until proven guilty by a competent court. I have washed my hands of any misdemeanour you and your masquerades might commit at Angelina's house. May *Urashi* be my witness."

Agodi left the grove with a resolve to be gentle on his son's teacher and her children. He assembled all the masquerades as instructed by Ezekwunna and the next morning headed towards the house of Polycarp.

* * *

As Ekene got to Titus's house, Titus was returning from tapping palm wine. When he saw Ekene running towards his house, he stopped, and in fear of what message the errand boy of the Chief priest of *Urashi* Deity might be coming with, said, trembling, "I am dead oo, what have I and my household done to merit this visit of the son of the gods this morning?" As he trembled, the calabash full of palm wine he was carrying slipped from his hands, fell on the rough ground and broke in pieces, and the wine splashed all around. "I said that I am finished, what a bad omen and a message from this calabash," he muttered to himself.

As Ekene came near him, he greeted Ekene with shaky hands and voice. Ekene recognized he was afraid and said, "Are you not a real man, do not pass urine on your shorts before your children.

There is evil in your brother's house. Angelina killed the python on the road and the gods are angry with her." As Ekene ended his message and turned to go, Titus broke down in tears, ran to his house, informed his wife and headed toward the house of Ikenga, his adviser.

As he went, he wailed at the top of his voice, "This Ngali daughter has killed us oo! This Angelina from Ngali has killed Akpu village! This Angelina from Ngali village has destroyed the Ibe family! She killed that python oo and the gods are after Ibe family!"

Everyone who heard his voice that morning ran out of the house or farm to see who was wailing, even children who were going to school joined the crowd and within a few hours, almost the entire Akpu village had surrounded Angelina's house where she was with her children. They were threatening to burn down the house and kill the widow and her children. Some people actually came with containers of kerosene and matchboxes.

A man named Ike*chi*, a native doctor and a wise man, saved the situation. He called the overzealous young men to order and told them, "If you kill the widow and her children, the calamity it will bring to this village will far outstrip the evil that the killing of the python will bring on us."

This statement saved the situation before the masquerades finally arrived. On sighting the *Oku Ekwe* and the *Achikwu* masquerades everyone took to their heels and ran away because these two categories of masquerades are rarely seen in the daylight, they only come out in the night. It is said that the last time they came out in the daylight was at the coronation of the late *Igwe* about forty-eight years ago. Moreover, young unmarried women are not allowed to look at them except by mistake.

Agodi, the leader of the masquerade cult knocked at Angelina's gate several times before she opened the house door, came out and headed towards the gate. Before this the entire household had held their hands together praying fervently for God to take control of the situation and see them through the expected barrage of persecution that would probably ensue if it were discovered that Angelina had killed the python.

Angelina had told her children, “My spirit is very strong and my faith is unwavering because I know the God in whom I believe.” She quoted Psalm 91 to them, “He that dwelleth in the secret place of the Most High shall abide under the shadow of the almighty … He is my refuge and my fortress … Surely he will deliver thee from the … noisome pestilence. He shall cover thee with his feathers and under his wings shalt thou trust … Thou shalt not be afraid for the terror by night; nor for the arrow that flieth by day.”

She also read out Psalm 23 to them, “The Lord is my shepherd; I shall not want … Yea, though I walk through the valley of the shadow of death, I will fear no evil; for thou art with me.” They all echoed “Amen!” She laid her hands on each of her children and proclaimed other promises of God in the bible that deal with divine protection and provision. She read to them from Isaiah chapter 41: “So do not fear, for I am with you; do not be dismayed for I am your God. I will strengthen you and help you… Do not be afraid, O worm Jacob, O Little Israel, for I myself will help you.”

Her prayers rejuvenated the family and the children made commitments to support their mother through her ordeal. Amaka also made a commitment, which made her mother laugh as she wondered what the little girl could do. She said, “My girl, pray for me, God honours little kids.”

They stood up and sang Ifeoma’s favourite song, “When peace like a river attendeth my way”. They were mid-way into this song when Agodi, the leader of the masquerade cult, knocked on the gate and Angelina went out of the house towards the entrance gate.

As she opened the gate, she saw Agodi Ndukwe, a middle-aged man with great strength and height. She looked around and saw so many masquerades, some facing her and others behind her. Ndukwe had instructed the *Oku Ekwe* and *Achikwu* to go to the back of the widow's house while the *Mgbadike* should face her house, because he did not want the *Oku Ekwe* and *Achikwu* to attract evil spirits on the house.

"Welcome Sir," Angelina greeted Agodi politely.

"Thank you, teacher Angelina Ibe," Agodi said.

"Who are you and can I help you?" Angelina asked Agodi.

"My name is Agodi Ndukwe from Akpana village, the leader of masquerades in the entire Umuocha community."

"Are you the father of Okwudili Ndukwe in class five at the Community Secondary School?" Angelina asked.

"Yes, he told me you are his wonderful teacher," Agodi said.

"Oh, thanks for the compliments." Angelina replied. "Now tell me why you are here with these masquerades?"

Agodi answered, "We are here on the instruction of Ezekwunna, the *Urashi* high priest, to arrest you and your children and take you to the police cell on behalf of the *Igwe* to be prosecuted for your alleged killing of the python near your house some days ago."

"That is interesting, you have come to arrest 'a mere woman' as you men normally say with these masquerades. Are we armed that you have come with this army of masquerades? Yes, I killed the python and I do not deny it. Nobody has asked me who did it. So, why the crowd of masquerades? The wisest thing to have done would have been to invite me to the police station for a chat and let me explain my actions to the authority, rather than wasting your precious time with your cult members this morning on this mission. This is like killing a fly with a sledge hammer," Angelina concluded.

Agodi felt sorry for the widow. He admired her while she spoke confidently and fearlessly. "Other women would have melted away on sighting the masquerades but not this educated woman," Agodi murmured as he turned to the lead *Mgbadike* and told them to retreat ten steps.

Angelina heard Agodi's murmur and told him, "Listen sir, it

is not education, but the Holy Spirit that gives me boldness." She politely excused herself to enable her to prepare with her children for the journey to the police station, which was about two and half kilometres from her house. Angelina and her children emerged after about twenty minutes clut*chi*ng their bibles. As Amaka and Ifeoma saw the masquerades, they ran back to their house crying for fear of those "dreaded beasts" as they called them. Angelina couldn't persuade her daughters to come out of the house. When he noticed what had happened Agodi ordered the masquerades to move about two hundred metres away from the house.

Obinna informed his sisters that the masquerades had gone far ahead of them. Ifeoma and Amaka opened the door and came out with tears on their cheeks. Agodi then escorted them to the police station amid the shouts of the young and the aged who lined the road heaping curses on Angelina and her children. Some people threw sand at her and an old woman ran out of the bush and spat at her. Angelina lifted her hands and glorified God saying, "Lord, I thank you for counting me worthy of suffering this shame in your name." Agodi held the woman, called on two *Mgbadike* masquerades and they promptly arrested her and took her along to the police station.

A fiery looking man ran towards Obinna with a machete with the intention of beheading him. His mother, on seeing the man shouted, "Jesus!" The shout drew Agodi's attention and he ran towards the advancing attacker, wrestled him to the ground and disarmed him. The masquerades came to arrest him, but he escaped into a nearby bush. Agodi and Angelina both became agitated by these incidents and Agodi motioned the *Mgbadike* to form a shield around them. This prevented further incidents and they were taken safely to the police station.

The state police officers received them and gave Angelina a notebook to enter her statement and that of her children. She did this, and passed the notebook to Agodi who did the same on behalf of Umuocha community. Agodi thanked Angelina for her cooperation and confidence and whispered to her that he was on her side. This surprised Angelina, and he told her that he could not work against Okwudili's best teacher. Angelina laughed and sent greetings to her student, Okwudili.

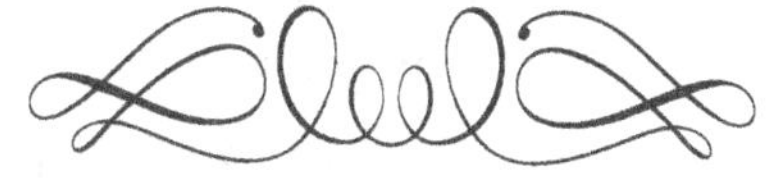

CHAPTER FIVE

My In-law, My Enemy

Back at Ikenga's house, Titus was rolling on the ground, crying and calling on his ancestors to help him out of the mess Angelina had put him and the entire Ibe family into. His crying attracted both the young and old folks. Some joined him in weeping while others consoled him by telling him to thank the gods who had revealed the criminal's identity.

Ikenga looked from his window and was full of indignation for Titus. His fury was a result of the attention Titus was attracting to his house that morning. He did not initially want to come out of his house to meet with Titus whom he felt should have come into his house and explained matters to him like a man. After about thirty minutes of wat*chi*ng this drama Ikenga decided to come out to confront Titus. He tied his traditional wrapper, put on his *Ozo* red cap with two eagle feathers and held a British staff, which he had bought in Liverpool when he visited the port city in 1955. He was bare bodied and frowned at the crowd. As he stood on the pavement of his home entrance, he ordered everyone out of his courtyard except Titus.

As the Traditional Prime Minister and the most senior *Ozo* next to the *Igwe*, Ikenga was highly revered and honoured by his people. In obedience, everyone left the courtyard, leaving a fearful Titus to his fate as he sat on the sandy courtyard with his legs folded. He looked very miserable and confused.

Chioma came out of her room and went to Titus and said, "It's a pity, Mazi Titus, get up and come inside."

Ikenga, who was still standing on the pavement, shouted at Chioma: "Leave that fool alone, he has no respect for tradition. You do not tell the deaf that war has commenced. When he is tired, he will get up. Our ancestors said, 'you do not advise a wise person to come out of the sun.' If Titus is wise he will come out before the sun rises on him."

On hearing this, Titus stood on his feet and followed Chioma who was now shedding some tears in sympathy with her father's friend. Ikenga went to the parlour and sat on his cane chair. Titus and Chioma followed him, and they sat down on separate seats opposite Ikenga. For some time Ikenga focused his embittered looks on Titus who turned his face away as they both remained speechless for quite a while.

Ikenga suddenly turned to Chioma and barked, "Get up from there, you girl! What have you come to hear or see where men are seated? Go to the kitchen, that is where you truly belong. Let today be the last day I will entertain this insult from you, toothless woman." Before he could end his last sentence, Chioma had dashed out of her seat into her room. Ikenga had beaten her once when she acted in a similar manner during the visit of another *Ozo* titled man and then revealed a secret that Ikenga and the *Ozo* man had discussed to her mother. Since that incident, Ikenga never gave her nor her siblings any chance of being around him whenever anyone visited.

After chasing out Chioma, Ikenga turned to Titus and screamed: "Now look at my face, you bush animal named Titus, or should I say a woman in a man's garb!" Ikenga looked up, shook his head in regret and again turned to Titus, "I am very disappointed in you," Ikenga said, pointing his finger at Titus. He went down memory lane: "In 1968, during the Nigeria/Biafra war, when we in Biafra lacked fighting personnel we were compelled to start conscription and I was in the Conscription Council commissioned by the then Head of state of the Republic of Biafra.

"I led a team to Umuocha to display my patriotism and that I loved Biafra not minding that this was my own community. Some of your mates came out and enlisted voluntarily while some of you ran away into the forest." As if his words were not having enough impact on Titus, he went closer to him and continued his verbal assault: "Titus, I remember you were one of those cowards who ran from the conscripting officers. While some agile boys dashed into the bush and escaped, you were running like a leprous woman and could not escape. The soldiers caught you and flogged you thoroughly while you cried like the fool you have remained until today.

"It was I who came to your rescue and pleaded that they should let you go. I lied to the officers that you were in fact a hermaphrodite and not a real boy. Your type could endanger others' lives, because when you hear the noise of shelling you could jump up to cry and call *nnem oo! nnam oo!* Many of your type were executed by their commanders when they displayed this womanish character. I wish you had been one of them, rather than continuing to live as a dreg among men, you are an insult to manhood and an everlasting fool! If slavery was still practised, you would be sold as a slave to foreign lands.

"You came to my house to show both the young and the old that, after all, a forty-nine-year-old man can cry. You came to embarrass me. When did my house become the weeping ground of Akpu village? Or did someone die in my house and I am not aware, and you came to herald the unfortunate incident?"

"Mazi Ikenga…" Titus interrupted.

"Shut up, you man-woman, do not interrupt an *Ozo* when he is talking. I am a real man and those who interrupt *Ozo* do not become *Ozo* themselves. Our forefathers said, 'He who respects the king becomes king one day'" an angry Ikenga advised.

"I am sorry." Titus said.

Ikenga shook his head in disappointment and continued his verbal assault on Titus: "Titus, 'the fool did not know when judgment was passed even though he was a part of the panel.' This is the saying of our forefathers," he said. He shook his head again, cleared his voice and continued. "The gods killed your enemy and instead of being happy that your enemy is dead, you are rather mourning the death of your enemy!"

Titus giggled at this and became more attentive.

Ikenga said, "A fool's prayer was answered by the gods, but he thought a problem was created for him. Now, hear me. Have you considered that Angelina and her children should die so you can take their lands? This has been your wish for a long time! Now your wishes are materialising and you are regretting it. How ignorant are you?"

Titus wiped his face with his handkerchief like one waking up from sleep. He nodded his head in agreement with Ikenga. "You are right," he said.

"I am right and you have been wrong," Ikenga replied, and continued, "Now go and report her to the *Umuada* and to the *Alutaradi*. Incite them and let them excommunicate her in all their dealings. This will put more pressure on Angelina and make her isolated. Do you know that on the morning she killed the python, she went for morning cry, defying her widowhood and mourning duration for Polycarp your brother. These are issues against her. She even called all of us *Osu*."

"What? I have not heard this abomination before now. She is a devil!" Titus exclaimed.

"Continue your pressure on her. Do not give her rest until she relinquishes that land to you. You have me as your backer and I will not fail. You alone will fail yourself. Finally, when she is out of the police cell, if anyone will risk bailing her, go to her and verbally threaten and intimidate her. A word is enough for the wise, but too many words make the fool more foolish. If you are a good pounder, pound inside the mortar, or pound on your feet if you are a bad pounder. I have exhausted my wisdom," Ikenga concluded.

These words of Ikenga resuscitated a dejected Titus. He stood up and bowed in submission, and said, "I have disappointed you so many times, but I will no longer disappoint. I have heard all you advised me, not even Solomon in the bible had this kind of wisdom, Mazi Ikenga."

"Stop teasing me, my friend. Go now and do all I told you and report back to me," Ikenga told him. Titus thanked him again and left Ikenga's house. Ikenga did not believe in the ability of Titus to make adequate use of this opportunity to deal with Angelina.

* * *

After a day in police cell with her children, Angelina was released on recognition as a responsible citizen with no prior criminal records and because of she was a widow. She went home with her children, a very happy family. She told them this was a step one victory from the Lord and admonished them not to relent in their prayers and faith.

The next morning, the members of Angelina's local church, The Word Pentecostal Ministry, led by Pastor Eke came on a visit of solidarity to Angelina's house. Her church members were few and most of the members were ordinary folks who had no voice in the affairs of the community. Some of them belonged to the *Osu* caste and had found solace in the open arms of the evangelical Christian believers. Most people in Umuocha hated and derided them as *Ndi uka akwa*. These church members used to cry while praying, a sign of penitence and grief for their wrongdoing. They also wept during intercession for the land of Umuocha.

Angelina was the most educated of its members and was the

Church Secretary and also served as an assistant pastor. She was a role model for other lowly members who would go to her for counselling and moral support. She was often derided by other graduate teachers for being too classless, that she had lost every sense of reasoning with regard to her achievements at Suka University. Perhaps, the most annoying part was her association with *Osu* in her Church whom she had so embraced that some slept overnight in her house, a trend that started when Polycarp was alive. She always insisted that before God there is no segregation and that the real *Osu* is that man or woman who does not believe in Jesus Christ, a view that was often frowned on by her listeners.

On the occasion of her church's solidarity visit, Pastor Eke read Psalm 34:19, "Many are the afflictions of the righteous, but the Lord delivereth him out of them all." He prayed with the small group of church members that visited Angelina and promised her the members' support in prayers. He also pledged financial support and informed Angelina of the members' preparedness to work on her farms free of charge as an encouragement to her.

Angelina was humbled by this show of love. She prayed that the Lord would bless them. She told them that persecution is just a sharpener to her faith. She read to them from St Paul's second letter to Timothy, 3: 12: "In fact, everyone who wants to live a godly life in Christ Jesus will be persecuted." She assured them that for every dose of persecution God will grant those who believe in Him matchless grace to stand up to it. They sang her daughter's favourite song, which had become her anthem since the death of her husband, and then the church members departed.

* * *

In the evening, Titus came to see Angelina and her children. He was very drunk. He arrived Angelina's gate on his rusty Raleigh bicycle, and dismounted but could not stand properly because of his drunken state. He staggered to the gate of his late older brother and, instead of knocking on the gate as was customary, he started addressing the gate as if it were a human being. "Hello why are you closed? Open! I say open now or I will pull you down! Idiotic gate, Angelina's ally. I will report the two of you to the *Igwe* and will send Angelina back to her Ngali people, away from our village." He staggered and murmured some indecipherable words and started calling on Obinna as if he had just realised his folly, "Where is Obinna the son of Polycarp! Come and open this gate or I will pull it down and beat up your recalcitrant mother, that python killer."

When Angelina heard the shout of someone outside the gate, she motioned to Obinna and Amaka who were arguing as siblings do to keep silent for a moment to enable her decipher whose voice it was. Amaka was the first to recognize it was her uncle's voice and wanted to run out to open the gate, but her mother stopped her when she observed the rage with which Titus was talking to the gate. Amaka was fond of her uncle because he used to buy char-grilled goat meat and sugar cane for her whenever he sold bags of ripe palm fruits, and on some occasions, she had spent her holidays in Titus's house.

Angelina decided to respond to the shouts of her brother-in-law. She greeted him, "Good evening Titus, you are welcome. I will open the gate in a few seconds, just let me get the key."

Titus responded, "I do not need any of those sweet tongues from you. If at the count of seven you have not opened this gate I will destroy it and you can make any trouble you may wish to … animal woman like you."

Angelina maintained her poise, but was beginning to wonder what could have gone wrong with Titus whom she had never quarrelled with since she married his brother, Polycarp, more than twenty years ago. Though the insults being rained on her and her children were becoming unbearable, she did not reply to the insults. She recited Isaiah 53:7, "He was oppressed and afflicted, yet he did not open his mouth; he was led like a lamb to the slaughter, and as a sheep before her shearers is silent, so he did not open his mouth." She found strength from this scripture and remained calm.

She opened the gate and smiled at Titus, and then she said, "Where is dear in-law coming from? You look so great this evening and must have brought some wonderful gifts to your beloved, Amaka. Please come in, the rest of the children are around and Amaka has been telling us that she wanted to come and spend the weekend with you and your family."

Titus did not utter a word as Angelina spoke. He was not interested in what Angelina was saying concerning Amaka. He had other things in mind. Titus followed Angelina into the living room where her three children were seated, agitated by their uncle's unusual quarrelsomeness outside the gate.

On seeing Titus, Amaka jumped up, grabbed him, and went straight for his handbag, expecting something good, but she found nothing that evening. Amaka, in her usual inquisitiveness demanded to know why her uncle had not bought her roasted meat. Titus smiled at Amaka and said, "My daughter, it is bad conditions that make crayfish bend."

Amaka did not understand this proverb. She became angry and withdrew herself from her uncle.

Titus tried to persuade her to expect something good from him next week, but Amaka did not want to hear that. "I have explained to you, Amaka, that if the crayfish had enjoyed pleasant conditions rather than passing through the fire it would not have bent. What I mean is that the economy of our nation is in a bad condition and that is why I am unable to buy anything for you at the moment."

"Amaka, that is okay, try and understand what Uncle Titus is saying," Angelina tried to persuade her daughter, but Titus who had not yet recovered from his drunkenness yelled at Angelina.

"Hey woman from Ngali village, just allow me and my brother's daughter to parley. Though you are her mother, you are from a different village and family, but I and Amaka are legitimate children of Ibe from Akpu village."

This differentiation amused Angelina and she chose to keep quiet while Obinna and Ifeoma watched speechless as Titus teased Amaka with various traditional names in order to make her happy. Finally, Amaka yielded. Titus was very happy and called her his late mother's name. Titus believed that Amaka was the reincarnation of his mother. It was this belief that explained the affinity between Titus and Amaka. This did not go well with Angelina who protested and told Titus to stop calling Amaka her grandmother's name, as her Christian faith did not believe in reincarnation.

Titus told Angelina that she was intoxicated with religious new wine, telling her she had gone mad because of too much reading of the bible.

Amaka, who was now leaning on Titus, on hearing him mention intoxication, replied to her uncle, "Uncle, if mommy is intoxicated with religious new wine, then you are intoxicated with palm wine."

Angelina nodded quietly in agreement with her daughter, but did not say a word.

Titus answered, "Amaka, I suspect your mother told you to say this to me. That is an insult."

"I did not insult you, uncle. I smelled palm wine since you entered this house" Amaka said.

The boldness Amaka displayed touched Titus and he bent his head down as if regretting his drunkenness. After a few minutes, he pulled Amaka closer to him and said, "If you were not my late mother's reincarnation I would have punished you with some lashes of cane." Amaka laughed, but the mention of reincarnation still did not go well with Angelina. She chose to keep silent in order not to escalate an already edgy situation.

Angelina's mind raced on so many issues concerning her family and the stand Titus had taken since the death of her husband. She remembered all the sacrifices Polycarp had made to establish Titus in various trades, which he mismanaged. She also remembered that her late husband had sponsored Titus's marriage and paid all the customary charges as demanded by his in-laws. It was a little over a month since Polycarp's funeral and Titus was visiting them for the first time with shouts of threat and intimidation.

Angelina could not hold back her emotions and she ran inside her room. She wept and cried to God for peace and the grace to love her brother-in-law who had neglected them since her husband's death. In all these tribulations, what almost broke Angelina's heart was the land case Titus initiated against her and Obinna a few days after the killing of the python. She thought, "Why didn't Titus raise this land issue while Polycarp lived? Why raise it now with me while I am under this burden of widowhood?" Angelina prayed, "O Lord God of grace, forgive Titus and touch his heart to repent and seek your face. Do not let him die in his sins; he is a precious soul that you made. Command the light of your word into his heart and turn him away from darkness. In Jesus' name I have prayed, Amen."

She wiped her tears, took her towel, which she dipped in water, rinsed it, wiped her face, and went back to the sitting room. Titus had fallen asleep and was snoring loudly after waiting for some minutes for Angelina to return. Amaka, who was leaning on him, had also fallen asleep, leaving Obinna and Ifeoma gazing at each other wondering what Titus's visit will eventually result in.

On seeing a sleeping and snoring Titus, Angelina decided to wake him by gently tapping his shoulder. She also called on Amaka with a loud voice and they both woke up, with Titus complaining, "Who is that fool disturbing my God-given sleep?"

Angelina did not reply to this insult, but simply said, "God bless you." Titus went to sleep again, this time snoring even louder.

Amaka was given a cup of water to wash her face to drive away sleep. She cleaned up her face outside the parlour, came in again and found Titus still sleeping. Amaka, who could say or do anything to Titus and get away with it, put her mouth to Titus's ear and screamed, "Uncle, wake up!"

Titus jumped and said, "Hey, my child, what have I done that Angelina your mother sent you to act mischievously?" He yawned several times and said, "Ifeoma, go get me a cup of water to wash my handsome face."

Ifeoma ran and got a cup of water for Titus. Trembling, she stretched out her hand to give Titus the cup of water. Titus was enraged and he barked at her, "I know where you got this bad character, it is from Ngali village, your mother's village. A good girl from Akpu village will kneel down or squat to give her uncle a cup of water; but look at you standing up and saying 'take'. It is from your mother's blood that you got this trait". Angelina and Obinna maintained a dignified silence.

Titus refused the water from Ifeoma and Amaka collected the water for him. He looked at Amaka, smiled and took the cup from her, then went outside to wash his face. After washing and wiping his face with a handkerchief, he asked Obinna and Ifeoma to excuse them. He said, "Amaka, remain here as my witness, because as my mother's reincarnation, you will be my witness to what I am going to tell Angelina today."

So Obinna and Ifeoma left the parlour and went to their rooms, leaving Angelina, Titus and Amaka, with no idea of what would come next. Titus cleared his voice and, for the first time in over twenty years called Angelina, "Angie." Angelina was surprised that Titus called her by her pet name, knowing that Titus had become more of an adversary in recent times. It raised her expectation for more surprises.

Titus was regaining his senses as his intoxication was fast fading. He stood up and walked round the sitting room. He looked up on the wall, which was decorated with several family pictures of Polycarp, his wife and children. He stopped at one of these portraits, which showed Polycarp standing in the middle, holding Angelina with his left hand, and Titus with his right hand.

He called Amaka's attention to it and Amaka asked him, "Uncle, you look so young in that picture, when was it taken?"

Titus laughed and said, "Amaka, do not ask because the answer is older than you are."

Amaka asked what that meant. Titus replied, "You were not yet born when this picture was taken but indeed you were around in the form of my mother, who was your grandmother. In actual fact, Amaka, you are older than the answer and not the other way round," Titus said.

Angelina frowned and reminded Titus that she and her family, as Christians, do not believe in reincarnation. She therefore ordered Amaka out of the parlour, but Titus resisted her. He said, "You, Angelina, have no right to order my mother, Amaka, out of this parlour. She is the mother of Polycarp, your husband, and therefore has more rights in this house and in the Ibe family in general than you have. That you are her mother does not nullify the fact that she is the reincarnation of your mother-in-law."

Amaka nodded in support of her uncle. Angelina, who did not want a direct confrontation with Titus on any issue, swallowed her words and allowed Amaka to remain with them. Titus climbed on a stool and took the portrait down. Angelina asked why he had taken the picture down.

Titus said, "I will explain later why I did what I have done. Do not count five when we are still at one or two. We count five after we have counted three and four. Okay?" He looked at Angelina straight in the eye and said to her, "You are a shame to the Ibe family and I have come to give you options with which to continue to remain in the Ibe family or pack your bags and go back to Ngali village where you came from."

Angelina smiled and said, "May I know those options, Mazi Titus?"

Titus adjusted his chair and said, "Number one, that land at *Ukpaka*nyi is no longer Obinna's alone. It has to be shared equally among us, the children of Ibe. It is too big for Obinna. Number two, in order to maintain the status quo in the first point I raised about the land, you must now become my wife as our custom allows."

"What!" Angelina exclaimed.

"Allow me to die before you bury me" (i.e. allow me to complete my statement before you speak), Titus told Angelina, who bent her head down and shed a few drops of tears.

Titus continued, "Angelina, I thought you know the bible very well, the book of Second Leviticus says..."

"Uncle there is nothing like the book of Second Leviticus. It is only one book of Leviticus," Amaka corrected Titus.

Titus said, "Yes, that is why I insisted that Amaka, no my mother, should be around in order to correct me when I err and also to be my witness in this just mission I have embarked on. Now, back to the issue. The book of Leviticus, as Amaka corrected me, says, when a man dies, his closest relation can help him raise more sons that will inherit his vast land like that land at *Ukpakanyi*. Angie, you know that that land is more than one hundred hectares and it will be too large for only Obinna to inherit. With me, you can have more sons who will join Obinna to inherit that land. Alternatively, you can keep yourself from me, keep only Obinna, but lose that land to me. I have concluded." He took the portrait and said, "Polycarp handed you over to me the day we took this picture, but you did not know it. Amaka you are my witness, I want you to have other brothers but your mother seems not to understand."

Amaka nodded in support of her uncle and said, "Mommy, I want to have more brothers who will play with me, go to the stream with me and fetch firewood with me."

Angelina ignored her daughter's ignorance and blinked at her. She took her handkerchief, wiped away her tears and said, "Titus, I do not blame you. Probably, you think that you are mocking a helpless widow. Let me tell you that if God did not put me in this situation, you would not have come into my house to talk to me like this." Her voice started to crack and she wept aloud. Her cries attracted the attention of Ifeoma and Obinna, who ran into the parlour from their bedrooms.

On seeing them, Angelina quickly cleaned herself up and said, "Go back to your rooms, all is well." Obinna left, but Ifeoma stayed. Angelina looked at her daughter who was dewy-eyed, smiled at her and said, "Ify, with God, it is well." Ifeoma knew something had gone wrong in the discussion between her mother and the uncle. She left the parlour but continued sobbing in her room.

Titus said, "I can see how your soldiers responded with dispatch when they heard your cry."

"Listen," Angelina interrupted, "My soldiers are heavenly hosts and they are invisible. They are greater than those with you and your advisers in this village. I warn you to desist from all your evil plans concerning that land. That is my husband's birthright, legally bequeathed to him by his late father, which he passed on to his only son, Obinna. Now you want to break order and take away what is not yours. My God, my soldiers and I will not allow you to a*chi*eve your paro*chi*al interest. I assure you that you will fail. Maybe you are the modern day Ahab, I do not care, all I know is that God will fight my battles for me and my family. The Lord said in Exodus chapter 14 verse 14, "'The Lord will fight for you; you need only to be still.'"

She put down her bible, stood up and said, "Lord Jesus I claim this promise from your word. Help me to hold my peace and be still in the face of this adversity." Amaka said "Amen." Titus looked at Amaka and frowned at her.

Angelina continued, "You quote the bible you do not know

in order to fulfil your lust for a widow. The bible says in Exodus 22:22-24," she picked up her bible again and opened to that passage and read aloud, "Do not take advantage of a widow or an orphan. If you do and they cry out to me, I will certainly hear their cry. My anger will be aroused, and I will kill you with the sword; your wives will become widows and your children fatherless.' Did you hear that warning, Mazi Titus Ibe? Your stand is not against me but against God almighty. I read the summons sent to me by the *Igwe*'s secretary and very soon I will reply to that summons and Obinna will also reply to his. You may have advisers among the *Igwe*'s cabinet and you may even have supporters among the *Umuada* and the *Alutaradi*. I do not care. One with God is a majority. Let me sound a note of warning to you, my body is the temple of the Holy Spirit and cannot be defiled by a nonentity like you,"

"Are you cursing me?" Titus asked Angelina.

"I am not cursing you, but I admonish you to look for your level. I knew your father, Mazi Ibe, my caring father-in-law. He was a gentleman who wanted you to be a reputable person. You chose to be useless in this village and refused his offer of sound education. You rejected it and preferred wine tapping and drinking, and today you want to defile me, a daughter of God and a notable graduate of Suka University. I pray you have a change of heart from your wickedness."

Titus got up and shouted at Angelina, "Sit down you common and ordinary woman! Who gave you the audacity to talk to me, Mazi Titus Ibe, like this? Are you the only woman university graduate from Umuocha? You may be educated, but I am a man and can marry so many of your types if I wish."

"That is daydreaming, a clear case of delusion, Mazi Titus. You cannot marry even a deaf and dumb Angelina. This issue is not just about education. It is about my rights as a woman. I may be an ordinary woman, as you said, but I am a human being, I have dignity and should be accorded some respect. You cannot buy my dignity even if you owned the whole of Umuocha community," Angelina responded. "You want to dispossess my son of his legitimate God-given right. Tell me in the history of Umuocha where such evil is recorded. You want to set an evil precedent and hence attract calamity on yourself and your children."

Titus interrupted her, "Wait, wait, so you know the history and culture of Umuocha, and yet you do not know that I have the right to inherit you from my late brother, Polycarp, a position even supported by your bible."

"That is what I said earlier, your knowledge of the bible is so corrupt that it starts and ends within your lust," Angelina said. "You cannot inherit me. I am not a property for inheritance, I am a heritage of the Lord and my body is not for a drunk like you."

Titus shook his head, pointing his finger at Angelina, and yelled, "You go on insulting me!"

"I do not insult you, our fathers said, 'when a man behaves like a rat, pussy cat pursues him,'" Angelina said.

"Yes that is insult number five. You are now Mrs. Pussycat, while I am Mazi Rat. You are pursuing me. Have you seen where you reduced me to and where you exalted yourself?"

Noticing that his subtle advances to Angelina have failed, Titus then thought he could exploit Angelina's killing of the python for his personal interest.

He looked her in the eyes and said: "Now hear me, you called me your enemy and now a rat. Your adversity is just beginning. You had the guts to kill the python on the road; you had the guts to leave the house three weeks after the death of your husband; you refused to have your hair completely shaven when your husband died and you refused to wear black attire and other mourning ornaments when my brother Polycarp died. Angelina, you have confronted men and the gods of this land, but you will not come out unscathed. You must submit to me, or I will send you out of Ibe's family and take care of my brother's three children, and you will be the loser in the end. I assure you that this house will be too hot for you that you will run out in the daytime naked. Our ancestors said, 'a green horn should not challenge a deft warrior to a fight for the sake of his life,'" Titus warned Angelina.

Angelina had listened attentively to Titus and after Titus had spoken, she replied, "I am proud to have killed the python and my refusal to obey all your funeral rites is not because I hated my husband, but I reflected my love for him and what he stood for in his lifetime. He fought against those anachronistic customs with vigour and I have to continue from where he stopped. I am not satisfied with reading history, but I want to make history. Let it be on record that in my lifetime I fought against python-worship and liberated the women of this community from male chauvinism. I went out to preach not because I disregarded Poly, but because he would have prepared me for that mission that morning if he was still alive."

"Now, I can see that you are unrepentant and not yielding to my demands. So whatever you see from the *Igwe*, the *Umuada* and *Alutaradi*, do not blame me," Titus said.

Angelina replied, "Go and muster them, I am ready to face them through the grace of God. For I can do all things through Jesus Christ who strengthens me."

Titus told her "Let your strength be ready." He removed a sleeping Amaka from his laps and left with both rage and some fear.

Titus was afraid because he thought Angelina might reveal his demands. Instead of going back to his house, he rode on his bicycle to the house of Gladys, his sister and the leader of the *Umuada* in Akpu village. On getting near the gate of Gladys' house, he noticed it was locked. He jumped down from his bicycle and headed towards the gate, not noticing that Jack, Gladys' ferocious watchdog, was lurking in the corner of the fence waiting for intruders.

As Titus made for the key of the gate, Jack jumped out of his hiding place, began to bark and advanced fiercely towards Titus. Titus called, "Gladys! daughter of Ibe, come and save your brother oo!"

The dog's barking and Titus's shouting immediately woke Gladys from her nap. She had fallen asleep on the bench on the balcony of her house after a tiring day at her farm. She recognized her brother's voice and shouted her dog's name, commanding him to stop barking. Instantly the dog stopped and retreated from Titus. As Gladys opened the gate, she saw a fear-stricken Titus and her dog almost at his leg, wagging its tail and lapping its tongue right and left.

A panting Titus was furious at his sister. He screamed at her: "Gladys, I have warned you several times to sell this your 'second husband' called 'Jack' and you won't take my advice. You do not even care to take it to the dispensary for anti-rabies vaccinations. You women are so stubborn! You are the same, the only difference is that you bear different names. It is the stubbornness of Polycarp's wife that nearly made this dog bite me this evening."

Gladys pleaded for pardon on behalf of her dog. "Come into the house, my brother, and let us talk, for the night will soon fall. I wouldn't want you to be going about in the night." Gladys said. She hurried into her kitchen and brought roasted yam and palm oil mixed with sliced and salted *ukpaka* (fermented oil bean seed). She knew the type of food that Titus liked.

When Titus saw it, he said, "Now I forgive you and your dog. You are a true daughter of Ibe. Where is your husband, my in-law?"

"He travelled to Onitsha for a conference," Gladys said. Titus was not happy because he had come to report Angelina to Gladys and her husband. He sat down and asked for palm wine. Gladys refused and warned him never to ask for any form of alcohol in her house.

Titus laughed and said, "It is as if you have also become 'born-again' like Angelina, our late brother's wife, that you now condemn alcoholic drinks?" Gladys did not reply.

Titus called his sister's attention and said, "The toad does not run at noontime in vain. There must be something pursuing it. This is the saying of our fathers. Angelina is that something chasing after me and I have run to your house as the *Isi Ada* in our family. If Angelina is stronger than I am, she cannot be stronger than you and the entire *umuada* in Akpu village who you lead in both war and peace times. Now it is war time in your father's house and you have to act fast."

Gladys interrupted him and said, "Go straight to the point, I do not want you to leave my house late, there are dangers on the road and your bicycle does not have lights."

"Now hear me, Angelina killed a python, she left her home three weeks after Poly's death to preach the gospel in the village square, she refused to shave her head during Poly's funeral, and she did not put on the compulsory mourning apparel. I expected you to take immediate action against her as the first daughter of Ibe, but your silence is a great disappointment to me. Our ancestors said concerning a situation such as this, 'The drum sounds twice for the warrior, either in life, or in death'. You are that warrior and you must act now!" Titus looked at his sister expecting a harsh and prompt condemnation of Angelina's deeds.

Gladys once again welcomed him and thanked him for coming to her house to discuss the worrisome situation in her father's family. After a moment of silence, she advised Titus to go back home and look after their late elder brother's family: "Remember that Angelina and her children are your own flesh and blood and let nothing on earth generate hate in our family. Angelina may have made some mistakes due to her faith but never put any pressure on her. Remember she is a widow and the God of heaven will protect her and her children. I repeat, do not stress her. We are great friends and I hope to meet her on those issues you have put before me. I will come with our younger sisters, Rita and Nkolika.

When the three of us speak to her, I believe she will retrace some of her steps."

Titus was not satisfied with Gladys' friendly disposition towards Angelina. He knew how friendly Angelina and Gladys were; he thought their friendliness would affect Gladys' judgment of the unfolding event. He got up from his seat, nodded his head and said, "One person cannot be greater than the whole family or the whole village. The earlier you, the *Umuada*, deals with Angelina, the better for us in the Ibe family." He dashed out of the house without saying goodbye to his sister, reversed his bicycle and headed home.

It is important to note that before Polycarp's death, Gladys and Angelina had been the best of friends. Their friendship started long before Polycarp married Angelina. In fact, it was Gladys who recommended her best childhood friend and secondary school classmate to her brother for marriage.

Angelina and Gladys were age mates and attended St. Anna's Catholic Convent School in Umudara town with the intention of becoming Reverend Sisters. After their convent days, they gained admission in the same year to the Suka University where Gladys studied Business Administration and Angelina majored in Agricultural Science. Gladys had always had a soft spot for Angelina. Not even Angelina's deeper religious convictions, which she experienced during their third year at the university was able to weaken her love for Angelina. They loved and respected one another deeply. Since the marriage of Angelina to her brother, Gladys had never called her by her name, but called her "My Wife" while Angelina called her "My Husband" according to Igbo tradition and the Umuocha community in particular. The friendship between Angelina and Gladys will be tested by the unfolding events. The following day after her meeting with Titus, Gladys invited her sisters, Rita and Nkolika for a meeting at her house to discuss family matters of urgent importance.

* * *

Although Gladys, Rita and Nkolika are sisters, they were not best of friends. While Gladys and Nkolika had cordial relationship, Rita always antagonised the two. The unfriendly relationship between the Ibe sisters became very apparent during this trying period.

The roots of the siblings' unfriendliness go back many years before the recent crisis. Rita was not as educated as Gladys and Nkolika, but was very beautiful. She is the tallest of Ibe's daughters, slim and fair in complexion. As recognition of her beauty, local women named Rita, "*Ada Bekee*," when she was a child. Rita knew she was a beautiful girl from childhood and often bragged about it. Incidentally, for some inexplicable reasons, she became pregnant when she was sixteen and had a baby by her teenage boyfriend. Rita and her boyfriend were high school students. After the pregnancy, she did not continue with her education. She had always looked at her older sister, Gladys, and Angelina with envy, and sometimes this envy led to aggression. She had never liked Polycarp and his wife, whom she felt had abandoned her after her teenage pregnancy, and her hatred for them increased because they had converted to the new brand of evangelical Christianity.

Rita and Titus were the best of friends and had never hidden their dislike for Angelina, their sister in law. They had once accused her of misleading their brother, Polycarp, into the "Weeping Church," a derisive phrase used to describe evangelical churches in Umuocha. The events that had happened to Angelina since the death of Polycarp had therefore provided Rita with the opportunity to vent her anger on her brother's widow. When the news of the killing of the python came to her, she had gone to Gladys and promptly demanded that Angelina be sent out of the Ibe family in order to avert the wrath of the gods. Gladys never subscribed to this idea. She also took the case to their youngest sister Nkolika in her husband's home.

Nkolika contrasted with Rita in different ways. Nkolika was the youngest of Ibe's children and, like Gladys, was a university graduate. She owed her education largely to Polycarp and his wife Angelina, who trained her and loved her for her humility and chastity. Unlike Rita, she was very obedient and deeply religious. She loved God and was a committed member of Angelina's Church, The Word Pentecostal Ministry.

Rita could not gain Nkolika's support in her move to eject Angelina from her home. She insulted Nkolika and went home very angry. Rita supported the idea of dispossessing Angelina and Obinna of their land at *Ukpaka*nyi and was the only person in the Ibe family that Titus informed of his plans.

Nkolika and Rita arrived Gladys' home very early the next day from their respective homes. Rita frowned and did not greet her older sister as custom required, and when Nkolika greeted Rita, she shu*nne*d and winked at her.

Nkolika, noticing Rita's mood, said to her, "My sister, I do not have any issues against you, so why are you keeping malice with me? This is against the word of God."

"Please keep that your God out of this. We have come to discuss how to punish that evil Angelina and not to talk about God this early morning," Rita countered.

Nkolika told Rita, "You must be born-again or you are heading to hell."

This angered Rita and she stood up and grabbed Nkolika by her hair and said, "If it were not for the sake of our late parents I would kill you and send you to hell first before coming to meet you there."

Gladys rushed and separated them. She looked at Rita furiously, pointed her finger at her and said, "Rita, our people say, 'He, who excludes himself from entering a car, should not say he was denied a seat in the car'. Stop acting differently, stop alienating yourself from us. Be careful, Rita! If you continue in this manner, you will alienate yourself from us, your family. Stop this aggressiveness and learn to tolerate other people. If you fail to heed this advice, I will charge you to the *Umuada* court where you will be fined and punished severely for disrespectful behaviour.".

The threat of fine and punishment frightened Rita who did not have any good source of income. Continuing, Gladys demanded, "Now, apologise to Nkolika for removing her headgear during your scuffle." Rita refused and accused Gladys of being partial. She pointed her finger at Nkolika and said, "Why should I apologize to this last born? She is the one who should apologize to me because I am her older sister! Rita looked contemptuously at Nkolika, winked at her and said: "Nkolika, Our mother used to say that, 'When a child is separated in a fight, he hungers for more fights not knowing that fights can lead to his death"

Nkolika smiled and told them, "I have become a different person since the Spirit of God took over my life." She went to Rita, knelt down and apologized to her. Nkolika's action touched Gladys and she said, "Indeed, Rita needs to be born-again!"

"You need it more than me," Rita replied her. Everyone remained silent, and after about five minutes, Gladys broke the silence.

She said, "*Umuada* Ibe, you know all the controversy at our late brother's home since he died." Rita and Nkolika nodded. "What are we going to do about it?"

Rita raised her hand, "We must flush out that evil woman called Angelina from our family."

Nkolika said, "Sister Angie is not evil. She is only facing persecution that is common to any heaven minded child of God. I suggest we meet her and encourage her financially and morally for the battles ahead."

This did not go well with Rita and she asked, "Support her for what? According to our ancestors, 'When the head disturbs the wasps it suffers a sting'. Angelina's head has disturbed the wasp, it must suffer a sting!"

Nkolika said, "I do not support your views at all."

Rita winked at her, shifted her seat and said, "I do not need your support. If the two of you fail to back my position, and if Gladys blocks it at Akpu *Umuada* village level, I will go on to the Umuocha *Umuada* level and get that evil woman out of the Ibe family."

Gladys motioned to Rita and said, "Our people have a proverb: 'when a woman is being scandalized, her husband's name is not immune from that scandal'. We are Angelina's husbands, our father's name is being scandalized, after all, she is Angelina Ibe and we are the daughters of Ibe. Our ancestors said that, 'It is the relations of the naked mad man on the street who are ashamed, not the mad man'. Angelina may not really know the implication of what she did, but we know and we have to protect our father's name and not escalate the already volatile situation."

Rita stood up and said, "*Tufiakwa*, I cannot support a widow who has not completed her mourning rites and has defied the gods. Let me tell you, people, that python was Polycarp that came out to protest Angelina's stupidity and instead of running away in fear she lifted her hand against the spirit of Polycarp. She killed Polycarp on the morning she went for her morning cry. Angelina is a daughter of Umuocha, she was born and raised in this community and so she understands all our customs. Why must we protect her?"

Nkolika said, "God forbid, my brother Polycarp could not have been that evil python and my dear Angie is not a husband killer."

This angered Rita, but she did not utter a word, she was waiting for the final word from Gladys.

Gladys thanked them for coming. She told them to come back in four days' time and accompany her to Angelina's house for a discussion with her and her children. She warned Rita to drop her aggressive stance, as she would not tolerate any insult to Angelina when they meet. She reminded Rita that Angelina was a widow.

* * *

On the fourth day, Rita and Nkolika arrived Gladys' house in a friendlier mood than the last time they met. They exchanged pleasantries and asked about their husbands and kids. Gladys was happy at this rapport between her siblings. She ushered them into her parlour and went into her bedroom to prepare for their meeting with Angelina.

Gladys came out of her room gracefully dressed in her Suka University alumni branded vest and matching fez cap. When Nkolika saw the vest and fez cap, she stood up and greeted her older sister in the Suka tradition. Both sisters were graduates of the famed University, although they had studied at different times, and they reminisced on the quality of education their alma mater delivered. They discussed the current state of education in the country, the low funding of research and reduced grants to universities and the effect on university education in Nigeria.

Nkolika, who had only graduated six years earlier, lamented how standards had fallen. Gladys laughed at her and jokingly told her that she was a 'half-baked graduate'. She said, "All of you that graduated from ten or twelve years ago are half-baked graduates."

This did not go well with Nkolika and she said, "Why not start from eighteen years ago when you graduated?"

"No, there was still sanity when we were there and that was when Suka produced great minds like Angie and her like. But as soon as we left, the campus fell apart," Gladys said.

"Please, enough of this nonsense talk," Rita interrupted the duo angrily. She never liked discussions of education, school or university because she was poorly educated as she did not complete her high school. Her fury also stemmed from the mention of Angelina as a great mind.

Rita continued, "Just explain who a great mind is, the one who insults the community in the name of religion, the elders and her husband in the name of education, and our customs in the name of enlightenment. I want to know what qualifies Angelina, that idiot, as a great mind."

Gladys answered and said, "Listen to me Rita, your problem is two-pronged."

"Mention my problems," Rita challenged Gladys.

"I will do so now," Gladys answered. "Number one, your major problem is jealousy, number two is illiteracy."

Rita laughed, lifted her legs and clapped her hands as some of the local women usually did when they spoke derisively of anyone. She nodded her head, looked at Gladys and said, "Look at yourselves, so-called graduates, and compare your looks with mine." She stood up from her chair and did catwalk for about four meters like a beauty model on a fashion parade. "Even as a mother of six children, I can still win the Miss World Beauty Contest. Look at yourselves, shameless graduates and ugly women." She sat down, crossed her legs and looked the other way.

Nkolika wanted to reply but was prevented by Gladys who did not want an already tense situation to escalate. She got up and said, "I thank you Rita for insulting us your sisters, it shows how mature you are. I will swallow all these insults but let me warn you, never dare repeat any of these words before Angie and her children. If you dare her, you dare me and that will spell danger for you because I will sue you at *Umuada* Akpu village and the larger *Umuada* Umuocha for insulting your older sister. You know what the penalty is."

This threat quietened Rita and she did not reply to Gladys but murmured, "Until I set my eyes on Angelina…"

Nkolika remained calm and said, "May God have mercy on Rita and touch her life for good."

Gladys called her last child, Emeka, and informed him that she and her sisters were going to their paternal home to discuss an important issue. She gave Emeka, a football lover, the leather ball she had confiscated when she noticed that the game was taking a toll on his class work. She advised him to fetch pasture for the domestic goats and firewood for the evening meal. Emeka was happy his mom was going out and felt relieved. He asked for money from his aunts, but only Nkolika obliged. Rita said, "Emeka, I am a poor illiterate village woman. Collect money from your rich mother and rich aunty, Nkolika." Emeka did not understand why Rita was so prickly.

"My son, do not mind her, she is joking," Gladys said, not wanting Emeka to be involved in their quarrel.

They left Emeka at home and he locked the gate after them. As they walked to their paternal home, Rita was left alone while Gladys and Nkolika discussed national and international issues. Nkolika had graduated in International Relations and Economics, and lectured "government" at the State College of Education and Economics. When she spoke, Gladys was proud of her and liked listening to her. She boasted of her grasp of contemporary issues and the flair with which Nkolika speaks the Queen's English.

Rita, however, would have preferred them to agree on a way to punish Angelina rather than discussing education and politics, which she saw as an insult to her. She kept a distance from them, singing and sometimes soliloquising.

When they got close to their paternal home, Rita stopped and called her sisters' attention to the spot where the python was killed. This did not interest either Gladys or Nkolika. They said, "We know it was here." Rita noticed their indifference, winked at them and continued walking.

She was the first to reach Angelina's gate. She picked a small stone from the ground and knocked on the gate while shouting, "Angelina! Angelina oo!!"

"That's alright Rita, you have tried, let me call that name with the respect it deserves," Gladys told her.

"Which respect? This house is Ibe's house and not your husband's compound. You do not have the right to tell me how to behave here. I repeat this is our late father's house which Polycarp inherited as his first male child," Rita said seriously.

Nkolika was not happy about the tensed atmosphere that was already building up. Whatever happened, she did not want a confrontation with Rita. She advised Rita to remember that Gladys was the *Ada ukwu* of the Ibe family while they were her younger sisters and should regard her as the head.

Rita looked at her and winked at her. Nkolika told her, "Whether you wink at me or you accept my advice, the truth cannot be changed."

* * *

As Nkolika was talking to Rita, Ifeoma and Amaka ran to the gate to see who was knocking. They were both excited to notice it was their aunties who had come to visit them that morning. "Open to us," Gladys said to Ifeoma. Ifeoma opened the gate and embraced Gladys, then she hugged Rita, and did same to Nkolika. Rita held Amaka tight: like Titus, she believed she was the reincarnation of their late mother. She refused to let Amaka go even when she wanted to greet Gladys.

"Please leave Amaka to greet the *Ada ukwu*," Nkolika told Rita.

Rita replied, "If you are *Ada nta*, I am not." She cuddled Amaka, calling her *Nnem, Nnem oo.* Ifeoma immediately ushered them into the parlour and went to call her mother, who was preparing their breakfast in the kitchen at the back of the main building.

"Mommy, aunty Gladys is here with Rita and Nkolika," Ifeoma told Angelina. She was excited at the mention of Glady's and Nkolika's names, but not Rita's. She quickly switched off the stove on which she was boiling water and ran to the parlour.

As she entered the room, Gladys and Nkolika stood up and with Angelina, they shouted, “Great Suka!” The visitors repeated “Great Suka!” Angelina responded “Great!” The trio then embraced, lifted up their hands and shouted in unison, “Great Suuukaa!!!” Then they sang the anthems of their university and Queen’s Hall, as all three women had been at the popular Queens Hall. Gladys missed a few lines of the hall anthem but Angelina ran through the verses as if she had left the hall only a few days ago.

“You are a genius, Angelina, that is why I recommended you for marriage to my brother Polycarp of blessed memory,” Gladys said.

“It is well,” Angelina told her.

Angelina looked to her left and wanted to embrace Rita who was sitting on the sofa with Amaka wat*chi*ng the three dramatise life at Suka University. Rita was not interested in what the other three were discussing; instead, she held Amaka and did not embrace her mother. Angelina acted maturely and said sarcastically, “Hmm, it’s like my body is too dirty to embrace Rita this morning.”

Nkolika said, “Angie is not dirty, even if you are, I enjoy embracing a worthy Sukite and a daughter of Zion like you.” They all laughed except Rita and all Angelina’s entreaties to Rita failed.

Gladys noticed Rita’s mood and insisted she must greet Angelina. She threatened her with expulsion and a fine from *Umuada* Akpu. It was only then that Rita reluctantly brought out her right hand to shake Angelina’s hand, while looking away.

Amaka made fun of Rita, saying, “Why are you always proud, Aunty Rita?” This drew general laughter from everyone.

Angelina was happy to have formally greeted Rita and jokingly added that “Today, I will add a few inches to my height for being permitted to greet my great in-law, Rita.” This drew another round of laughter with the exclusion of Rita.

Amaka, who was now entering the fold of her seniors, asked,

"Mommy, how many inches will you add to your height?"

"Amaka, shut up. Who invited you to this adult joke?" Angelina rebuked her daughter.

Rita countered, "Answer Amaka, how many feet will you add today?" Angelina, noticing that further discussion on this topic might degenerate into quarrels, quickly changed the subject. She asked Nkolika about her lecturing job, her husband and his banking career. Nkolika, beaming with smiles, gave satisfactory answers. Angelina was very pleased with Nkolika, especially with her faith in the Lord Jesus Christ and the boldness she exuded whenever she talked about her faith and the veracity with which she quoted the scriptures. Angelina was particularly pleased because she had led Nkolika to the knowledge of Jesus Christ when she was a teenager. She lived with Angelina and Polycarp and was a very obedient and aspiring young girl, always ready to accept corrections. As a teenager she was committed to church activities, especially Sunday school. Polycarp made sure she had a sound university education, unlike Rita, who was very obstinate and aggressive to her older siblings.

Having welcomed her early morning guests, Angelina knew why they came, but she feigned ignorance. She wanted to hear them say it. Before they could do so, she excused herself and asked for a few minutes to prepare breakfast for everyone. Gladys and Nkolika readily agreed, but Rita opposed the idea insisting she had other plans for the day. Angelina humorously said, "Now we shall vote. Those who want their breakfast prepared now should raise their hands." Gladys and Nkolika raised their hands, and Angelina raised hers, but Rita did not.

Amaka was amused, and asked, "Aunty Rita, why are you always in the minority?"

Gladys jumped at Amaka's question. She responded, "Our ancestors said, 'the voice of men is the voice of God.'"

Nkolika said, "Sister Gladys, how I wish you knew the bible.

Psalm 8 verse 2 says, 'Out of the mouth of babes and sucklings hast thou ordained strength because of thine enemies, that thou mightest still the enemy and the avenger.' So God has used a babe like Amaka to ask Rita an important question." Rita pretended that she was not part of the discussion.

Angelina shouted, "That is my Nkoli! The bible says in St Paul's letter to the Colossians, chapter 3, verse 16, 'Let the word of Christ dwell in you richly in all wisdom; teaching and admonishing one another in psalms and hymns and spiritual songs, singing with grace in your heart to the Lord."

Nkolika nodded in agreement and said to Gladys, "Please stop quoting our ancestors all the time and learn how to address issues based on the bible."

Gladys, who was a very disciplined woman and a committed Roman Catholic, did not feel slighted. She said humorously, "The two of you should take me to a bible school in order to learn how to recite these biblical verses."

"No." Nkolika said. "We did not learn them from Bible schools, but the Holy Spirit which dwells in us is the greatest teacher and if you make a decision for the Lord Jesus today and forget these traditions of men, He will also teach you in all things."

Rita was very uncomfortable and began to wonder whether they had come for a jamboree or for business. She looked at Angelina and said, "Hasten up, if you want to prepare breakfast. We must save time for other engagements."

Angelina then went to the kitchen. She came back within five minutes beaming with smiles. She said, "I have a wonderful 'mother' in my daughter, Ifeoma. While we were here debating about breakfast, she was preparing *Akamu* and *Akara* for our breakfast.

"That is great and very commendable. Ifeoma, you will marry a wonderful husband," Gladys said, and the other women echoed "Amen!"

* * *

After they had eaten their breakfast, Gladys said, "My dear Angelina, our forefathers said, 'The toad does not run in the daylight in vain.' Something must be after its life that forced it out of its abode. We have been forced out of our abodes this morning, leaving our families and businesses to be in our father's house in order to douse a flame that will consume all of us if it is not checked. Therefore, we are here to take a stand on the python killing. The act in itself is an abomination according to the tradition of our people, but this is not the time for blame. I know your religious convictions, having been your closest friend right from our days at the convent. It is also my duty to stand by you as someone who brought you to the family of Ibe, having recommended you for marriage to my late brother. We are like David and Jonathan in the bible, but I must not fail to point out that I was disappointed by your action.

"This is a crime committed by no less a person than a best friend, a sister-in-law, a classmate and a former roommate. This is the greatest test to my office as the leader of the *Umuada* in Akpu village. I really do not know how to protect you and your children before the *Umuada* Umuocha in general, the *Nze-na-ozo*, and the various age grades that have summoned me for explanations. I need your prayers because this matter is capable of attracting the wrath of the entire community or even the gods if I do not handle this matter with the wisdom and maturity it demands.

"Now, I and my sisters have decided…" She looked at Rita, who winked at her and shook her head in disagreement. Gladys continued, "We shall do our very best to give you the protection you need to the best of our ability. I do not also mind losing the position of that office in order to stand by a friend and family member in her hour of need." She burst into tears and wept loudly, lamenting the death of her older brother, Polycarp.

Her emotional outburst also moved Angelina who was close to tears while Gladys spoke, and Nkolika also wept. They cried and held hands, except Rita who was inwardly happy at the travail her enemy, Angelina, was going through.

After about ten minutes, the three wiped their tears and Gladys continued in an emotion-laden voice, "We shall support you; and may the God you have trusted since your childhood not let you down in this trial."

Nkolika said, "AMEN!"

"Do you have any contribution to make to my speech?" Gladys asked her sisters.

Nkolika raised her hand, stood up and said, "History and even the bible are full of cases of revolutions that changed the face of the world. I do not need to labour us with examples, but I am convinced that Angie is boldly making a name for herself as a heroine, whose stories, future generations shall read. She will be remembered as one who alone transformed our retrogressive cultural beliefs with the support of the bible. She will be remembered as a woman who fought the wickedness of male chauvinism and liberated the widows from the fetters of tradition. She will be remembered as the one who fought snake worship in a society that pretends to be Christian, but is actually bound by idolatry. I want to be associated with that General called Angelina. When your history is read, my name will also be mentioned as one of the few who carried your shield and amour and encouraged you to ride on in the battlefield of change."

Rita jumped up and said, "I am standing alone in this matter! I want to be remembered as the one among the many who stood against an evil woman who desecrated the custom of our land, poured contempt on our ancestors and rebelled against the gods of our land. I want to be remembered as the person who arrested evil before it germinated to grow into a mighty tree."

Gladys shouted, "Rita, shut your mouth and sit down before I give you the beating of your life." Gladys was furious. She hardly ever spoke like this. She got close to Rita and dared her to speak again and be beaten up. Rita kept silent.

Angelina pleaded with Gladys to go back to her seat and allow Rita to vent her vituperations on her. She told them that she expected such behaviour from Rita and those like her in the Umuocha community. She said, "Their persecutions will fire me up rather than discourage me. Not even the horrors of the cross could deter Jesus Christ. He did not renounce his mission on earth when He faced the cross. I have a mission, which Nkolika mentioned in her speech earlier. If I should run away for fear of Rita and her likes then I will be a coward and the punishment of Revelation chapter 21, verse 8 will catch up with me. I have put my hands on the plough: there is no going back, even if it means chasing me out of my husband's house, or worse, stoning me to death. I am ready to die with Christ, after all St. Stephen did it. God bless you for standing by me. We shall overcome."

Immediately Angelina finished her speech, Rita took her handbag, dashed out, and headed to the house of Mgbeke Okafor, a highly respected woman of substance. She was not formally educated, but was gifted with leadership skills, intelligence and wits. She was also rich through her palm oil business, which had brought her into meetings with businesspersons of all classes and government officials. She was the leader of the entire *Umuada* Umuocha, which exercised powers almost at the same level as the *Nze-na-ozo*, although they did not participate in the crowning of an *Igwe* as this responsibility was the exclusive preserve of the all-male *Nze-na-ozo*.

Meanwhile, immediately Rita left, Angelina, Nkolika and Gladys encouraged each other and affirmed their resolve to fight together irrespective of Rita's position, Titus' or any other individual.

Angelina thanked them for their visit and asked Nkolika to

pray. Nkolika opened her bag and took out a small bible. She opened it to Psalm 34 verse 19 and read, "Many are the afflictions of the righteous: but the Lord delivereth them out of them all." She also opened to the first epistle of Peter, chapter 3 verse 12, and read, "For the eyes of the Lord are over the righteous, and his ears are open unto their prayers, but the face of the Lord is against them that do evil." She led the others in singing:

What a friend we have in Jesus,
All our sins and grief to bear;
What a privilege to carry
Everything to God in prayer.

CHAPTER SIX

Trial at The Palace

On arrival at the home of Mgbeke Okafor, Rita asked one of her maids, Maria, for permission for a meeting with her. As Maria was initially reluctant, Rita asked her to inform the leader of *Umuada* Umuocha that a daughter of the community needed her attention. Maria told Rita, "Mgbeke will possibly meet you at 1 PM. "Please tell her, it is an urgent matter that drove me to her house this morning," Rita pleaded to Maria, who conceded and informed Mgbeke. Mgbeke agreed to meet with Rita at noon.

It was about midday and the titled woman was in her lounge singing a folk song to two of her several grandchildren. As a good leader, she gave utmost attention to all matters involving any daughter of Umuocha whether married within the community or outside the community.

Mgbeke quickly called another maid, Ngozi, to take the children away while she attended to Rita. She asked that Rita be ushered in to state her reason for coming. Rita was somewhat apprehensive. She knew that she ought to have brought tapioca and sliced oil bean seeds to the elderly woman as a mark of respect and tradition, but she did not have the money to buy these items and the impromptu nature of her visit did not help matters.

Rita came into the large sitting room of Mgbeke Okafor, fidgeting. It was the first time she had met the much-respected elderly woman whom the whole of Umuocha called "*Ugwumba*" (the

Pride of the land). She was wealthy and held in high esteem by the male folk, and was the only woman allowed to see the *Igwe* of the land without any prior notice. To demonstrate her importance in the community, no important decision was taken by the *Nze-na-ozo* council without her knowledge and input. If such a thing ever happened she could mobilize the entire women of the land to ask for redress.

On getting closer to the *Umuada* leader, Rita greeted her, "Good evening, *Nne anyi*."

"My daughter, be confident, it is not yet evening; it is still noontime," Mgbeke replied.

"Thank you ma. I am sorry that I missed it. It is because of the pain in my heart," Rita told her host.

"My daughter, did I hear you talk of pain in your heart?" Mgbeke asked Rita.

"Yes ma, I am in serious pain because of the impending calamity that could befall me and my father's house," Rita told Mgbeke.

Mgbeke looked at her and said, "My daughter, sit down." She also took her seat. As she was about to continue the discussion, one of Mgbeke's grandchildren, a three-year-old boy cried and entered the lounge to complain of a wrongdoing by another child. Mgbeke excused herself, took her whip and went outside to confront the offending child.

Rita shook her head as she looked round the spacious lounge with innumerable decorations and artefacts dating from pre-colonial and colonial days as well as the recent past. There were portraits of Lord Lugard, the great British explorer and colonialist who unified different parts of Nigeria into one entity in 1914. Rita had learnt about him in primary school. There were also paintings of other colonial staff, especially from the colonial Eastern Nigeria civil service. There were also military swords made in the nineteenth century, which Mgbeke's father-in-law had bought in 1906 when he visited Lagos Colony. He was part of the Native Select

Committee sent by Sir Kessington, governor of Eastern Nigeria, to study elements of indirect rule for application in Eastern Nigeria as proposed by Lord Lugard. There were also many certificates of honour, which Mgbeke and her husband had received from both within and outside the country. Of all the paintings and artefacts, Rita particularly admired the lion skulls and several elephant tusks arranged in a most impressive manner. The room, Rita thought, looked like a museum of monuments, and this made her even more intimidated.

"Sorry my daughter, these children can keep you talking for a whole day, judging and settling quarrels that you do not even find in our law courts," Mgbeke said, smiling.

Rita smiled back at her and said, "That is the beauty of being a grandma." "It is a blessing indeed. I enjoyed it once when my husband and I visited England in 1947 aboard a merchant ship. We spent between six to seven months on that journey, and when we came back, my mother-in-law had become emaciated from the worries of my children. Now these kids are here for their holidays from the city. Their parents are the ones that troubled my mother-in-law when we holidayed aboard the merchant ship in 1947. Today, their parents are holidaying in the Caribbean Islands and their kids are troubling me in the village. That is how life rolls in circles," Mgbeke said.

"Now, my daughter," Mgbeke adjusted her seat and pulled it towards Rita. "Who are you? Who are your parents? And from which village of Umuocha do you come? So many questions in one!" Mgbeke said humorously. They laughed as Rita giggled in her seat, looking towards her host. She answered, "My name is Mrs. Rita Uwakwe, the daughter of the late Ibe and Alice Ekwe, both of Akpu village."

"Hey my daughter!" Mgbeke exclaimed. "When I was young, I was a good friend of your mother. We were age mates. We used to go to the stream together and we did our initiation into adulthood the same day at the Eke market square. It was because of my friendship with your late mother that made me choose your older sister, Gladys, to be the village leader of *Umuada* in Akpu village group. She is a great thinker and a godly person too. I respect her so much and will nominate her as the General Secretary of the entire *Umuada* Umuocha community next August Meeting."

Rita did not like all these encomiums heaped on her older sister whom she disliked because of her closeness to Angelina. However, she feigned approval, smiled and nodded twice.

"Now tell me why you are here in Ajalla village to meet with me." Mgbeke requested.

Rita cleared her voice and said, "*Nne*, he whose house is on fire does not hunt for rats." Mgbeke nodded in agreement. Rita continued, "I know you must have heard how the evil woman, my late brother's wife, Angelina, killed a python on the morning she broke our mourning code while returning from her early morning sermon." Mgbeke nodded, and Rita continued.

"Now, I am here to report that she should be brought to the palace of the *Igwe* to explain to all and sundry why she decided to be an outlaw. Secondly, I am here to dissociate myself from any wrath that might befall the Ibe family, especially on her supporters within our family. Thirdly, it is unfortunate that my older sister whom you love so much is Angelina's supporter..."

Mgbeke screamed, "Are you sure of what you are saying?"

"I am very sure. They have formed an evil alliance to support a python killer who dared the gods of our land. *Nne*, I am done with my complaint," Rita concluded.

Mgbeke bent her head, and shook her head in utter disappointment with Gladys but she still had some doubts over Rita's allegation. She remained speechless for about a minute and then called her secretary, a female employee who had newly obtained a certificate in shorthand and stenography. The secretary came in with a piece of paper and pen. Mgbeke told her to sit down and draft a letter to Gladys, the head of *Umuada* in Akpu village, about what was happening in her father's family. After addressing the secretary, she read out the letter as follows:

From Mgbeke Okafor,
The pride of Umuocha.
22nd of Feb. 81.
Dear Gladys,

Your Actions

May I know your position on the abominations perpetrated by your sister-in-law, Angelina. Your clarification is needed urgently before her arraignment at the Igwe's palace on the 5th of March.

Thank you, good daughter of Umuocha.

The secretary folded the letter, put it in an envelope and handed it to Rita but she refused to deliver it. She requested that one of Mgbeke's maids be sent to deliver the letter to Gladys. Rita stood up, greeted Mgbeke by kneeling on the ground and asked to go.

Mgbeke obliged and led her to the second gate from where a security guard led her out of the large compound. Rita was fulfilled. She beat her chest and said, "Our fathers said, 'All heads are equal is only in words.' They also said, 'A green horn should not challenge a deft warrior for the sake of his life.'" She smiled and continued her soliloquy, "Go and tell Angelina and her cohorts that our heads are not equal and that I am a deft warrior. They should not challenge me for the sake of their lives." She smiled as though someone had amused her.

* * *

From Mgbeke's house, Rita headed towards Titus's house to brief him on the developments. When she reached Titus' house, she was told by his son that Titus had gone to the farm, and so she decided to go to the farm to brief him.

When Rita arrived, Titus shouted, "Ibe's only true daughter is here! The gods of this land have replaced Gladys with Rita. You are the only woman from my mother's womb who is not intimidated by Angelina's so-called educational achievements. Gladys and Nkolika are cowards!"

Rita smiled and said, "Leave them to their foolishness."

Rita then briefed Titus on their mission to Angelina and how her two sisters sold out to Angelina's wiles and how she withstood them. Rita also told him about her mission to Ajalla village to inform the "The Pride of the Land" on Angelina's evil deeds and Gladys' position.

After about an hour of discussion, Titus was pleased with Rita. He gave her a cup of palm wine, for which she thanked him and then drank it. She also encouraged Titus to keep up the pressure for the land at *Ukpaka*nyi. "It must be taken away from Angelina and Obinna," Rita stressed. She cautioned him to work closely with Ikenga to perfect all strategies on the land issue, while she worked with the *Umuada* and the *Alutaradi* to deal with Angelina. Titus agreed, thanked her for her concern for her father's house and bade her farewell.

* * *

Meanwhile, Mgbeke's maid, Maria, had just arrived at the home of Gladys with the letter from Mgbeke. Gladys' son, Emeka, ushered Maria into the sitting room. Gladys came into her parlour and recognized Maria as one of Mgbeke's maids.

"Good day," Maria greeted her.

"Good day, wonderful lady, you are welcome from *Nne*'s house, I guess?" Gladys smiled at her.

"Yes you are right, she sent me with this letter," Maria answered, handing the letter to Gladys.

Gladys knew something was in the offing but exercised poise. She unfolded the letter, read it, refolded it and remained silent. After a few seconds, she told her guest to sit down. She took her seat and Gladys relaxed the tense atmosphere and became very informal with Maria. She asked Maria so many questions and teased her about her dress, her boyfriend, and so on. She wanted to play on the lady's mind to get to the root of the letter. After a long time of friendly chat with Maria, Gladys said, "Now that we are such great friends, I hope you know that friends do not lie to one another." Maria nodded in affirmation, but did not know why Gladys said that.

Gladys then said to her, "Tell me all you know about this letter."

Maria opened up and revealed all that she knew about Rita's visit and what she had heard them discuss, the praise that Mgbeke had showered on Gladys and all that Rita had gossiped about her. Gladys thanked Maria and asked for few more minutes to reply to the letter. Gladys was annoyed with Rita but did not show it.

She picked up a pen and a ruled sheet of paper and wrote.

From Gladys
Akpu village.
22nd Feb. 01

To: the Pride of the Land

Dear Nne,

May you live longer than your ancestors. On your letter, I choose to stand on the truth and with the poor widow of my late brother Polycarp. I shall be glad to stand before the whole community of Umuocha on the 5th of March 1981 to make this position known to all and sundry. If the office of the leader of Umuada in Akpu village is the price, I wish to vacate it because I have a living conscience. Once again, may you live longer than your ancestors.

She folded the letter, put it in an envelope, sealed it and gave it to Maria.

* * *

As the date of Angelina's trial drew near there were elaborate preparations at the palace. The *Nze-na-ozo* council had asked Ezekwunna, the Chief priest, to list all the materials for the funeral rites of the python to be presented to Angelina when she stood trial. In addition, the Palace secretary had informed Agodi Ndukwe to m*obi*lize at least seventy-five Oku-Ekwe and *Achikwu* masquerades and one hundred *Mgbadi*ke masquerades to maintain peace.

The *Umuada* were also mobilized to appear at the *Igwe*'s palace in their various uniforms and to sit according to their various villages – seven villages in all. The *Igwe* had directed the secretary to invite the state police force to be present to complement the masquerades with the maintenance of order. The secretary argued that it was purely a customary matter and that the state police had no hand in it, but the *Igwe* insisted and overruled the secretary. He then drafted a letter inviting the Superintendent-in-charge with his men to come as observers and help to contain a possible outbreak of lawlessness.

The secretary drafted a summons to Angelina to appear at the *Igwe*'s palace as follows:

The secretary of the Igwe*-in-council*
25th Feb. '81

To: Angelina Ibe (Mrs.)
Akpu village.

Woman:

You have been summoned by the people and the gods of Umuocha to appear before the Igwe, the Nze-na-ozo, Umuada, Alutaradi, etc., to explain to all and sundry your actions against our cherished traditions. You must be seated by 11 AM. Your trial will commence at 12.30 PM

Do not fail. Date is 5th March 1981.

Ifeoma received the letter from one of the palace guards and handed it over to her mother. She knew what the likely content would be. Angelina refused to open it before her children. She took the letter and her children to her church, The Word Pentecostal Ministry. She requested the pastor to be present before she could open the letter. The pastor, Reverend Eke, and Elder Chukwuka were holding a meeting in the parsonage to iron out some church issues.

After their meeting, Pastor Eke and Elder Chukwuka then entered the church auditorium, a small wooden hall with asbestos roofing and a well-decorated altar bearing an inscription from St Paul's letter to the Hebrews, chapter 10 verse 38: "The Just Shall Live by Faith". Elder Chukwuka was first to see Angelina and her children seated quietly in the front row. He did not like their mood and decided to raise their spirits. He shouted, "Praise the Lord!" and the hitherto quiet hall came alive with the responses of "Hallelujah!" from the pastor, Angelina and her children.

Pastor Eke asked, "Sister Angie, what is the matter?"

Angelina in her characteristic faith manner replied, "It is well." The Pastor said, "May it ever be well with your soul." The children echoed "Amen."

Angelina brought out the letter of summons, handed it over to the pastor and said, "Man of God, this is a letter written to me by the *Igwe*, his council and the entire land of Umuocha to appear before them to defend my action of killing of the python. As one under authority, I have come to you, my spiritual father, to open this letter. Read it and let us pray about it and cancel any evil imprint and wickedness against my family and me."

The pastor took the letter from Angelina, and looked at Ifeoma, who was a chorister in the church. Seeing that she looked shaken, the pastor said, "Ify, cheer up, it is well with your soul. The devil has no right to steal your joy and peace, for the joy of the Lord is your strength." He opened the letter and said, "I present this piece of writing to you, dear Lord, and no pronouncement made against the family of Polycarp Ibe shall stand in Jesus' name." He quoted from the book of Numbers, chapter 23 verse 23, "There is no sorcery against Jacob, no divination against Israel. It will now be said of Jacob and of Israel, 'see what God has done!'"

He read aloud the letter from the palace secretary to Angelina in which she was summoned by "the people and the gods of Umuocha" to appear at an open trial on the 5th of March, a few days from now. The pastor laughed and enjoined the others to laugh and make a caricature of the devil. They all laughed except Ifeoma and Amaka. Angelina also laughed and jumped up as if she had just won the jackpot. The Pastor commended Angelina's resilience in the face of trial. Pastor Eke admonished the children to be strong and to encourage their mother in times like this. He then called on Elder Chukwuka to lead them in prayer.

Elder Chukwuka was a member of the *Mmiri* Cult and had been a diabolical individual prior to his conversion. According to his story of conversion, his diabolical powers failed him when he went to an evangelical crusade ground one night to nullify the powers of a well-known evangelist who came to the Umuocha playground to hold a deliverance crusade. He became very committed to proselytising among his former cult members so that some people now referred to him as Apostle Paul, in testimony to his complete turnaround lifestyle. He belonged to several traditional groups and was about to qualify for membership of *Nze-na-ozo* before his conversion.

He had become an asset to the church in Umuocha and was the leader of the prayer group of The Word Pentecostal Ministry.

When the Pastor called him up to pray for Angelina and the family, he got up from his seat looking very sober as usual. He picked up his New International Version of the bible, his usual companion. Chukwuka requested the letter of summons and it was given to him. He read it again, now silently, and then he began speaking a mysterious indecipherable language which evangelical Christians believe is inspired by the Holy Spirit.

Chukwuka spoke in this manner for over ten minutes during which time the Pastor and Angelina also joined him in this unknown language. He was believed to have the gift of revelation. He suddenly stopped praying, and said, "Listen to me" pointing at Angelina, "the Lord says, 'This trial is for your promotion.'" They shouted "Amen." He said, "Listen woman," still pointing at Angelina, "the Lord says, 'I shall write your name with an indelible ink if you hold unto the end and a great Iroko in this town shall be won over to the Lord through your travail.'" The people shouted a louder "Amen!"

Elder Chukwuka had not yet finished. He opened the bible to the book of Isaiah chapter 37, verses 14-20. He told Angelina and her family that all who seek their downfall would experience remarkable disappointment. He told them the story of King Sennacherib of Assyria who threatened Hezekiah, King of Judah, with his gods and army, and how God turned the tide against the mighty Assyrian King and his nation. He assured his listeners that those who sought the life of Angelina and her children or wanted to take away their land would be like Sennacherib and his army. They echoed, "Amen!"

He read the bible passage to them in order to strengthen their faith. He placed the letter on the altar of their church and told his hearers to listen as he read from the book of Isaiah, chapter 37, :14-20: "Hezekiah received the letter from the messengers (of Sennacherib) and read it. Then he went up to the temple of the Lord and spread it out before the Lord: 'O Lord Almighty, God of

Israel, enthroned between the cherubim, you alone are God over all the kingdoms of the earth, you have made heaven and earth. Give ear, O lord and hear; open your eyes O Lord and see; listen to all the words Sennacherib has sent to insult the living God. It is true, O lord that Assyrian Kings have laid waste all these peoples and their lands. They have thrown their gods into the fire and destroyed them, for they were not gods but only wood and stone, fashioned by human hands. Now, O Lord our God, deliver us from his hand, so that all kingdoms on earth may know that you alone O Lord, are God.'" The rest of the people shouted "Amen!" in agreement.

The reading of this passage was like an awakening tonic to Ifeoma in particular. Her spirit was lifted and she raised her hands towards heaven and began praying in similarly unknown language as a few tears ran down her cheeks.

Elder Chukwuka led them in a few songs to charge their spirit in preparation for a time of prayers. They sang a few songs and a hymn and then went into a period of prayers that lasted for an hour and a half. At the end, everyone in the hall looked electrified and was beaming with smiles like soldiers just back from a very successful campaign. Only Amaka looked drowsy she had dozed off a few minutes into the prayer session.

In conclusion, Pastor Eke read Exodus chapter 14 verse 14 to them: "The Lord shall fight for you, and ye shall hold your peace." Everyone responded with a loud shout of "Amen!" The Pastor made the position of the church known to Angelina and her household: "We are solidly behind you in the morning, noontime and at night. We cannot abandon you because your action in challenging godlessness represents what we believe and preach. Do not let your heart fail you, trust in the Lord and upon his word.

"On 5th March 1981, the members of this church will be at the palace premises at a corner with our bibles as our swords. We shall be singing Christian songs when the unbelievers will be singing to glorify their gods. The ears of the Lord shall be wide open unto our praises and his eyes shall see our hearts and grant you a remarkable victory.

"Secondly, may we know any way that the members of this church can support you in your farms. I can m*obi*lize our members to work on your farms, as this trial is capable of distracting you from certain duties at home. Feel free and let us know how we can help you in times like this. God bless you all," the Pastor concluded.

"Praise the Lord!" Angelina shouted.

"Hallelujah," they responded.

Angelina beamed with smiles, her radiant looks betrayed any iota of stress. She looked more like one preparing for a Community Award of Excellence than one preparing to defend herself against allegations of crime against the community and the gods of the land. She burst into song:

He is Jehovah
He changeth not
He is Jehovah
He changeth not
He is Jehovah
I know his name

In her usual way Angelina maintained her poise all through the period of ministrations by Elder Chukwuka and Pastor Eke. In her vote of thanks, she began by thanking God for counting her worthy to bear the cross of Jesus in this case and promised never to let God and the faith down. Angelina was very knowledgeable about the bible, and drawing from several portions of the scripture, she encouraged herself, the church and her children to "Stand up for Jesus and be counted in times like this."

She quickly opened the bible to the epistle of James, chapter 1 and read verses 2-4 which say, "My brethren, count it all joy when ye fall into diverse temptations; knowing this, that the trying of your faith worketh patience. But let patience have her perfect work, that ye may be perfect and entire, wanting nothing."

Obinna, who had not said a word since arriving at the church, jumped up from his seat and told his mother, "Mommy, I am proud of you."

Angelina behaved as if she did not hear that statement and quickly turned to St Paul's second letter to Timothy, chapter 3, and read verse 12 with emphasis, "Yea, and all that will live godly in Christ Jesus shall suffer persecution."

Finally, she quoted from St Paul's first letter to the Corinthians, chapter 10 verse 13, and explained that God knew her ability beforehand that she would be able to bear the cross of the community's persecution and that is why He allowed it to come to her. She thanked the Pastor and Elder Chukwuka for their support and willingness to m*obi*lize hands to work in her farms.

She promised to identify her areas of needs before inviting the church members to help her. She liked the idea of gathering her church members to a corner in the palace on the day of her trial, but referring to Apostle Peter's reaction when he cut off the ear of one of those who came to arrest Jesus, she cautioned that "Everybody should sheath his or her sword as I wouldn't want anyone to cut my persecutor's ears." They all laughed, and she continued, "When they slap you, turn the other cheek, but if you lack the grace to turn the other cheek, please run away like a gazelle." This brought more laughter.

Angelina was not done yet. "Please tell all our members to pray and not cry for me. The Lord has assured me of victory, and a sweeping change in this community through the mouth of his children and I am emboldened by this assurance. God bless you all. Remain strong in the Lord. We shall overcome!" she concluded.

It was getting dark and the Pastor and Elder Chukwuka accompanied Angelina and her family a distance from the church exchanged good night wishes, waved to each other and continued in their opposite directions. Angelina and her children walked to their home, which was about two kilometres from the church.

* * *

On the night of 4th March, Angelina and her household, and Nkolika, who had returned to the village from the city where she lived and lectured, held a night vigil of songs of praise and prayers. It was a night the entire neighbourhood would not forget in a hurry. Starting at 11 PM on the 4th, they sang and prayed till 4 AM on the 5th of March.

Nkolika, who was a very zealous and vibrant young lady, had told them that the whole of Umuocha was like a prison yard held bound by myriad of irrelevant customs and demonic activities. She declared that they should use that night of praise to free the people of the land just as when Paul and Silas praised God in the prison as described in the Acts of the Apostles, chapter 16 verses 25-27. Nkolika emphasized: "O Lord let the prisoners of Umuocha, my community, hear us tonight and be freed from their evil ways in Jesus' name!" "Amen!", the worshippers responded.

All the members of the family participated in the vigil, even Amaka did not doze off as she normally did. At the end of the vigil Angelina told them all to go to bed and rest for about three hours. She reminded them that the summons stated that they should be at the *Igwe*'s palace by 11 AM and that the trial would commence at 12:30 PM. They all agreed and retired to their various rooms. Nkolika slept in the guest room.

* * *

Angelina woke up from her sleep around 7:45 AM but decided not to wake up anyone including Nkolika who was enjoying her rest in the guest room. She went to the kitchen and got their breakfast ready within a few minutes. At 8:25 AM she woke them all up and asked them to clean up and come to the table for breakfast.

Nkolika and Ifeoma were surprised that Angelina had done so much work in the kitchen that morning. They gathered, ate and prepared for the walk to the palace. Angelina took only her bible without her handbag as she used to do. Everyone including Amaka had their bibles. Before they left their house, Nkolika asked Obinna to pray for their journey to the palace. Obinna prayed for their safety. He remembered how his head was nearly chopped off by an attacker the day they were being taken to the police station by the masquerades. He prayed to the Lord to grant them special protection. They all agreed with him.

Nkolika, Angelina and her children arrived at the *Igwe*'s palace gate in good time at exactly 10:45 AM and were booed by the various youth age grades that had been loitering around since the early morning, chanting war and provocative songs against the killer of the python. The booing of the widow and her family attracted the attention of Agodi Ndukwe and his masquerades, who immediately swung into action to protect the widow and her family.

When Angelina saw Agodi approaching, she smiled and exchanged pleasantries with him. "How is your son?" Angelina asked Agodi.

"He is fine and doing well at home. He has been praying for you all night with his rosary," Agodi whispered to Angelina.

"Thank you," Angelina replied. Agodi then led Angelina and her family with the masquerades shielding them through the open field inside the palace to an enclosure prepared for them to stay before the trial began.

Not long after the widow's arrival, people of all walks of life started trooping into the open field within the palace. This area of the palace is larger than a normal football field. They were taking their seats in their group canopies erected by the palace servants.

In all, there were over thirty-five large tarpaulin canopies bearing inscriptions of the names of each group. The *Umuada* Umuocha had five of those canopies, while the *Alutaradi* had three.

The *Umuada* appeared in their uniforms of white lace on top with red "George" wrappers, and they wore black armbands to signify a mourning period for the python. The *Alutaradi* also came in their uniforms of blue tops and brown "George" wrappers, with the black head tie worn during mourning periods.

There were different male age grades, too numerous to mention and several musical troupes from Umuocha in attendance. In addition, Umuocha's neighbours, such as Kpulu and Kokwa communities, sent their representatives in solidarity with the Umuocha people. Ezekwunna, the Chief Priest and his seminarians came with long brooms made from palm frond to sweep Angelina and her types out of Umuocha. The seminarians went round the field making incantations and enchantments throughout the duration of the trial.

The various musical groups entertained the people before the heralded arrival of the *Igwe* and the *Nze-na-ozo* council. The long cortege of the royal majesty of Umuocha came in as soon as the field was filled to the brim with at least six thousand people.

When the traditional twenty-one trumpeters sounded their trumpets (made from elephant tusks), the echo was deafening and could be heard several miles away. The *Otimkpu* climbed a tall palm tree with an ability that baffled most of the observers, from where he announced the imminent arrival of the *Igwe* and his council.

For the next twenty-five minutes, the *Otimkpu* eulogized the *Igwe* with graceful words and called him names that could best describe an immortal being. He said, "Here comes the one man we welcome as a crowd; the shadow that protects Umuocha, the mighty iroko tree, the feeder of Umuocha whom death cannot kill, the wisdom of the world, the one who speaks and no one contradicts him, the mighty lion that protects his people, the light giver, the unchangeable one…"

As Angelina heard these names she shook her head in pain, turned to Nkolika and said, "Nkoli, there is so much to be done in our land. Did you hear those names? These names belong to the Almighty God, not to a mere mortal. I shall fight on, but if I die in the process, you must carry the sword and continue." Although Angelina sees the *Igwe* as mere mortal, in Umuocha's mythology, the *Igwe* is mystical – a representation of Chukwu (God almighty) – hence, an immortal who only ascends to the pantheon of transited ancestors.

Nkolika responded, "You shall live to be crowned when the victories are finally won."

After the *Otimkpu* had finished his eulogy there was a graveyard-like silence everywhere. The *Otigba* then began to play mystical, transcendental tunes with his *Igba*. His mastery of the drum was beautiful to see, and the young cheered him on while the elderly nodded in agreement.

It is believed that the *Otigba* communicates directly with the spirits of the ancestors. No one can interpret the drumbeats, not even the *Otigba*.

Suddenly the *Otigba* fell to his knees and raised the drumbeat to a crescendo. As the crowd joined in the frenzy of his beats with their dancing steps, he lowered the beat of the talking drum. No one knew why he did it. They supposed the gods must have directed him to do so. The beat became quieter, and then ceased completely. Unexpectedly, the *Otigba* fell onto the floor in a trance. One of his assistants rushed forward with the masquerades following behind. More masquerades thronged around him, lifted him and carried him away.

"The spirits have called him for a message," Ezekwunna whispered to one of his seminarians, who looked baffled like most of the crowd.

Otigba's assistant picked up his master's drum and resumed the tune, but he did not have the skill that earned his master the alias *Onu ndi mmuo*. As he beats on, the *Igwe*'s train of *Nze-na-ozo* from the seven villages of Umuocha danced to the tune. Behind the train of the *Nze-na-ozo* was Mgbeke Okafor, dressed all in black, also dancing with the titled male chiefs. She was the only woman allowed by tradition to join the *Igwe*'s train on such an occasion, not even the *Lolo* would join the royal train.

Immediately after Mgbeke came Ikenga, and then the secretary of *Igwe* and his council. Both of them wore red flowing traditional gowns over their green "George" wrappers. They were gorgeous to behold, especially with their well-decorated red caps, which had white eagle feathers pinned on them.

Lastly came the *Igwe* himself. The present *Igwe* does not like too many adornments. His ruling council, however, oppose his love for simplicity; they see the adornments as a display of the wealth and riches of Umuocha and the office he occupies. The *Igwe* does not feel comfortable putting on many robes especially the thick royal attire. They made him feel hot, since he had lived much of his adult life in temperate Europe. He also felt that since he now lived in the tropics he should not burden himself with heavy attire as if he was in wintery Europe. The *Igwe* had been seen on many occasions wearing a simple shirt and tie, a dress code considered an abomination by some hard-line traditionalists.

On this day, the palace secretary and Ikenga, the traditional prime minister, prevailed on the *Igwe* to put on the adornments befitting the *Igwe* institution of Umuocha. He acceded to their demands and was as well decorated as the day of his coronation. His red cap was long and pinned with several types of eagle feathers and gold chains purchased by his great-grandfathers from European slave merchants over two centuries ago. The *Igwe*'s staff, a gold-plated structure about nine feet long, was held by his *onye nche eze*, while he held his woven fan with the inscription "The glory of Umuocha". He danced the *Otigba*'s tunes awkwardly, as he was not properly schooled in dancing traditional music.

The *Igwe*'s entrance signified the formal commencement of the open court session. Everyone in the audience stood up as the *Igwe* danced to his throne, another structure well crafted with gold and silver ornaments. He took his seat amid shouts of "*Igwe* live forever oo!" As soon as he sat on his throne facing the crowd, he was greeted by twenty-one *Mkpo n'al*a (large musket shots) that shook the ground while his guards, also in a military fashion, released another twenty-one Dane Gun shots.

The Chief Priest, Ezekwunna, was invited by the Secretary to pray before this grand trial started. He took seven kola nuts representing, the seven villages of Umuocha, made some incantations, raised up the nuts, ate one, took a cup of palm wine and one kola nut, threw the nut on the ground and poured libations over it. He turned round and said some indecipherable words. He then invited the spirits of Umuocha, their gods and ancestors to come and witness the trial. The whole assembly echoed "*Iseee!*"

The secretary thanked Ezekwunna and then called on the accused widow to come out and stand before the gods and the people of Umuocha to answer to the charges against her. Agodi Ndukwe and some of the masquerades guided a radiant Angelina to the wooden dock set up for the day's open trial. As she came out, some elderly women chanted curses against her. One of them, a ninety-five-year-old woman called Mgbafor, came out with her walking stick and headed towards the dock to strike Angelina. The masquerades prevented the old woman and took her away gently. Agodi, then called in more masquerades to encircle Angelina. They came in their numbers and did as their leader instructed them.

For the first time in many days, Obinna burst into tears and cried, "God, why my mom?" His scream and tears moved Ifeoma and Amaka to weep also. Their aunt Nkolika consoled them with some quotes from the scriptures.

The secretary read out the charges. "This case is between you

Angelina Polycarp Ibe and the land of Umuocha which comprises the people, gods and our ancestors," the Secretary said, looking directly towards Angelina. "The charges are as follows:

1. That in the early morning of 27th of January 1981, you, Angelina Polycarp Ibe of Akpu village, three weeks after the death of your husband, wilfully left your house to disturb your neighbourhood with your early morning evangelism;
2. That on the 27th of January 1981, you, Angelina Polycarp Ibe of Akpu village, wilfully killed a royal python, adored as a gentle god in the land of Umuocha.

"*Igwe*, these are the charges against your subject, Mrs. Angelina Polycarp Ibe, a daughter of the land," the secretary addressed the *Igwe*. He went close to Angelina and served her with a copy of the charges. The *Igwe* stood up, greeted the people and said, "My people of Umuocha, no sitting *Igwe* prays to experience a day like this during his reign. However, it has come and the gods are not to blame.

"The charges that the secretary has read are not for the *Igwe* alone to hear and judge. As is our custom when such an issue arises, everyone gathered here, who is a freeborn of the land of Umuocha has the right to question the accused person.

"However, because of time constraints, these thousands gathered here cannot question her. Therefore, let the *umuada*, *alutaradi*, the youth age grades, market women, and the priests of our gods, make representations and bring one question each for the accused person to answer.

"Now let me sound this note of warning to all and sundry. As a trained lawyer, I emphasise the word *accused*, because our customary law does not operate in a vacuum. It is subject to the laws of our country and our legal system assumes that an accused person is innocent until he or she is proven guilty to the charges made against him or her in a competent judicial structure. Therefore, we take this setting as a competent judicial structure because our statute book recognises it, yet its judgments can be appealed in the higher courts of law in our state or the nation in general.

"Having said the foregoing let me also remind us that this woman is a widow, and as we know, in our culture it is believed that the spirit of her husband is with her. Umuocha people are noted for their civility, so let us behave in a commendable manner and not take the law into our hands to prevent the wrath of her departed husband. Once again, I greet you, the people of Umuocha. I hand over to the Secretary for further proceedings."

There was a deafening applause from the crowd. Meanwhile Angelina was busy jotting down some points as the *Igwe* spoke those intelligent words. All the representatives of the groups mentioned by the *Igwe* came up with their judgments rather than questions as the *Igwe* had requested. The *Igwe* glanced over these judgments, smiled and handed them over to the secretary. The *Igwe* stood up again and warned his subjects that hasty judgments could be preposterous, and then he asked if they would withdraw those written judgments, and submit questions as he had directed. They all refused.

The *Igwe* then said, "Since tradition bestows on me the authority to pronounce a person guilty or not guilty, I will withhold that pronouncement until I know it is right and proper to do so. Any judgment that I pronounce must be based on verifiable evidence that cannot be contradicted. He then warned certain highly placed *Nze-na-ozo* members whom he observed were the brains behind the deadlock to desist or face the wrath of the *Igwe* some day. The *Igwe*'s decision did not go well with the people, especially the group of non-conformists led by Mazi Ikenga. Ikenga left his seat, and went round the various groups to canvass for punitive measures against the widow and her family. The *Igwe* initially pretended not to have noticed his movements.

The *Igwe* insisted that he could not pronounce Angelina guilty without hearing her voice on the charges, as this would put his reputation as an erudite lawyer both at home and abroad in question. The *Igwe* gave the people one more hour to come up with questions and they bluntly refused. During this period, there was confusion everywhere.

Angelina watched as all the people quarrelled among themselves and argued over the *Igwe*'s position. The temperature had risen intensely, and she was sweating profusely under the tropical sun. She had no visible supporters: her church members, numbering fewer than forty, were sandwiched in a corner. They were attacked by a group of youth when they tuned a Christian song of praise. The attack was however quelled by the masquerades. The enraged youths warned them to remain silent or risk being lynched. Pastor Eke, being a man of wisdom, asked his members to exercise restraint and pray inwardly.

Finally, when the deadlock could not be broken, the *Igwe*, who refused to alter his position, stood up from his throne and waved for silence. The whole throng kept the noise and he threatened to invoke thunder in his ancestor's names against noisemakers. It was only then that they became quiet. He directed the Secretary to call on Angelina to address the people of Umuocha.

The Secretary then formally called on Angelina Ibe to address the Umuocha community. It was one of Angelina's finest moments. She said silently to herself, "God has turned my foes against themselves. Now God has provided me with the chance of a lifetime to preach the gospel of Christ to thousands of my people. What a great evangelical opportunity for me!"

Angelina, beaming with smiles waved to the angry crowd, bowed her head to them and told the gathering, "My people of Umuocha, I greet you in the name of Jesus Christ." There were pockets of murmuring in the crowd, however the majority of the people remained silent because no one wanted to incur the thunder the *Igwe* threatened would come on him or her.

Angelina continued, "Our world is like our great Eke market place. People of different communities come to buy or sell their wares and afterwards they go home. Some go home early while others go late, but all the sellers and buyers must return home at one time or the other. Whether or not you traded well in the Eke market is not an excuse for you to remain at the market. You must go home." When Angelina observed the rapt attention with which the crowd listened to her, she was fired up. "As those who are trading in a market setting like the Eke market, what preparations are you making for your returning home?" She opened her bible to the gospel according to St Matthew, chapter 16 verse 26, and read "What does it profit a man if he gains the whole world and loses his soul? Or what shall a man give in exchange for his soul?" She closed her bible and continued, "Our life is like the Eke market, we will go home to our maker some day. So start now to consider how you will return to your maker because you must go home one day. Now, for you to return to a better home when you leave this world, you must do one thing. Our saviour Jesus Christ said, "You must be born-again" to be able to return to the heavenly home where he has prepared mansions for us. Why not give your life to Jesus now and be a partaker of that heavenly mansion?

"We all believe there is a supreme God and it is Him who gave us his only begotten son that whomsoever believes in Him will not perish but will have everlasting life, as St John said in his gospel, chapter 3 verse 16. The name of Jesus Christ is the only name that God has given the world for its salvation. So receive Jesus now and be saved from your sins."

"You must have gone mad," Mazi Okwute interrupted her from the crowd. He stepped forward, pointing at Angelina, and said, "This is the reason our forefathers refused to train you women in school, because when you are sent to school you graduate into madness like Angelina whom her father sent to school. She came back with certificates and this brand of madness called 'Born-again.'"

The *Igwe* was furious and ordered his guards to arrest Mazi Okwute and take him to the state police and remand him in their cell for one week. They promptly apprehended him and left the arena with him.

The *Igwe* asked Angelina to summarize in one minute. She thanked the *Igwe* and concluded: "My people of Umuocha, why will you not surrender your lives to this Jesus who was given by this Supreme God we all recognize. Surrender to him and settle the issue of your home going once and for all. Decide now, for tomorrow may be too late. *Igwe*, I thank you for this opportunity and I thank my people for listening to me." Angelina masterfully avoided any mention of python and the offence she committed There was grumbling everywhere with some insinuating the *Igwe* was conspiring with Angelina. However, no one dared criticise the *Igwe* loudly. It is forbidden in Umuocha tradition.

The *Igwe* motioned the Secretary to come forward. He whispered to the Secretary that he was adjourning the trial indefinitely. The Secretary was not happy with this opportunity given to Angelina to express herself, but he had no authority to oppose the *Igwe*'s instruction. He did not look Angelina's way, for he felt disappointed by the *Igwe*'s seeming clemency. The *Igwe* mounted the rostrum, and the guards fired twenty-one Dane Gun shots. He then announced the indefinite adjournment of the trial. The *Otigba* resumed his drumming and the whole assembly echoed "*Igwe* live forever! *Igwe* live forever!" The *Igwe*'s train left the arena in reverse order with the *Igwe* and his guards in front.

The masquerades escorted Angelina and her family home. Her church members joined them, singing choruses as they went. Surprisingly, members of the Umuocha Widows Association, a suppressed group of dispossessed widows whose voices were scarcely heard, joined the church members in their singing. These widows lived in peril as their more powerful male in-laws dispossessed them of their husbands' earnings and lands and subjected them to all forms of abuses. They now saw Angelina's ordeal as a possible pathway for their emancipation.

While it has become apparent that there is now a clear division between the position of the *Igwe* and his traditional council on what Angelina did, *Nze-na-ozo* members, led by Ikenga, insisted they will not change their position on the widow. Their ruling was that Angelina should be ostracized from any form of contact with the people of Umuocha. Their strictures included that she should not come to Eke market to buy or sell, she should not go to the Iyioma or Oka streams to fetch water, she should not partake in any public function, and she should not relate with the *Umuada* or *Alutaradi*. However, they hid this decision from the *Igwe*. Ikenga feared that if the *Igwe* found out what they had decided and circulated in the community, he might strip him of all entitlements as the traditional Prime Minister, exile him and suspend other members of *Nze-na-ozo*.

CHAPTER SEVEN

Signs of The Cross

"Woman, you are just an idiot! Do not display your items close to mine. I warn you to pack up what belongs to you and leave this market before I raise the alarm. I give you the next twenty minutes to pack your stuff and leave Eke market or you will be lynched by the people of Umuocha," Nweze, Angelina's aunt, threatened her.

As Angelina looked at her aunt with surprise, Nweze continued. "You shameless lady, I doubt if my late brother was your real father. Your blood does not react like ours, you are a shame to us and your late father will be weeping right now in the land of the dead; I know that very well. We sent you to the University; you came back with good results but lost your mind there and embraced this Jesus Christ who has defaced you. Angelina, I am sure you are certainly under a spell that has made you lose every sense of good reasoning; if not, tell me why you are the only one in your age grade who is ostracized from the rest of the community, *tufiakwa, tufiakwa,*" she concluded and sat down on a chair, sobbing quietly and tears running down her face.

"Aunty, I have heard..." Angelina said inconclusively.

Nweze stood up and in fury spat on Angelina's face. Angelina bent her head, leaning on the wall facing her, and then pulled out her handkerchief to clean up the saliva. But Nweze was not done yet. She went closer to her, as though she wanted to apologise, grabbed her shirt and threatened to tear it into shreds. Angelina did not say a word. Nweze then slapped Angelina's face repeatedly, tore her gown and pushed her to the ground. Angelina was still on the floor when Nweze poured a handful of sand on her face and into her eyes. Immediately Angelina's eyes turned red and she could hardly see. This assault attracted a large crowd of people who knew the two as relations. Nweze was the younger sister of Angelina's father.

Nweze was a heavily built tall woman of about seventy years old. Her physical strength and agility bellies her old age. She was a known farmer in Umuocha, a woman of relative wealth, who with her husband, Mazi Onyekwere, owned one of the largest yam barns in Umuocha. Apart from their yam farming, Nweze was also a major trader in palm oil. The riches Nweze and her husband owned brought them much respect. Nweze was a traditionalist to the core. Although, she was a communicant in the Catholic faith, she never compromised her beliefs in ancestral worship, a sore point in her relationship with Angelina.

Nweze had travelled out of Umuocha on the day that Angelina went for her morning cry, and later that morning, killed the python. When she came back from Onitsha where she had gone to be with her youngest daughter who had a new baby, she was informed of Angelina's atrocities in her absence. Nweze wept the whole day for what she called "a family shame" that Angelina inflicted on her natal family. She vowed to deal with Angelina ruthlessly, but kept her plans close to her chest without revealing it to anyone, not even her husband Mazi Okoli.

Angelina regarded Nweze like a parent, because Nweze was the only surviving close relation of her father who had died some years earlier. They related to each other like daughter and mother until this turn of events.

On that fateful Eke market day, Angelina had gone to the open market area where Nweze rented a shed to display her food crop and sell bunches of improved variety plantain she harvested from her farm. It was Angelina's regular practice and Nweze loved seeing her niece around her. When Angelina arrived, Nweze was not at her shed, and when she came back, she saw Angelina displaying her plantain at her shed as she normally did. Nweze saw this as a great insult, and her rage could not be assuaged by Angelina's pleas.

The people that trooped to Nweze's shed did not know what had gone wrong between Nweze and her niece, Angelina. They first poured a litre of water on Angelina's head and face to help revive her. When she regained her strength and could see more clearly, she thanked them for their concern, looked at her raging aunty and then wept. Angelina cried aloud, calling "Jesus! Jesus!" Her plight made many women who had rushed to Nweze's shed weep in sympathy with Angelina. Many of them showed even greater compassion when they were told she was a widow.

As this was happening, Nweze went to collect ashes from the place where the sanitation officers burned market rubbish. She pretended to want to console Angelina, then she poured the whole container of ash on Angelina's head so that she was literally covered with ash. This action attracted attention from those around them. There was uproar and it was as if the entire market of over ten thousand sellers and buyers was to experience a kind of stampede.

People were running in different directions for safety. They shouted as they ran. Many in the market did not really know why those who were running and shouting did so. Some of those who saw the ashes blown by the harmattan wind thought a bomb had been detonated in the Eke Umuocha. The commotion in the market brought back memories of what had happened at the same Eke Umuocha market during the Nigeria-Biafra War when the Nigerian Air force bombed the Eke market. The bombing on that day claimed innumerable lives. While many people reminisced that unfortunate incident, others thought a fire had broken out in the market.

Some women, mostly widows who recognised Angelina and

her travail since killing the python, came immediately and 'smuggled' her out before Nweze could explain herself. They took her out of the market arena to a nearby bush, and got a bucket of water and soap so that she could clean herself. One of them whose house was nearby and whose daughter Angelina had taught Agricultural science four years earlier, ran to her house and got her an old blouse and skirt so that she could change her torn dress.

Angelina thanked them and prayed that none of them should experience the kind of assault she had just experienced. One of the women, a widow, advised her, "Do not to come to the Eke market again, or even go to the streams to fetch water, or go to a funeral, or to any gathering in Umuocha in order to avoid being lynched by the overzealous members of the community who have put you through this ordeal. I was told the community have ostracised you." "Really, ostracised me!" Angelina said with astonishment. She is hearing this for the second time. One of the women told her, "Please take the bush path to your house, do not let anyone see you until you arrive your home. Do not go through the main road. The sparrow said, "Since children learnt how to shoot without missing; he has learnt how to fly without perching," Please run and do not look back. I am afraid that some young men may have gone out searching for you." Angelina, once again thanked them for their kindness. She then went home unnoticed through the bush path as advised. She left behind the plantain she had gone to sell in the market. She had also lost her handbag, which contained her cherished bible, gospel tracts and the key to her house.

In the market, Nweze was very annoyed that some people had taken Angelina away. She was searching for her in the crowd that gathered around her. She raged, "Where is that accursed girl, Angelina? Come out let me tear you into shreds. She killed a python and left her home only three weeks after the death of her husband." Nweze continued to swear and curse Angelina with the names of deities in Igbo land, such as *Ibini-Ukpabi*, *Agbala* and *Kamalu*

When the crowd heard that Angelina had killed a python and left home before the expiration of her post-bereavement period, they shouted, "*Aru*!" (Abomination); some said "*Tufiakwa*!" Many of those who expressed surprised at her actions were people from neighbouring communities who were not aware of the incident in Umuocha in the past weeks. Some of them regretted that she had escaped the market alive.

Nweze told them that she had come back from Onitsha in order to teach her niece the lesson of her life and that she was partially satisfied. She said, "My only regret is that she left this market place clothed. I wanted her to leave this market like *Onugo*. That Angelina is evil and very stubborn, imagine defying the voice of the masses of this community to come to the market after we have ostracized her!"

The crowd numbering in their thousands hailed her as a great daughter of Umuocha whose love for her community surpassed her family interests. Some said that Angelina's husband whom she had dishonoured by leaving the house three weeks after his death had revenged by disgracing her in the market place. Others ascribed her market ordeal to the gods of the land who came to fight for the python on the road. They discussed this as they returned to their individual businesses.

When Angelina got home, she was very emotional as she sobbed quietly, not letting her children notice her. Her children who were expecting her to return home with some foodstuffs saw her coming back empty handed, not even with her handbag, and worst of all wearing strange clothing. Amaka did not initially recognize her mother until she came into the house.

Obinna asked, "Mommy, what happened to you?"

Angelina waved at him and tried to feign a smile, although she could hardly do that because of her sobs. She asked in a very low voice, "Where is Ifeoma?"

"Mommy, what happened to you? Please tell me," Obinna

persisted.

"It is well," Angelina could hardly complete her usual catch-phrase, before she wailed at the top of her voice, drawing Amaka and Obinna into weeping as well.

As they wept, Ifeoma came in from the church where she had gone for choir rehearsal. She could not understand why everyone was crying. She had had a nice time in church, but the mood in her home was a complete contrast. Ifeoma shouted, "Praise the Lord." Nobody responded, not even her mother.

Surprisingly, Ifeoma did not show any emotion, even though she did not know why everyone was crying. The last time she experienced that was in January when her father died. She looked at her mom, went close to her, took out her handkerchief and wiped her mother's face.

Angelina was surprised at Ifeoma's courage and poise. She did not utter a word, as she had not recovered from the shock. After about fifteen minutes of silence in the room, Obinna decided to break the silence. "Mommy, please tell us why you came back from the market in another woman's clothing, without your hand-bag and your most cherished bible? Ifeoma, did you notice that our mother is wearing another person's clothes?" Ifeoma did not answer Obinna's question.

Angelina cleared her voice, looked up to the ceiling and muttered some words of prayers, smiled at her children, and then said, "It is well with us." Only Ifeoma responded, "Amen." Angelina continued, "My children it is true that I came back without my handbag, my cherished bible and in another person's clothing…" She kept quiet for some time, overwhelmed by emotion, she used her hand to wipe the tears from her cheeks. Angelina was not often so emotional no matter how serious events might be.

"My children," she said in a broken voice, "I thank God that I came back with my life." This caught everybody's attention. She told them, "Today, I was assaulted in the open Eke market by no other than my only aunt whom I call both mama and papa. Someone who should clothe me sought to expose my nakedness, someone who should oil me poured a whole container of ash on me, and someone who should wipe away tears from my eyes has broken my heart. That is why I am weeping. She did it because I believe in Jesus and his finished work on the cross. She did it because she feels I am defenceless, she did it because according to her the people and the gods of Umuocha have ostracized me. She has rejected me, the only daughter of her older brother. On my father's deathbed, he pleaded with her to help me feel well, he told her to give me all the protection I needed in life and not abandon me to be maltreated.

"Today she has joined the world to do me evil, she has preferred a python to her only niece, and she has preferred a python to a poor widow with three children. She did not even mind the persecution and deprivation of in-laws I am facing presently." Angelina stopped suddenly, looked up, raised her hands and prayed, "Lord, I do not hate mama Nweze; help me not to hate her and please open her eyes of understanding to realize her ignorance and repent from it. You know my wish for her is that she becomes saved from those unprofitable practices that will damn her soul."

Angelina continued, "Father, have mercy on all my persecutors and tormentors in this community and beyond. Forgive them for they do not know what they are doing, give them true wisdom and direction to know your son Jesus Christ whom you sent to redeem man and set him free from unfruitful works of darkness. Heavenly father, remember the *Igwe* and his ruling council members, the *Nze-na-ozo*. As it says in St Paul's first letter to Timothy, chapter 2 verses 1 to 3, 'first of all, supplications, prayers, intercessions and giving of thanks, be made for all men; for kings and for all that are in authority; that we may lead a quiet and peaceable life in all godliness and honestly. For this is good and acceptable in the sight of God our Saviour.' My children, the Lord will hear and answer this prayer for all that are concerned."

Her children echoed "Amen."

"Listen," Angelina continued. "I have not been crying because the shame was too much to bear for the Lord Jesus. No, I have been crying because of the medium through which this shame came. After all, Jesus was not ashamed to bear the cross for us. So, why should I be ashamed to walk back home naked for the sake of the cross? He went to Calvary with boldness, though he was injured, yet he bruised the head of the serpent and came out victorious. We shall be victorious in Jesus' name."

"Amen," responded the children.

"Listen, my children," Angelina told them, as she began to recover from the assault. "Those people of God whose stories we read in Hebrews chapter eleven are real historical personalities. They suffered worse shame than I have suffered today and they have a new song after all. We shall sing a new song in Jesus' name."

"Amen," the children echoed.

Ifeoma, who had been it*chi*ng to talk, said, "Mommy listen to me, I have put on a thick skin and I am ready to die for what I believe in. As mama Nweze was beating you up at Eke market, some children were mocking me, throwing sand at me and shouting 'Daughter of python killer… hey! hey!! hey!!!' They almost mobbed me as they followed me to the village playground and stopped at the *Udara* tree. I merely smiled and continued home. I remember the message you preached in church two years ago. Mommy, do you still remember that popular sermon you preached at church that revived many weary souls?"

Angelina smiled and said, "Which of the sermons? I preached many sermons two years ago and have preached a lot since then."

Ifeoma laughed and asked Obinna, "In the light of these incidents, can you still recollect Mommy's sermon two years ago that fits into our ordeal presently?" Obinna could not remember.

Ifeoma made fun of their forgetfulness, putting them all in

suspense. "Please tell me my daughter, I am forty-eight years old and so many things are occupying my mind right now," a curious Angelina pleaded with her daughter.

"Mommy, you titled that sermon "Signs of the Cross," Ifeoma reminded her.

Angelina embraced Ifeoma and said, "That is why I call you Adannaya because you reflect my darling husband in so many ways. Though you are a girl, you are just like my husband, Poly. In his lifetime, he remembered what happened to his grandmother when he was barely four years old. It is good you reminded me of that message in times like this. Yes, in this family, right now, we are all wearing signs of the cross on our bodies. Isn't that a privilege? I guess it is." Obinna and Ifeoma nodded in agreement.

"So, you should all be prepared not only to wear signs of the cross on your bodies, but to have it embossed on your bodies if need be, since you may be attacked and wounded for the sake of the your Lord and saviour Jesus Christ."

Obinna thanked his mother and then told her, "Mom, I fear for your life, but because of your implicit faith in God, you will enjoy divine protection all the days of your life."

Amaka also complained how Chidi, her best friend, had suddenly withdrawn from her and she did not understand why. Amaka complained, "When I asked Chidi, why she no longer plays with me, she said, her daddy warned her not to play with me again because my mother committed an abomination."

Angelina laughed and said, "Even Amaka has the signs of the cross on her body, she too is persecuted for Christ's sake. Rejoice, my children! If they refuse you, do not worry, you have brethren in the church and you have me to play with."

As they were talking, Elder Chukwuka, one of their prominent church members, arrived on his motorbike and knocked on the gate. Obinna ran out and opened the gate for him. "Good evening, elder", Obinna greeted him. "Good evening" Obinna," Elder

Chukwuka responded with a reassuring smile. He rushed into the house where Angelina and her other children were seated and in his usual manner said, "Shalom! Peace, be unto this house." Angelina and Ifeoma responded in unison, "peace be unto you, welcome, elder." He sat on the couch, looked straight at Angelina and said, "The Lord says, 'It is well with you.' Do not be afraid, He is with you and will fight for you. Your aunt is just ignorant and does not understand the implications of her action. We will not report her to the state police, but we will report her to the heavenly police where she will not be bailed or appeal the case unless God decides to let her go." He stopped as Angelina and her children nodded in agreement at every pause.

Elder Chukwuka continued, "The news in this community right now is that you have been ostracized by the Umuocha community. That is a lie of the devil. We are part of Umuocha community and we have not ostracized you. Even if you lose friends, in-laws and relations in this community, you have all of them among the brethren in the church. Therefore, you do not have to fear.

"I have met the pastor about the market incident, and we have jointly decided to detail our members to visit your house regularly, to pick whatever you have for sale at the market. They will sell such items and return the proceeds to you. Do not go to the streams for water, the youth in our church have been directed to supply you with the quantity of water you need. Your children should not go to the stream alone, for their safety they should go with some of the youths in our church. They should also go to school in the company of our youths who are in the same schools as them. We are praying and believing in God for an immediate resolution of this crisis.

"I informed you the other day that God will soon write your name in the Annals of the Greats of the faith in our time. So do not give up. In fact, I envy you. Goodbye to you," Elder Chukwuka concluded. Angelina and her family greeted him back, and he stood up and left the parlour. Angelina and her children offered him some oranges from their orchard and accompanied him to their gate. Chukwuka thanked them and told them he had other errands to run for the church that evening.

The following morning, Angelina prepared and left for school. She decided not to attend the general assembly of students and teachers, which was held every morning before the commencement of classes. She walked quietly into the staff room. She took her seat, bent her head over her desk and prayed as she normally did. She brought out gospel tracts and distributed them to all the desks for other teachers to read when they came in after assembly.

She took up her lesson notes and revised a topic she would teach in the senior class, 6A, that morning. Angelina waited for about an hour and the teachers had still not come back to the staff room. She was confused about the delay in dismissing the assembly, as morning assemblies did not normally last more than 30 minutes. "Why has today's assembly taken more than the normal twenty-five to thirty minutes?" She said to herself. She then decided to go to find out.

On reaching the ground, she discovered that the assembly had been dismissed and the students were already in their classes, but surprisingly no teacher had entered the staffroom to sign on for the day and to collect his or her teaching materials.

Angelina came back to the staff room confused. She stayed for about five minutes and said, "My God what is happening to my colleagues? Where are they? This is very strange." She went out again, yet could not locate them.

"Okay, let me pick up my notes and go to the class," she said. She met a colleague on her way. The colleague is Madam Agnes, a widow from Ngali village and a senior history teacher. Agnes, looking forlorn, said to Angelina, "My sister Angie, the teachers foolishly decided to relocate to Hall B when they noticed you were in our usual staff room. They said you have been ostracized, and therefore, they will not sit in the same staff room with you."

Angelina nodded and asked, "Where have you been since the assembly ended?"

"I have been with them, but after a second thought, I decided to look for my fellow widow," Agnes answered.

"Thank God, you realized your mistake early enough. I wonder why educated people like you do not reason properly. What does a school environment have to do with community politics and traditions? What has a state owned institution to do with a damn python? When did a citadel of learning become an island of ignorance? It's a pity," Angelina lamented.

Agnes was penitent and apologized. Angelina told her that she would be very happy to have the whole staff room all to herself while the rest of them struggle for space in Hall B. She told Agnes jokingly, "Agnes, please pick up your instructional materials and follow the others." They laughed, exchanged their usual greetings and Angelina continued to class 6A for her lecture.

On getting to the door of the classroom, one of the students shouted, "She has come o!" Every student in the classroom left with the exception of three students who attended the same church as Angelina. Angelina was baffled and could not understand who was behind all this. "Is it the principal or their parents that instructed them to walk out on me?" she wondered, as she stood speechless for two minutes.

Finally, she entered the classroom. The three students stood up and greeted her, as students are required to do when a teacher enters their classroom. She called them by their names and asked, "Why didn't you leave with your peers?"

Okechukwu, the son of Elder Chukwuka, answered, "Ma, you have the knowledge we came to acquire, that is why I did not leave." Ngozi, the daughter of Brother Uwa, another church member, answered, "Madam Angie, of what value will it be to us if we left?" The last one, Chike, answered, "Even if they rejected you I will not reject you."

"God bless you all for staying behind." Angelina had her normal lecture with the three students for about forty-five minutes and then ended the class.

She was troubled and headed straight to the principal's office. The principal was seated and reading a novel when Angelina knocked on his door, "Please enter," the principal said.

"Thank you sir," Angelina replied as she opened the door and entered his office. The principal had always been fond of Angelina as a fellow alumnus of Suka University. He often called her "Mrs. First Class," because of Angelina's first class grade at the university.

On seeing Angelina, he sighed and said, "Madam Angie, sit on that chair. The Lord you serve will give you victory. You know I am not a native of this community, I am from Kokwa community and what I am seeing here is disturbing. It does not happen where I come from and I do not know how to handle it. Tell me, what do local beliefs and tradition have to do with this school? This is state government property, and funnily enough, our staff has joined in this mess. It is really a pity."

He brought out a letter written and signed by Mazi Ikenga and the palace secretary on behalf of the *Igwe* and *Nze-na-ozo*, and he gave it to Angelina to read. In fact, the *Igwe* did not authorize the letter. The secretary, with the influence of Mazi Ikenga had used his access to the palace stationery to write the letter and endorse it with the *Igwe*'s official seal. Angelina read the letter, which instructed the entire staff and students of the community to ostracize her, and if possible her children, until further notice.

Angelina pleaded with the principal to make a photocopy for her. The principal initially refused for the sake of his life but later agreed when Angelina reminded him the Suka university dictum, "All are one in the spirit of great Suka." The principal smiled and said, "What on earth can I deny a woman who set a record that has lasted unbroken for two decades at Suka Varsity."

Angelina thanked him for his compliments and explained her ordeal to him since coming to school that morning. The principal advised her to keep her cool. He told her that he would order every teacher back to the staff room and would instruct the students to remain for their Agric classes or return home on indefinite suspension.

Angelina thanked him again and left the office fulfilled. As she left the office, the theme of that sermon, "The Signs of the Cross," continued to ring in her mind. Angelina remembered telling her listeners that one of the signs of the cross is rejection by friends, family and associates.

As she arrived home after work, she saw her little daughter, Amaka, crying in the sitting room. "Amaka, what is the problem with you?" Angelina asked.

"Mommy, they called me names and also said you hated daddy, that is why you left the house and killed him as the python on the road," Amaka replied with a cracking voice.

"My daughter, do not believe the lie of our enemies. I loved your dad until death and if I will come back again to this life I will marry him the second time, okay? Now listen, I killed a python; that was not your daddy. Your daddy was a man and not a snake. Do you understand what I am explaining to you?"

Amaka answered, "Yes mom."

Angelina continued, "When they call you names, do not cry, after all they called Jesus 'Beelzebub', the prince of demons, instead of the Son of God that He is. He did not cry. At the cross, they mocked him by calling him 'king of the Jews.' They derided Him and flogged Him repeatedly. Today, He is glorified and St. Peter told us as Christ's disciples in his first epistle, chapter 2 verses 21-23, "To this you were called, because Christ suffered for you leaving you an example that you should follow in his steps. He committed no sins, and no deceit was found in his mouth. When they hurled their insults at him, he did not retaliate; when he suffered, he made no threats. Instead, he entrusted himself to him who judges justly."

Angelina then narrated her own experiences to Amaka and told her not to retaliate if she was insulted or even beaten up for no just reason.

Amaka asked her mommy, "Is that a sign of the cross also?"

"You have said it, my daughter. That is it!" Angelina exclaimed.

As they were talking, Elder Johnson's son and a fellow church member, Nduka, came into their compound with the handbag that Angelina had lost at Eke Market when her aunty Nweze assaulted her. Angelina ran out, grabbed the handbag and to her amazement, her most cherished bible and the tracts were still inside but the money was gone.

"How did you come about this bag, Nduka?" Angelina asked Elder Johnson's son with a smile on her face. The young boy explained that his dad returned from the market yesterday with the bag but because of his farm work could not send any of his children to bring the bag to her. "My daddy will explain better when you meet today at the midweek fellowship," Nduka added. Angelina burst into song and danced as the boy left. She sang with Amaka:

God is turning my mistakes into miracles
He's turning my losses into gain
Yesterday trials and today triumph
And my desert is bringing down the rain
Now I am knowing why he's turning my whole life around
His power and mercy I depend
God is turning my mistakes into miracles
He's turning my mistakes into miracles
He's turning my losses into gain.

CHAPTER EIGHT

Midnight Cry

"You are alone
You are a widow
You are single."
These, they say to me
Children *laugh at me*
Adults jeer at me
The society shuns me
The world hoots at me

No, you made me so
I told them
How could I be alone in your midst?
Are you not supposed to be my "husbands?"
Oh, how could I be "single" and "lonely?"
For I live in the midst of thousands
Are you not my parents?
Are you not my children?
Am I not human like you?

Why am I ostracized?
I breathe the same air with you
I eat the same food with you
I walk the same road with you
I dwell in God
He fellowships with me
I talk with him
I am not ostracized
I feel humans around me
I smell humans around me

You made me a widow
God loves me
I am pleasant to him
He shields me
He "marries" me
He provides for me
He cherishes and covers me
No, you made me a widow
I am not, for God has "married" me

Please let my children *live*
Do not kill them
They are humans like you
Do not heap my sins on them
Let them live, I plead
Their lives are precious to God
They are not alone
Cos' they dwell in your midst
You made them lonely

I do not hate you
Though you seek my life
I wish you well
For so did my master
He wished them well that nailed him
Children *don't laugh at me*
Adults don't jeer at me
Society don't ostracize me
I came for a change
Yes, I came for a change

Angelina said these words as she sat in her parlour and reflected on the ordeal she and her children have suffered since the morning she killed the python. The reflection was part of her preparation for the all-night prayer meeting she had pla*nne*d with Gladys and Nkolika.

It was about 10 PM with just an hour until Angelina and her family, with Gladys and Nkolika, would commence their night vigil. They wanted to pray all night to seek divine intervention in the travail Angelina was going through. Nkolika had initiated what she termed, "Ibe family all-night prayer meeting," when she heard the news of the maltreatment her sister-in-law, Angelina received from the hand of her aunt Nweze in the public glare of the Eke Market traders.

Nkolika lived in the city with her family and lectured in the state College of Education and Economics. She had several female lawyer friends and was a notable member of an advocacy group, Action For Women's Rights (AFWR), an organization that is committed to the protection of the rights of the marginalised in Nigeria, especially widows and orphans.

Nkolika had pla*nne*d to come to the village with a team of police officers from the State Criminal Investigation Department (SCID) to arrest Nweze for prosecution for assaulting Angelina at the market place. The penal code stipulates that assault is a criminal offence. If convicted, Nweze risked spending up to seven years behind bars without the option of fine. Some of Nkolika's lawyer friends advised her to also sue the *Igwe* and his council for 'social ostracism', a crime defined by the Nigerian constitution as segregation, and therefore illegal.

Nkolika could not take such a serious decision without seeking Angelina's views. She therefore wrote an elaborate letter to Angelina, explaining the need to use the ma*chi*nery of the state to seek redress against all the injustices meted out to her and her children in the community. Angelina read Nkolika's letter with interest, shared Nkolika's views with her children and her pastor, and then sent her this reply.

16/06/81

My dear Nkoli,

Grace and peace from our Lord and Saviour Jesus Christ abide with you all the days of your life. I read your elaborate letter detailing the need for us to explore state machineries to fight our enemies who have resorted to using all overt means to fight against me and my children *in this community. Thanks for your concern for our safety. We deeply appreciate it.*

My dear Nkoli, my silence over my predicament does not in any way suggest weakness or lack of knowledge of what to do to seek redress legally. I am sure you know this very well. I know that I have committed no crimes against humanity or against my community or against anyone.

I am being subjected to ridicule because my people are ignorant of what is right and acceptable both to God and to modern civilization. Take note of this. My mission to this community is to open their eyes to Christian values and modernity. Make no mistake about it; customs that have been rooted for ages may not be uprooted so easily with just a few years' effort.

Secondly, I recognize that such customs and traditions are supported by certain reactionary forces of wickedness that are bent on foiling any revolutionary move that is capable of toppling their strongholds. Mind you, no kingdom gives up its sovereignty so easily to an invader. There is usually a fight and our situation is not different.

Nkoli, using any other means to fight against a spiritual case is vanity. It may not achieve the desired result. I feel it is defeatist in effect. On the contrary, I have decided to continue warring against these forces using the fruits of the Spirit of God, which include love, patience, faith and steadfastness.

I shall continue to love my persecutors because Jesus did the same. He rebuked Peter when he slashed the ear of one of those who came to arrest him. He put back the ear that Peter chopped off from his persecutor. He had the authority to take out his persecutors using Angelic forces at his disposal as the son of the Most High God; but for His work on earth to yield the desired result, He never did this.

As St Matthew said in his gospel, chapter 9 verses 9-12, Jesus, preaching *the sermon on the mount, said, "Blessed are the peacemakers: for they shall be called the* children *of God. Blessed are they who are persecuted for righteousness' sake: for theirs is the kingdom of Heaven. Blessed are ye, when men shall revile you, and persecute you, and shall say all* manner *of evil against you falsely, for my sake. Rejoice, and be exceeding glad, for great is your reward in heaven: for so persecuted they the prophets which were before you."*

I shall continue to bear, not that it is convenient suffering ostracism. I will no longer go to the stream to fetch water or go to the market to sell my farm products for fear of being lynched. I endure because the word of God says I should keep on enduring and loving them. St Paul in his first letter to the Corinthians chapter 13, verses 4-8, writing on the mystery of love says "Love is patient, love is kind, it does not boast, it is not proud… it is not easily angered, it keeps no record of wrongs… always hopes, always perseveres. Love never fails." Nkoli, this is why I tarry with God.

Apostle Paul, writing as inspired by God in his letter to the Romans, chapter 12 verses 17-21, instructed them, "Do not repay anyone evil for evil. Be careful to do what is right in the eyes of everybody. If it is possible, as far it depends on you, live at peace with everyone. Do not take revenge, my friends, but leave room for God's wrath, for it is written: 'It is mine to avenge; I will repay says the Lord. On the contrary: If your enemy is hungry, feed him; if he is thirsty, give him something to drink. In doing this, you will heap burning coals on his head. Do not be overcome by evil, but overcome evil with good." And in chapter 13 verse 8, Paul says "Let no debt remain outstanding, except the continuing debt to love one another. For he who loves his neighbour has fulfilled the law."

I shall not cease praying for those who persecute me to repent and accept Jesus and a new way of life. Through prayers we communicate our heartbeat to God and receive on our knees what we may not be able to receive through much struggles or rancour. Through prayers we will be able to pull down strongholds, cast down imaginations and every high thing that exalts itself against the knowledge of God, bringing every thought into captivity to the obedience of Christ.

My prayer is that they be saved from their sins and idolatry. My prayer is that they should open the various institutions of our community to the cleansing power of the blood of Jesus Christ. If they refuse after my efforts then, like St Paul according to the Acts of the Apostles, chapter 20 verses 26-27, I shall be able to proclaim, "Therefore I declare to you that I am innocent of the blood of all men. For I have not hesitated to proclaim to you the whole will of God".

I exercise faith also, knowing that faith in God over every hard situation honours him and tells HIM to take over the situation. It tells God, "I am not able; you are able." Faith decreases a man, but lifts God; faith brings light and vision when a man is blind and visionless. I look forward to a brighter tomorrow, after today's crucible through the eye of faith.

Nkoli, pray that my mustard-seed-faith will grow to a giant Iroko tree, touching the skies where the winged will nest and obtain shelter and succour for their weary souls. In the words of St Paul's letter to the Ephesians, chapter 6 verse 16, pray that I be protected with the shield of faith with which to extinguish all the flaming arrows of the evil one.

My dear Nkoli, I have known you from childhood *and know that you have a great faith in the saving grace of our Lord Jesus Christ. Do not relent. I invite you home to come so we can talk about the way forward. May the Lord bless you richly until his appearing. Bye.*

Yours truly,
Angie.

After reading Angelina's letter Nkolika broke down and wept for a long time. She prayed, "God forgive me for fighting this battle with mortal weapons. I am challenged by Angie's life. She has uplifted my spirit and Lord help me to walk in her path and build in me her type of faith and love towards those that seek my downfall."

After this, Nkolika travelled home the following morning. On reaching Umuocha, she went to Gladys' home to share with her, her vision of holding an "Ibe family all-night prayer vigil" in the house of Polycarp's family. Gladys did not oppose the idea of holding the prayer meeting. She always wanted to promote peace in her paternal home. After about two hours of discussions on family and community matters, both women were ready to go to their paternal home. Gladys took her chaplet and left for their paternal home with Nkolika.

They arrived to the warm embrace of Angelina and her children. After hours of discussion on the assault in the market and incessant harassment of Angelina's children, they arrived at the conclusion that a more proactive approach was needed to battle this behaviour. Nkolika then shared her views on the all-night prayer vigil. Angelina was very happy. She said, "Nkolika, it is the same Holy Spirit that works in both of us. He had prompted me to call for this night prayer meeting in this house, but I hesitated. That is why He put it in you to initiate it, knowing you are more forceful than me."

Gladys added her support for the night prayer meeting, believing that God could do something to save the situation. At about 7 PM Ifeoma served their dinner. Angelina explained that the early dinner was to enable all to sleep briefly before the start of the all-night prayer vigil at 11 PM.

Amaka did not like the idea. She dreaded keeping awake at night and usually slept whenever they went for all night prayers in their church. Obinna and Ifeoma were used to it and were happy that it would be held in their home. After their supper, Angelina asked everyone to go to bed and have some hours of sleep in order to be awake during the night vigil. Angelina had set her electronic alarm for 10 PM when she intended to wake up and get ready for the vigil.

At exactly 10 PM, she woke up as the alarm sounded. However, she waited until 10:30 PM before waking the others. Amaka and Gladys took longer to wake up. Gladys was not used to vigils, although she attended them when it was a funeral ceremony for a dead *Umuada* member and this was usually an all-night singing and dancing event until dawn, not for prayers.

At exactly 11 PM, everyone was seated in Angelina's parlour, Nkolika lifted her hands, the rest followed her, and she started with songs of adoration. Nkolika was an excellent worship leader and one of the best in both her local and city churches. She could sing non-stop for several hours and whenever she led in worship songs there was often contriteness and godly sorrow among her fellow worshippers.

As Nkolika led in songs of worship, all the worshippers wept loudly. Some of them confessed ancestral sins, village and community sins and pleaded with God to forgive their community all manner of sins they had committed, knowingly or unknowingly. Angelina asked everybody to kneel down as the atmosphere became charged, with some of them speaking in tongues (indecipherable words).

After about an hour of songs of worship and adoration, Nkolika called on Ifeoma to give thanks to the Lord. Ifeoma, who was already dazed in her spirit, stood up, wiped her tear-drenched face and prayed: "Oh Lord our great father, hallowed be thy name. You made the heavens and the earth to your glory; the stars and all the heavenly bodies exhibit your wondrous beauty. Who can compare to your matchless worth?"

"Nobody!" Angelina shouted.

Ifeoma paused and continued after a few seconds: "That is why we recognize you as the only one worthy of our worship, praise and adoration. We say thank you Lord for whom you are to us; for saving us through your son Jesus Christ and for opening our eyes to the mysteries of your kingdom. Lord, we thank you for the beauty of the universe, the animals and the trees. They praise you and show your glory every minute of the day. Be exalted now and forever more." The whole house echoed "Amen."

Nkolika told them to clap for Jesus. They all stood up and did as Nkoli had directed and sat down. She called on Obinna to pray for the *Igwe* and the *Nze-na-ozo* for a right sense of judgment and God-fearing leadership. Obinna started to sing:

All powers belong to Jesus
All powers belong to him
All powers belong to Jesus
All powers belong to him

He spoke in tongues for about three minutes and then prayed; "Oh Lord we recognize you as the King of kings and the Lord of lords. You set up and dethrone kings and kingdoms. There is no ruler in all the nations that ever ascended his throne without your consent. Your word says that the heart of the king is in your hand and you turn it wherever you wish.

"Lord, this day we remember the leadership of our land, the *Igwe* and his ruling council. We set them before you this day, asking that you visit them, not in wrath, but to give them the right sense of judgment in all they do. Lord we pray that our *Igwe* should forsake the gods of his ancestors and recognize the only one who reigns in the heavens, the Almighty God and his son Jesus Christ.

"Father we pray that his council members be saved through your living word. Deliver them from the spirit of lust for money and power. Pull them out of bribery and give them right understanding and wisdom in all their ways.

"Lord, we pray that they should always give the *Igwe* the right advice he needs to govern the land of Umuocha in thy fear. We pray that you purge the council of evil members such as Ikenga and all others who are evil minded.

"Father in this case of ours, we receive favour from the *Igwe* and his council in Jesus' name. You said that we shall possess the gates of our enemies and you shall turn every counsel of the wicked to naught. Lord do it for your children and let your name be glorified now and forever more." The whole gathering echoed "Amen."

Nkolika came up again and enjoined all to give Jesus a clap offering and they did. She sang some worship songs and they all clapped and danced. After about twenty-five minutes of praise and worship songs led by Nkolika, Amaka was called to pray for the children of the land.

Initially Amaka looked startled and would not pray. Ifeoma was amused by Amaka's looks. She asked, "Amaka can't you pray?" Amaka complained about Ifeoma's interest in her prayers and looked the other way. Gladys held Amaka's hand and pleaded with her to pray for those children of her age group who had suddenly deserted her or who jeered and hooted at her when she went to the stream to fetch drinking water.

Amaka then smiled at her aunt and prayed, though inaudibly: "In Jesus' name." Others responded "Amen." She continued, "Jesus, you love little children and do not want them to go to hell. Lord Jesus, save them from evil advice from their parents and bring back all my friends to me. Deliver me from those who want to beat me up for no reason." Amaka paused as if the words had exhausted. She looked round and observed that everyone still had their eyes closed and were waiting for her to continue. She went on.

"Lord even at Mommy's school, grant forgiveness to those children who insulted her. We pray in Jesus' name." "Amen" they echoed and then opened their eyes. "Who says Amaka cannot pray?" Gladys asked rhetorically. Amaka covered her face because she was often shy among her elders. They all clapped for Amaka and encouraged her to always pray for her peers who had now become enemies since her mother was ostracized from the community.

Nkolika then called on Gladys to pray for the *Umuada* Umuocha to change their ways and turn to Jesus Christ en masse. She told her that history would judge her as one of the leaders of *Umuada* if they failed to bring the much-needed godliness in the land. Gladys thanked her younger sister and raised a supplication song:

God hear your children,
God hear your sons and daughters,
We are unworthy to even call your name,
We come in faith,
Lord, hear us as we pray.

The song really touched Angelina and she burst into tears and sobbed through Gladys' prayer. Gladys prayed: "Lord of hosts, you created us and placed us on this land and called us a great name, *Ala* Umuocha, which means The Land of the Children of Light. What a beautiful name, but unfortunately we have forsaken light and embraced darkness and unsavoury practices. Lord, forgive us; Lord, pardon us; Lord, judge us with your mercy and do not be angry with us.

"Father, we bring before you the daughters of this land, *Umuada Ala* Umuocha, the Daughters of the Land of Light. Jehovah, deliver us from all forms of evil practice. Make us the epitome of godliness, good mothers, good partners to our husbands and good citizens of our great country.

"Lord, may we always abhor evil that threatens our very survival as a people, in Jesus' name." They echoed "Amen!" She continued, "Such evils include abortions often committed by our daughters with the full support of their mothers. Lord forgive us in Jesus' name." "Amen" they shouted. "Lord, give us the right sense of judgment in our *Umuada* association. We lack divine wisdom and are controlled by traditions and customs that have for long needed changes. Give us leaders in *Umuada* the fear for your holy name and respect your divine laws with added decorum" Gladys ended her prayers with "Hail Mary" (she was a Roman Catholic). The whole house clapped their hands as Gladys ended her prayers.

Nkolika asked, "Is it not a contradiction for a people who do not punish the termination of pregnancies, which involves in reality the killing of unborn children, to ostracize a widow for killing a mere snake? God forbid this evil in Jesus' name!" "Amen," they supported her view. She thanked her older sister, Gladys, for her expository prayer and called on Angelina to pray for their safety and changes in the land of Umuocha.

Angelina commenced her prayer at 3:45 AM and ended at exactly 4:42 AM. She prayed with contriteness that most of them wept through the period she prayed. She started by singing

Thou art worthy,
Thou art worthy O Lord,
To receive glory, honour and power,
For thou has created
All things and for thy pleasure,
They are and were created.

She sang about five such songs and then she took up her bible and read from the second book of Chronicles, chapter 7 verse 14, which says, "If my people, who are called by my name, will humble themselves and pray and seek my face and turn from their wicked ways, then will I hear from heaven and will forgive their sins and will heal their land."

She exhorted her listeners to always make their ways right with God. It is the only condition for God to hear their prayers. She also told them that a sinner's prayer is an abomination in the sight of God; hence, it is only the children of God who can receive answers to their prayers from God. She also admonished her listeners to be consistent in their prayers as the only way that God would deliver the land of Umuocha from idolatry and ancestral worship.

After this exhortation, she prayed, "Oh Lord, the maker of the universe and all that is in it, we humble ourselves before you this early morning, asking that you accept us in your presence with open arms and do not reject us. Lord, as we pray, hear us; do not close your ears against us. We do not have any person or gods to go to. We have you as our father and we pray that you hear us and shower upon us answers to our requests that the whole world may know that you are God and we are your children.

"Lord, we challenge you concerning the words of your mouth. You said if we who are called by your name should humble ourselves and pray to you concerning our land you will hear us and effect a change in our land. Lord, we have bowed our hearts and heads before you and we believe you will receive us into your throne room and empower us with answers for our land in Jesus' name.

"Lord, we pray against the spirit of totemic ritual in the land. All forms of totemic practices are religion in themselves. Lord, we stand against them and we pull their strongholds down in the spirit while we erect the worship of the one and only true God and his son Jesus Christ. We dethrone all forms of idolatrous practices and we erect a reign of godliness, respect for the downtrodden, the deprived, the pariahs and all those regarded as the wretched of the earth such as the *Osu* people. Lord, forgive our land for such discriminations based on status as there is no stratification in your kingdom.

"Lord, as we pray for change, we bring before you once again the *Igwe* and his council. Change their hearts and turn them over to your side. Remove anyone whose heart is hardened and made up for evil and grant them your free salvation through your son Jesus Christ.

"Lord, we pray concerning all the gods, deities, shrines, groves and totemic poles in the land – the *Agbala*, the *Amadioha*, *Urashi*, *Ogwugwu*, *Ibini-Ukpabi*, etc. We set them ablaze and reclaim their sites for the worship of the one true God in Jesus' name. We confuse their priests and deliver them from the captivity of the evil one in Jesus' name. Thank you Lord for answering us.

"Concerning our security in this community, we are not afraid. We are secured in the hollow of your hand." She picked up her bible again and opened it to Psalm 91 and read some verses: "He who dwells in the shelter of the most high will rest in the shadow of the Almighty. I will say of the Lord, He is my refuge and my fortress, my God in whom I trust."

She put down her bible and continued, "Father this is your word, confirm it in our lives. We cannot secure what we do not have. You have our lives in your hand, so secure it to your glory in Jesus' name. As it says in Psalm 127, unless the Lord watches over the city, the watchmen stand guard in vain. Lord, watch over us and send your angels to shelter us in this land in Jesus' name.

"Deliver us from fear. As it says in St Matthew's gospel, chapter 10 verses 28-29, 'Do not be afraid of those who kill the body but cannot kill the soul. Rather, be afraid of the One who can destroy both soul and body in hell. Are not two sparrows sold for a penny? Yet not one of them will fall to the ground apart from the will of your father.' Lord, perform your word in our lives. Help us to fear only you and not any man who threatens us. We know you will never fail us. Give us faith and everlasting hope in you, in Jesus' name we pray." "Amen," they all responded, except Amaka who had fallen asleep.

Nkolika checked her wristwatch with the fast dimming lantern and it was 4:42 AM. She said jokingly, "It must be an Angel of the Lord that stopped Angie. She is a prayer warrior of note and give her the next two hours she will still be on her knees calling on heaven." They all laughed. Nkolika called on Obinna to take the lantern out and refill it with kerosene as it was becoming dim. He got up immediately and left with the only lantern that gave them illumination and the sitting room was momentarily thrown into darkness.

While they waited for Obinna to re-join them, Ifeoma tuned a song of praise:

Jesus is the winner man,
The winner *man,*
The winner *man,*
Jesus is the winner man,
The winner *man all the time.*

They sang this song repeatedly until Obinna came back and the room was once more lit up and Nkolika signalled a stop to the song. She stood up and everyone stood up with her. She promised them that in less than an hour the vigil would be over. Amaka heaved a sigh of relief and Obinna noticed it and said, "Amaka is now a happy person." Amaka smiled and kept silent and waited patiently for that "less than an hour".

Nkolika sang, "I have the God who never fails." They all joined in, clapping their hands and dancing to the tune. She again motioned them to stop, and she said, "Now I am going to take the last prayer topics. Firstly, we must pray that evangelical Christianity would grow in this community." She started, "Abba father, we your children in this community who have identified with you are calling on your name to be raised over and above every name, pillar or mountain that is erected in the physical or spiritual realm in this land of Umuocha.

"We dethrone every mountain that has cast a shadow upon the power of evangelism and repentance in this land. We raise your ba*nne*r in this community. We pull down every opposition to the progress of our brethren and our church, The Word Pentecostal Ministry. Lord, we shall prosper according to your word and purpose for our lives.

"Father, unite us in one spirit, for it says in Amos chapter 3 verse 3 that two cannot walk together except there is agreement. Lord, give us love for ourselves in this community so that those outside the fold will be attracted to us. Father, increase our numerical strength and let our imprint be found in all areas of life in this community."

Nkolika prayed for all the villages of Umuocha mentioning all their names one after the other. She mentioned their peculiar problems and asked that the Lord intervene and deliver them from all spiritual bondage afflicting them. She prayed for progress for the youths of the community and against ungodly lifestyle and untimely deaths. This was the final prayer of the night vigil. As Nkolika ended her prayers, everyone shouted the name of Jesus three times, as she had requested from them.

The night vigil was a refreshing moment indeed for all that participated in the vigil. Nkolika thanked them one after the other, mentioning them by their names. She said, "Let me sound prophetic, soon you will see the fruit of this labour. We have not been playing all these hours, we have not spent our comfort just for fun. The Lord will certainly reward us, wipe our tears and comfort us as we continue to seek his face in holiness and righteousness, loving our persecutors and praying for their repentance rather than for their damnation. May the Lord abide with all of us." They all echoed "Amen!"

Angelina stood up, gave a vote of thanks to all who had participated and said, "You have all come to share in my bond. The Lord will reward you according to your needs."

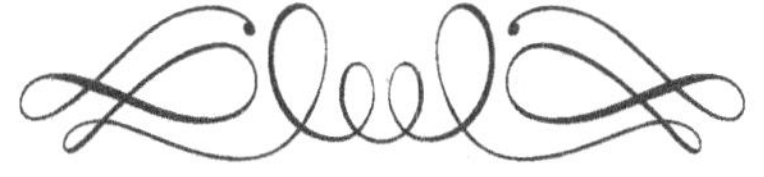

CHAPTER NINE

She is Our Flesh and Blood

"Angelina Ibe is from Akpu village because she married a man from Akpu. Let us not forget that her parents came from Ngali village and that it was in Ngali village that she was born, and it is there that her umbilical cord was buried. It is in this village that she was breast-fed, educated and then sent to Suka University where she dazzled the whole world and set records. Her records at Suka University have remained unbroken for the last two decades. Therefore, she is our flesh and blood." These were the words of Barrister Okey Ndubisi to his mother when she informed him of the face-off between Angelina and the Umuocha community.

Barrister Okey was Angelina's classmate at both primary and secondary schools. He was a notable lawyer in Nigeria, based in Lagos, and served as the secretary of the Ngali Enlightened Society (NES), an association of professionals and university graduates from Ngali village of Umuocha that acted as a pressure group in their village specifically and the entire Umuocha community as a whole. They attracted development projects from the state and federal governments to their village first and then to the Umuocha community.

Ngali village was the first of the Umuocha villages to make contact with Christian European missionaries in the mid 19th century. The people of Ngali showed hospitality to these missionaries and liberally gave them lands to establish churches, schools, hospitals and recreational facilities. Hence, Ngali village, from the early times had always come first in every area of socio-economic life in Umuocha. For instance, they produced the first university graduate, the first medical doctor, the first lawyer, the first male and female engineers, and the first teacher, among other firsts in Umuocha community. It was no wonder that Angelina, with her academic record, also came from Ngali village.

Chief Okey Ndubisi visited his rural home to attend to his aged mother who was ill. In a conversation with his mother on the state of affairs in Umuocha community, his mother, a traditionalist, expressed her unhappiness with Angelina. She told, Okey, "Your childhood friend and classmate, Angelina, has descended from being the pride of Ngali village to the shame of Ngali village."

Okey adjusted his seat as his interest in his mother's words increased. "Why do you describe my childhood friend with such unpalatable language, mama?" Okey asked his mother.

His mother initially did not want to bother her son with the details because they often had arguments when it comes to customs, especially concerning certain customary practices that seemed to contradict modernity. Okey's mother knew that her son was a member of the Amnesty and Rights Organization (ARO), a very vocal human rights organization that fought for disadvantaged groups in various states within the country. Okey served as its National Secretary. This made his mother reluctant to elaborate on why she described Angelina as the "shame of Ngali village", even when Okey prodded her to open up.

After much prodding and teases, Okey's mother opened up but warned Okey not to argue much as he knew that she was unwell. She asked Okey, "Since you were born, have you been aware of the duration a woman must stay indoors, before coming out after her husband's death?"

Okey responded, "The reviewed duration is now three months."

"Thank you my learned son," his mother said.

"Another question, since you were born in this village, are you aware that no one kills a python even if it enters your house and kills your chicken?" his mother asked him.

Okey laughed and said, "Mama, let me be honest with you, if a python enters my house and kills a chicken I will slash its head and burn its carcass."

"Then you will become another Angelina," his mother said in anger as she turned away her face from her son.

Okey smiled and said, "Mama, if these two cases are Angelina's crimes, then she committed no crimes at all."

"You, keep quiet, Mr. Lawyer and judge," his mother told him in anger. Okey, sensing an ensuing tension, decided to mellow the fragile situation. He cracked some old jokes about his mother's youthfulness. Okey's reminiscences got his mother smiling and even laughing.

"You boy, you do not forget anything, even things that happened when you were only two years old are recorded in your memory," Okey's mother said, laughing.

Okey was enjoying the jokes and said, "Mama, how come you still call me boy. You know I am forty-seven years old this February. I have a wife and four children."

His mother looked at him with contempt and said, "Your problem is too much education and travel. Your contacts with Western Civilization have whitewashed your 'Africa*nne*ss'. I am frightened by that, because I do not want my grandchildren to lose their Igbo identity. Listen, my son, in Igbo culture, you are always a little child as long as your parents are alive. We have a proverb, which says that, two Iroko trees do not grow on the same piece of land." Okey's mother smiled, looking fulfilled. Noticing that Okey looked cowed, she follows up, "So, what do I call you when I am still alive? Do I call you *Nze* or Chief? Those titles are not for me. I remember vividly when you were in my womb, I remember the day you came out of my body, naked and crying. I bathed you and clothed you, sent you to school and trained you until you became a lawyer.

"The government did not help me, and your father died young. So, as long as I live, you are not just a boy, but my little boy even if you are seventy years old." Okey covered his face and looked intimidated, and almost regretted initiating this discussion. He thanked his mother for taking him down memory lane but pleaded that his mother should not call him "boy" when his children or wife were present. "You must tell me what to call you when my daughter-in-law and grandchildren are around," Okey's mother replied.

Wanting to change the topic of discussion, Okey said, "I will tell you, but mama, let's go back to your first and second questions. I have never said that our customs should not be respected, but it baffles me that we still want our women to stay at home for a whole three months mourning their husbands on empty stomachs.

"In the case of Angelina, she has three children, with herself, that is four in all. If she should stay at home for a whole three months, who takes care of their needs? Come on Mama, please answer me!" Okey's mother remained silent, looking the other way.

Okey went on, "I am surprised when women like you with wealth of experience talk in respect to issues like this and take sides as you have done. Angelina was right in leaving the house, and if I found myself in her shoes, I would also have done so, Mama."

Okey's mother then said, "All right, that is enough on that issue. What do you have to say about the second crime? She killed a harmless python on the same day she committed the first sacrilege. She went out to preach her Jesus and her late husband appeared in the form of a python and in spite of her ability to interpret sciences she could not read the writing on the wall in front of her. She stupidly killed her husband in thc form of a python."

"Mama!" Okey called his mother, "Do not say that. Do you imply that Angelina's husband was resurrected and became a python? It does not happen that way. Firstly, Angelina has every right as a citizen of this country to communicate her faith as long as she does not breach the sensibilities of others. Having said that, nobody has any legal authority to stop her, as long as, she does her morning cry with respect to other people's feelings. Secondly, if the python posed a threat to her safety, then she has every right to kill the snake. I think she did well."

His mother looked at him, shook her head, spat outside the balcony where they sat, and said, "*Tufiakwa*!" She quietly left her son, grumbling to herself as she went into her room. "This is why I don't like discussing such matters with him, because you will never convince him, he will never accept your position, he is the only wise person in this world."

Okey continued as his mother walked out on him, "We, the Ngali Enlightened Society, will defend one of our own, she is our flesh and blood. We will fight for her human rights and save the poor widow from the teeth of anachronistic and dying customs."

Barrister Okey was fuming at his mother's lack of understanding. He went into his room, took a piece of paper and then said to himself, "The earlier we act to save Angie and her kids the better for us." He drafted a circular to all the members of the Ngali Enlightened Society (NES) to attend an urgent meeting in a fortnight. The circular read:

URGENT

As a matter of urgent importance, you are cordially invited to a meeting to discuss the welfare of one of us who is being persecuted by the entire Umuocha community. Failure to attend will attract a serious penalty.

Date: 22/03/1981
Venue: Ngali Progressive Hall
Time: 12 Noon.

Yours in service,
Barrister Okey Ndubisi

He first sent the notice to the president of NES who lived and practiced his profession as an architect at Orlu. He also attached a letter that detailed the community's grievances against Angelina and expressed the need to address these concerns. Upon receipt of the letter, the president was full of thanks to the secretary and gave his full support to the meeting. The president then photo*copie*d more *copie*s of the circular, addressed them to the members and dispatched them to their respective addresses.

On the following day, Okey visited Angelina at Akpu village. He had sent a letter of condolence to her when she lost her husband, Polycarp. He brought beverages and some cash in an envelope as gifts to Angelina and her children.

He drove in his sleek Mazda car to Angelina's house. Angelina was going to her farm when she saw a car that looked like Okey's driving toward her. The car stopped on the other side of the road and Okey alighted from the car. There were no jokes and childhood reminiscences as there always used to be when they met.

They looked at one another seriously for a few seconds with neither of them speaking. Angelina broke the silence when finally she smiled and said, "Okey, it is well. You are welcome, how is your family, and your legal practice?"

Okey nodded, as Angelina turned and entered her courtyard, and followed her. He did not enter the house with her, but stopped outside. He requested that she bring chairs outside, as it would be very hot inside because of the weather.

Angelina obliged and brought a wooden bench outside and a small leather seat for her guest. She sat on the bench facing Okey. Okey smiled, shook his head and said, "My dear Angie, as you usually say, it is well with your soul. I heard the sad news of Poly's death. I would have come to see you but ARO executive members were travelling to Kenya for an international conference and as the national secretary, I had a paper to present at the conference. Mama's illness brought me home and my ears are full of the pains you have been subjected to since you lost your darling husband. That is too much for a widow. It has to be fought with all the seriousness it deserves."

Angelina smiled and said, "I didn't believe I still had friends in this community until I saw your car coming close to my house. I thought you were also ostracising me, and honestly it would have baffled me if you had joined them."

"No, no! Angie, it's like time and space have made you forget the stuff I am made of and my relationship with you since childhood," Okey interrupted. "You know I wouldn't have been part of this conspiracy against you in a million years. If I were there on that Eke market day when Nweze attacked you, I would have used all my strength to protect you from her or anyone who wanted to harm you. You know I would defend you any time, any day, anywhere, even at the Supreme Court of this country, and I will m*obi*lize my colleagues to defend you there. Angie, do not include me or any of the members of the Ngali Enlightened Society in this evil alliance.

"We are setting ma*chi*nery in motion that will produce a common front to confront the leadership of this community. By this, I mean the *Igwe*, the *Nze-na-ozo*, the *Umuada* and the *Aluta-radi*. We shall seek redress on your behalf and shall work towards expunging from our values, all these obsolete customs that amount to brazen idolatry and intimidation of the less privileged.

"Just pray for us, it could be that the Almighty God has finally answered your prayers for a change in this community. Listen, we shall not give up until there is change in this land. We shall broaden the fight and take the heat off your neck. We have the resources and personnel to prosecute this fight to the end.

"Angie, you are our flesh and blood, you are a member of the

Ngali Enlightened Society and a remarkable one for that matter. We shall not let you down."

As Barrister Okey was speaking, Obinna and Ifeoma came in from the bush where they had gone to gather firewood for cooking. They embraced Okey. Obinna said, "Mommy, I am going to Lagos with Barrister Okey."

Angelina said, "As soon as your university matriculation examination result is released, I will let you travel even to London if you have a visa."

"Obinna, you know your mother is a nerd and would not let you go until you pass your matriculation exam. Just let me know when your result is out so I can come home and take you to Lagos," Okey said.

Ifeoma said to Okey "I wish you had visited us before now." Angelina intervened, "My daughter, that issue has been settled."

Okey smiled, brought out his car key, gave it to Obinna and said, "Go, open the front passenger door and get the carton of beverages for the household." He then took out the envelope containing a large sum of money and handed it over to Angelina as his contribution towards the upkeep of her family.

Angelina thanked Okey for his kind gesture as the children headed towards the car. Angelina again expressed her gratitude to Okey for identifying with her in her hour of need. She said, "It is not easy to opt for a different direction when the whole community has opted for an opposing direction. No one wants to be in the minority against the majority. However, today, you have written a minority report before me and you are willing to defend it before the people of this community. You have also decided to do it with your strength and the might of our associates in NES. That is great, please go on and let us cleanse our land of this decay that has held us captive."

"They ostracized a widow and almost lynched me at the market. I wept bitterly because my only living paternal relation, my aunty Nweze, championed this heinous act. That was the only time I wept and I know that my tears have reached the throne of God and are raising my compatriots to join in this crusade against the evil forces of darkness that have left Umuocha far behind her neighbours in Christian values and growth in development infrastructure. I will gladly provide any information that NES might need in its crusade."

Okey thanked her for her courage and greeted her in the Suka alumni tradition. Although he was not a graduate of Suka University, he tried to sing Suka's anthem to one of its prominent graduates. Angelina laughed and told him, "Please Okey, do not mess up my school's anthem." Okey laughed and asked Angelina to sing it correctly. Angelina obliged and sang it correctly. Okey clapped for her and called her the pride of Ngali village. It was a fun time for them. Finally, Okey gave her a notice of the forthcoming NES meeting and requested that she bring along all the evidence that might be needed in this campaign. She agreed and thanked Okey.

While they were still talking, Ifeoma had made yam porridge garnished with dry fish and crayfish, which was a popular meal in many Igbo communities. Okey was surprised at Ifeoma's thoughtfulness. He said, "I am surprised that you could reason so fast and prepare a meal for a visitor without anyone asking you to do that." Turning to Angelina, Okey said, "Angie, I can't wait any longer, the aroma of this meal is irresistible." Angelina and Ifeoma laughed as he guzzled the delicious yam porridge. After eating, Okey turned to Ifeoma and said, "Ifeoma, may God give you a wonderful husband who will appreciate you all the days of your life." Angelina lifted her hands and shouted, "Amen!"

Okey literally licked the plate. Angelina made fun of him, "I know you will always fall to any temptation that comes with yam porridge." "Are you not the one who told your daughter to tempt me with this porridge?" Okey asked, laughing.

After about three hours of discussion and reminiscences, Okey left Angelina and her children at 11.30 am. He drove to the home of Nweze where he dropped a letter of invitation to attend the meeting of NES in a fortnight. He also visited all the seven *Nze-na-ozo* members representing Ngali village and gave them their invitations to the meeting.

CHAPTER TEN

The Meeting Day

It was noon at Ngali Progressive Hall, and hundreds of NES members were assembled, exchanging pleasantries, as some of them had not met for several years. Its members were professionals in various fields who lived in cities and towns across Nigeria. The membership of NES also included several professionals from Ngali who lived overseas. This group did not participate in meetings at short notice; often they attended the December or August Meetings. This day, members had come home to save one of their members who had been maltreated by what most of them called "outdated practices." Some of the attendees have come to the meeting with anger against the traditional institution in Umuocha, while others have come to listen before making an informed judgment. There were also some villagers sitting in the gallery who had come to witness the verdict of their highly respected intellectuals. The gathering was scheduled to last two days but the secretary, Barrister Okey Ndubisi tactfully squeezed the program to fit into a day, leaving room for a possible spill over to the next day.

After the exchange of pleasantries, the president, Architect Duru, called on one of their members, a Catholic priest, to say the opening prayers. Rev. Fr. Venatius Uwakwe prayed for a smooth, orderly meeting and the members responded "Amen."

The president asked that the invited non-members such as Nweze and the *Nze-na-ozo* members be led into the waiting room and be served with their choice of drinks while they proceeded with their deliberations. The class of the "Guild of A*chi*evers" was also called to take their exalted seats. This included members who had a*chi*eved firsts in their chosen fields of endeavour. Among these a*chi*evers was Angelina. She got the highest ovation when she stood up to take her seat. She was the first woman to be admitted into this hallowed body. Angelina smiled and waved back at the crowd.

After the guild members had taken their seats, the secretary, Barrister Okey then read a joint Chairman/Secretary's welcome address, which he titled, "She is our flesh and blood". The address was meant to inspire passion against certain practices the writers considered backward. As he read the lengthy address, there were occasional ovations from the crowd and suggestions by the more radical members to pull Ngali village out of the confederate Umuocha community.

Concluding his address, Barrister Okey said, "As we meet today heaven is asking who will heed this clarion call to change the face of our community for good." He raised his hand and said, "I heed." Everyone in the hall raised their hand and echoed, "I heed!" The crowd gave him a standing ovation for five minutes as he ended his address and took his seat.

The president asked the society's warden to call in the invited guests. Nweze and the *Nze-na-ozo* came in and took their seats in front of the massive hall. They looked terrified and edgy. They were reminded of the reason they had been summoned by NES and asked to feel free in the midst of their brothers and sisters.

Angelina was then called up to give an account of her ordeal since her husband's death. As she stood up, she had only her bible in her hand. The rest of the NES stood up for her, giving her an ovation that did not stop even when the president motioned for a stop.

"Thank you, thank you and God bless you," said Angelina,

motioning the crowd to stop. However, the more she motioned them, the louder the ovation lasted, and for the next ten minutes, Angelina stood before them, beaming with smiles. It was reminiscent of her graduation day at Suka University when the entire staff, students and even the president of the country who came to receive a doctorate degree (*Honoris Causa*) stood for over twenty minutes, cheering her and clapping for her as her citation was read. That day she delivered the greatest speech ever made by a best graduating student. Her brilliance earned an invitation from the president and his wife for lunch at the presidential villa.

When the ovation ended, Angelina said, "May I once again thank you for your uncontrollable ovation." This drew much laughter and some clapping. Angelina resumed her speech, "Today we have gathered to make right what we did not make right as a community. I do not want to start this address by making wrong what I ought to have made right." She smiled at the crowd. There was another standing ovation for her.

She continued, "Therefore let me first thank you again for the third time for accepting what our community rejected; for exalting what our community debased; for your friendship and open hand when our community has shut me out and ostracized me – preferring a python to a daughter in the name of culture. What a shame!" There were intermittent sighs and shouts of "*Tufiakwa*!"

As Angelina spoke, the *Nze-na-ozo* and Nweze became more jittery. At one point, Nweze started shedding tears, sobbing loudly, but they ignored her. Angelina gave an account of what her life had been like since the death of her husband; how out of her love for God she went to preach in the morning and on her way to her house she was unable to get past a mighty python that had crossed the entire width of the road. She had summoned her courage and killed the python, and since opening that Pandora's Box, there had been no peace in the Umuocha community.

Angelina turned round, pointing to her aunty Mrs. Nweze,

she said, "Look at the only relation of mine alive. She gave me the greatest insult and physical assault of my life and invited the whole world to witness an open market assault on me. She held my clothes and shredded them, pushed me down, poured ashes on me and got me beaten up. Is that the Ngali way?" She asked and the whole assembly shouted "No!!!" Nweze bent her head low, crying. Angelina tendered those torn clothes as evidence.

She turned to the *Nze-na-ozo*. They all hid their faces from her. Angelina said, "I respect you all as elders of our village but I had expected you to be custodians of human life rather than custodians of totems. She brought a letter of summons from the council of *Nze-na-ozo* and tendered it.

The origin of that summons, she explained, came from the threat of her brother-in-law, Mr. Titus Ibe of Akpu. She said, "Titus took me to the *Igwe* and his council of which these *Nze-na-ozo* are members and reported that he was going to deprive me of my late husband's land at *Ukpaka*nyi on the advice of his mentor, Mazi Ikenga. This august body of *Nze-na-ozo* Umuocha summoned me to appear before it to answer to frivolous charges made against me by Mr. Titus Ibe.

"Before proceeding, let me tell you why Titus went to the *Igwe* and his council to report me. He came to my house and requested that as his late brother's wife he reserved the right to inherit me, and sleep with me to raise more male children for his late brother since I had only one son with Polycarp. He gave me this selfish condition as the only reason why he would leave that land, otherwise he would dispossess me of the land." There were hisses of disapproval and anger over this revelation.

Angelina continued, "I also have a complaint to make concerning Mazi Ikenga." Angelina tendered Ikenga's letter to her school principal, a native of Kokwa, asking that the whole school should ostracize her. She narrated to them her embarrassment the day she waited for other teachers in the staffroom only to discover the other staff had deserted her, just because Ikenga had directed them to do so. The same Ikenga influenced parents to ask their children to vacate their classes any time Angelina entered the classroom to teach. She called out Elder Chukwuka's son, who had remained in the deserted Agricultural Science class, to stand as her witness.

She narrated countless other attacks, assaults and intimidations that her children had suffered at the hand of their peers in the course of her ostracism. The secretary recorded all her accounts. Angelina spoke for over an hour and a half, as the whole assembly remained calm with occasional sighs of regrets from the members.

"My fellow members of NES, this has been my ordeal at the hands of our people. I do not ask for your vengeance, however, I am asking for recruits in my army that will fight against this mess and root out evil from our midst. I have forgiven all my tormentors. God bless you richly for being my husbands, brothers, sisters, friends, fathers and mothers." She bowed her head in salutation. There was another thunderous ovation from the assembly. She went to her seat, took a glass of water and sat down.

The assembly then sat down and the Secretary stood up and thanked her again: "I can assure you that if Angelina is in a debate or oratory competition with some us of lawyers, she would beat us silly. Thank you, Angelina."

There was general laughter as the members discussed Angelina's account in groups. The secretary asked the members to take a 15-minute recess and return with questions for Angelina, Nweze and the *Nze-na-ozo*.

At the resumption of sitting, the invitees, Nweze and the *Nze-na-ozo*, were asked if they had any questions for Angelina, who stood facing them. Nweze, Angelina's aunty, was the first person called up to question Angelina. She broke down and wept, asking that Angelina should forgive her for the assault and ascribing her actions to the work of the Devil. Angelina gave Nweze her handkerchief to wipe her tears. She embraced Nweze, saying "I have forgiven you, aunty." Angelina's gesture moved many of the members, especially the more elderly women, to tears, but the youthful members were calling for Nweze's head.

The secretary turned to the seven *Nze-na-ozo* members from Ngali village and said, "Do you have any questions or defence to make on the evidence given by Mrs. Angelina Ibe?" In unison they said "No." Angelina stepped forward, put out her hand and shook each of them by the hand, saying "I hold nothing against you."

The secretary sat down. The president stood up and said, "Who among the members has any question for Angelina?" Over a hundred of them raised their hands. The president told them he needed only one of them to ask Angelina a question. He restricted the number of questioners to one because the meeting was running beyond the time pla*nne*d for it. A geologist, Dr. Chinedu Umeh working in the Niger Delta with an American multinational oil company, came out first and said, "Angie was my senior at Suka several years ago and she is a lady I have admired for a long time. You are like a custodian of morality and Christianity in this village and our community in general. Please, could you tell us what you want this body to do to your tormentors? Thank you."

Angelina came up again and said, "Thank you. Sorry, I cannot fully recognize you, my great Sukite." She smiled at Dr. Chinedu and continued, "Now to the question, firstly, I have said during my speech that I have forgiven my persecutors. Therefore, the NES should equally forgive them, especially as they have shown remorse. Secondly, they should be made to get involved in this war against anachronism." She ended her answer there, but there were hisses of rejection of Angelina's view.

The secretary stood up, motioned for order, and said, "Now we shall put this to vote. How many of us support Angelina's views on general amnesty for Nweze and these titled men?" Surprisingly only fifteen members out of the hundreds that were present raised their hands. Okey looked at Angelina, shook his head, smiled and said, "If you reject Angelina's view on forgiveness and amnesty say REJECTED!" The hundreds who did not accept Angelina's view, thundered, "REJECTED!"

The President took his gavel, hit it on the table, and quoted a proverb, "The verdict of the people is the verdict of the gods." He turned to Angelina and said, "Distinguished member, your position is rejected. We are proceeding to the *Igwe*'s palace with our communiqué, which we shall read in the next hour. Everyone should go on break and come back in an hour's time for a communiqué following executive deliberations. Thank you." Angelina sat speechless.

As the assembly dispersed for their break, many members of NES crowded around Angelina, consoling her over the death of her husband and her ordeals. She beamed with smiles and told them "God bless you for your care; God will reward you all." Angelina was not comfortable with taking the matter back to the *Igwe*. She would have preferred to settle everything there and pardon her offenders. However, she did not have the authority as an individual to change the decision of the body.

She thought, "Could it be God who is working in these men and women? Lord, if you are behind their action, take it to the very end, let it sweep through the entire community and bring the changes long needed."

As the crowd around her increased, she could no longer afford to stand with them; she then sat down on a chair while she responded to their greetings and condolences. After about an hour and a half, the warden asked that the bell be rung for a formal announcement of the resumption of the last phase of the meeting.

Within half an hour, the hall became full again as members settled back on their seats. The assembly was quite calm with random discussions among friends as they waited for the twenty-man executive committee to appear from over two hours of deliberations.

There was heightened tension when some of the members

of the executive committee appeared clut*chi*ng their files to their chests. The appearance of Nweze and the *Nze-na-ozo* members was sombre. They could not interpret what the meeting of the executives had concluded, and they felt that their fate was uncertain.

The executives were duly seated and the president stood up, cleared his voice, and picked up a piece of paper containing the communiqué. He bowed to the assembly in his usual manner and the members stood up in respect for their elected executive members.

"You may be seated, honourable members of NES," the president said, and they all sat down, wondering what might be the content of the piece of paper in their president's hand.

"Good afternoon once again, distinguished members of NES," he said. He looked at the gallery and at the invited defendants and greeted them in their traditional manner. The members responded with a clapping ovation. The president said, "Ladies and gentlemen, as I stand before you, my heart bleeds that our community, the land of our ancestors where each one of us was born, has become the scum in this country, because we have decided to maintain anachronistic customs and traditions that have for a long time needed revising.

"We have played into the hands of the privileged but mis*chi*evous cultural apologists who are living in this community, exploiting the defenceless and mistreating the very ones they are empowered by our custom to defend." The assembly members stood up and gave him an ovation because the direction of the president's speech was going as they expected.

The president motioned for silence and continued, "This order of events must change forthwith in this community or Ngali village will be forced to secede from the Umuocha confederacy!" This brought an even louder ovation from NES members, some of whom favoured having an Ngali autonomous community.

"We shall not fold our hands and watch our sons and daughters traumatized by these men of greed," Architect Duru, the president said. He pointed at Angelina and said, "How do you fathom their rationale in preferring a python to this icon of a woman, or tell me the justification in giving a veiled licence to their immoral girls who regularly commit abortions, spilling the blood of innocent unborn children that are now crying daily against our community. How many of these girls and their parents do they ostracize? Let me ask, the murderer or the snake killer, who is guilty before God?" There were shouts of "the murderer!" The president continued, "But we have allowed the murderers to live and have ostracized a widow who killed a snake, just because she refused certain conditions set by selfish men.

"I thank God we are Ngali people. We first received the European evangelists in the early 19th century and gave them unhindered access to our land and through that action of our ancestors, our village has become a model of justice, truth and progress in the entire Umuocha community.

"Our ancestors in this village rejected evil practices. They were the first in this community to reject the killing of twins and human sacrifice. They preferred to be Christians, were educated, set up schools and hospitals. They helped evangelize other communities around us and even went across the *Urashi* River with the white missionaries to plant churches and build schools. Their efforts took us to the height we have attained and we must not let them down.

"If we go back to what they vomited then we are wayward children. Angelina noticed the tendency of our people to go back to the practices our forefathers rejected, and it spurred her to pick up the light of the gospel and fight against retrogression. She aimed to continue what our fathers left off, but some wicked men in this community are bent on quenching her lantern of change. Listen to me, ladies and gentlemen. History is about to be made a second time, and a second book of social transformation in Umuocha is about to be written. Already Angelina has taken the driver's seat.

I have signed up as her first passenger, I do not know about you?" Virtually everyone in the hall stood up, saying, "I am the next passenger! I am the next passenger!"

The president continued, "If you are really the next passenger, then show it by your deeds. I am proud of the executive council members. They unanimously voted to free Angelina from her problems and to fight with her to cleanse the entire Umuocha of all manner of evil. We shall do this with the support of other six villages in Umuocha.

"In pursuance of this act of cleansing, this august body has arrived at these decisions as our ground for agitation. As a rule in our society, all members debate the resolutions read by the secretary. Subsequently, corrections are made where needed and then adopted as a policy of NES.

"The second phase is that the NES executive will forward her policy to the *Igwe* and lobby for its adoption as an Umuocha Bylaw, which will be binding on all and sundry in our community. As I take my seat, one more time, I salute the courage and resolve of our great daughter, sister and friend, Mrs. Angelina Ibe, the pride of NES and Umuocha, for standing for change, women's rights and equality in the face of a life-threatening situation. God bless you all." He waved to the assembly, bowed, and took his seat as all the members rose with a standing ovation for their president whose power of oratory was not in doubt.

The secretary, Barrister Okey Ndubisi, stood up, collected the same piece of paper the president held and enjoined all the members to get ready to note down all the points in the communiqué. He allowed them some time to get ready and after about five minutes, he asked, "Are you ready?" They replied, "Yes!" He then read out the resolutions of the Ngali Enlightenment Society as follows:

1. That Angelina be accepted back to the community immediately.

2. That Angelina be compensated hugely by the Umuocha community.
3. That Ikenga be expelled, and de-robed from the *Nze-na-ozo* council and then exiled to wherever it may please your Majesty.
4. That the python be removed as a totem and that totemic poles be dismantled from our land.
5. That an enlarged committee be set up to work out modalities on how to free our women from certain customary practices that tend to put them in bondage.
6. That Titus withdraws his land suit against Angelina and her son, that he be reprimanded and pay compensation to Angelina.
7. That Nweze be fined and exiled for at least two years.
8. That abortionists and those who assist them be punished and exposed for all to see.
9. That the freedom to practice and communicate one's faith without hindrance be emphasized. We recognise that the freedom of religion must be exercised within the bounds of the law of our country.
10. That the seven *Nze-na-ozo* members from Ngali on the *Igwe*'s council be de-robed and new eligible ones installed.
11. That the palace secretary be suspended or replaced with a non-partisan person.

Distinguished members, this is our communiqué to be discussed with the *Igwe* tomorrow morning. We are thankful because we have the most enlightened *Igwe* in this local government area and, perhaps, in our state. He is a legal luminary with a sense of humanity. We shall press for the adoption of all the points or a minimal review where necessary as an edict for the whole Umuocha to observe. We shall also add a proviso that if our stand on these issues is ignored, Ngali will have no alternative than to use its wealth of human and material resources to seek recognition by the state and local government area as an autonomous community independent of Umuocha. Thank you and God bless."

The assembly rose in applause with the shouts of "Able secretary! Able secretary!" The president once again stood up and asked for a debate or an outright adoption. Some members led by Barrister Chukwuma favoured a debate, arguing that the language of the communiqué sounded like a military fiat, an imposition on the *Igwe* and an intimidation of the other six villages.

Dr. Umeh, a National Merit Award Winner because of his exploits in gynaecological medicine, supported an outright adoption of the communiqué as read by the secretary. In his short speech, he said, "Let the *Igwe* argue for himself, he is a lawyer of international repute. Let the six other villages see light through Ngali people. This way, the whole world will know that Ngali people, who were once derided for their acceptance of the Christian faith, have overcome the reverence of pythons and other forms of idolatry."

His statement drew a resounding ovation and the two views were put to the vote. The warden, Mr. Louis Agu conducted the count and only thirty-five members supported the views of Barrister Chukwuma. The Secretary was happy as he looked at Angelina and smiled at her.

Then he took the gavel and said "If you oppose the adoption of the communiqué say "oppose." Only Barrister Chukwuma shouted "oppose" as the others who had voted for debate immediately switched camps. The secretary jokingly said, "Let my professional colleague come forward and shout 'oppose'. We are waiting." This attracted general laughter as Chukwuma did not turn up and so his view was defeated.

The secretary raised his voice in a crescendo, like an American ringside announcer, "And now, if you support the adoption of these resolutions, lift your hand and shout, "Adopt!" The noise of their shouts of "Adopt!" could be heard a kilometre away. Someone humorously raised his legs as well saying, "Not only have my hands, but my legs also adopted the communiqué." The secretary then knocked the gavel on the table and said, "Adopted," as the assembly sat down clapping their hands and congratulating one another for a job well done.

The president once again stood up and promised to end the meeting in a few minutes. He gave a vote of thanks and promised the entire body that none of the executives would return to his base in the cities until the *Igwe* acceded to their demands and progress was made in line with their demands.

He then called on an Evangelical Minister, Reverend Emmanuel Uba, to say the closing prayers. Reverend Uba stood up and prayed, "Oh Lord let your peace abide in Umuocha, that its people may grow from strength from to strength and live in togetherness. Bless NES members and let a wave of revival based on Christian and modern lifestyle sweep through the whole of Umuocha. Help us overcome backwardness occasioned by traditional practices. In Jesus name we have prayed." The whole assembly echoed "Amen" at the close of his prayers.

There were several mini gatherings as friends who had not seen each other for years embraced each other, exchanged addresses and telephone numbers. The day was fast fading into night and Barrister Okey instructed one of the young members of NES to take Angelina home to Akpu village in his car.

CHAPTER ELEVEN

A Shining Crown

The day after the meeting of the Ngali Enlightened Society and the issuance of the communiqué, the NES executive committee members, having written and obtained permission to meet with the *Igwe*, drove in a convoy of fifteen cars to the palace at Akpu village.

The convoy was a remarkable sight as children and farmers came out of their schools and farms waving their hands to the highly respected men and women from one of their villages. They drove the over four kilometres road from Ngali Village Square, where they assembled, to the palace at Akpu village. On approaching the palace vicinity, the outer guards directed them to stop and park their cars at Ukwu-Orji about a hundred metres away from the first main gate.

According to palace tradition, nobody was allowed to drive into the expansive palace except the *Igwe* and his family members. In 1979, when the military president of Nigeria visited Imo state, he paid a courtesy visit to the *Igwe* of Umuocha. Surprisingly, the president and his convoy were dropped off at the Ukwu-Orji, although they were provided with a red carpet upon which the president walked from the Ukwu-Orji to the *ime-obi* where he met with the *Igwe*.

On this particular day, the chief security officer in charge of the outer gate, a retired Superintendent of Police, was detailed to receive the NES executive members on behalf of the *Igwe*. After a brief ceremony, which involved an introduction of the members by the president of NES, Architect Duru, the chief security officer introduced himself as Retired Superintendent of Police Nwude Chudi, a native of Akpana village in Umuocha. He recognized a number of them and reminded the president that he had been on the committee that awarded the contract for the design and construction of St. Luke's Anglican Church to his firm, Duru & Associates. He saluted them and led them to the inner gate security chief, who was an ex-major in the defunct Biafran army. He had organized a guard of honour for the president of NES, which he inspected on arrival to the admiration of the other members of the executive. It looked like a full military compliment paid to the president and his team that morning. There was no person-to-person introduction this time. After the brief ceremony at the Inner gate, he then led the team to the secretary of the palace who was waiting to lead the NES executive to the *Igwe* in his *ime-obi* where he had opted to meet with the NES executive committee members.

The secretary was full of smiles as he recognised some of his former students among the NES executive who were now heavyweights in various trades. He paid glowing tribute to Mrs. Adaku Mba, a chartered accountant and the Executive Director of Operations in one of the leading banks in Nigeria, who served as the treasurer of the society. She was a primary school student of the palace secretary in 1961. The palace secretary mimicked the way Mrs. Mba used to cry in his class many years ago. His jokes and mimicry made the other executive members burst into laughter and teased Mrs. Adaku Mba. She also joined in the general laughter whenever anyone joked about the mimicry. This became a reference point for Mrs. Mba's colleagues throughout their outing that day.

When they reached the door to the *ime-obi*, two special guards conducted searches on them except for the female members. It is an abomination in Umuocha for a man to touch the body of a married woman, it is only the husband who has the right to do so. After the searches, the guards led the NES executives into the *ime-obi*.

The *ime-obi* was something most of them had never seen before. The building was a perfect circle with a glassy high dome, stained with green and blue decorations that reflected royalty and power. The walls were panelled with interwoven oak and mansonia woods that were crafted by the Italians in the early 1950s. Apart from some sections that were covered with Oriental rug carpets of very high quality, the floor was laid with stained glass-like tiles that reflected many colours at the same time.

However, the most astonishing of all was the throne, which was plated with gold layers, designed in the shape of an eagle but standing on three horse-like legs. The interior, where the *Igwe* sat, was covered with sumptuous red satin. The throne had been brought from England in 1951 when the then *Igwe* was knighted by the British monarch.

The members of NES were seated in their beautiful glass seats in the circular *ime-obi* waiting for the arrival of the *Igwe*. After appreciating the beauty of Umuocha's royalty, the president of NES jokingly asked his secretary, "Okey, are you intimidated by this opulence and pomp?" Much laughter greeted the president's question, and the secretary replied "I am not, but I am rattled by the portraits on the walls of this throne room of our majesty."

The walls could be described as a 'gallery of pictorial flaunt'. Some of these pictures had been photographed with early black and white cameras and some of these were fading badly. They showed the coronations of the *Igwe*s over the last nine decades, the various overseas trips of the different *Igwe*s, courtesy visits by presidents and heads of states of different nations, and visits to the presidential villa in the nation's capital by sitting *Igwe*s, different festivals, etc. There were over four hundred portraits, in different shapes and sizes, neatly arranged in a way that would baffle the best interior designers.

Okey insisted that it was only those pictures that rattled him. Okey was an art enthusiast and collector, and dreamt of setting up an art gallery in Ngali village that would display the bravery and exploits of the Ngali people, especially in the field of Christianity and education.

Other members were standing and appreciating the portraits when suddenly a large trumpet made from an elephant tusk was blown by one of the *Igwe*'s guards. The palace secretary asked everyone to return to their seats and to stand up when the Elephant tusk was sounded again. After about three minutes, the tusk was blown twice and the handsome, tall and heavily built *Igwe* entered the hall with his first son, a lawyer practicing in England and had come home for a holiday. They appeared in simple shirts and could pass for any commoner.

The NES executive had expected a well-decorated *Igwe* in his royal outfit and felt somewhat surprised when their expectations were not met. The *Igwe* did not bother to sit on his throne but personally carried one of the seats close to the throne to where the NES executives were seated, shook their hands and said, "Do not be surprised that I am defying traditions. Sometimes it is permissible to defy traditions when you are with people who defied traditions to be at the top of their chosen fields of human endeavours." They laughed and clapped at his remarks and sense of humour.

The *Igwe* greeted everyone including the women in their midst. He was the first *Igwe* of Umuocha to shake the hand of a woman other than his wife, his mother or his sister. Since his ascension, he had brought in many social changes, such as allowing women into the *ime-obi*. He was currently drafting an edict that would ban all forms of discrimination, including the *Osu* caste system. While these changes were acceptable to most of the educated members of the community, the core traditionalists opposed these changes, revealing the socio-cultural fault lines in Umuocha. The traditionalists believed that the radical reforms the *Igwe* initiated might attract the wrath of the gods on Umuocha, but they could not oppose him because it was only the *Igwe* who was permitted by tradition to initiate such changes. In addition, they were also not allowed to oppose the *Igwe* because he was seen as the revered intermediary between the living members and the ancestors of Umuocha community. In fact, in pre-Christian Umuocha mythology, the *Igwe* did not die: it was assumed that he had 'travelled' to rest in the land of the ancestors because of old age and worldly troubles. He would be reincarnated in another prince who would be born immediately after the *Igwe* had travelled. Hence, even in modern day Umuocha, the names of the reigning *Igwe* was usually the name of the *Igwe* who died immediately before he was born. While some of these beliefs are no longer popular with the evangelical Christians and the educated, the traditionalists still hold tenaciously to them.

Having taken his seat with the people, he introduced himself humorously as "Barrister *Igwe*". This brought general laughter among all present. He asked for their names, professions, and the towns and cities where they live. After the lengthy introductions, the *Igwe* again said, "All of you live outside Umuocha community, enjoying the facilities in the cities. You guys were among the people who literally dragged me home from England where I had all the facilities as well." Once more, they laughed and clapped for the *Igwe*.

After an hour of jokes and informal exchanges the *Igwe*, who had other engagements that day including a meeting with state officials at Owerri, the state capital, asked that they settle down to business. He asked them: "Ladics and gentlemen why are you here?"

The President of NES rose up, bowed to His Royal Majesty and said, "We come to drink from the wisdom of our very own King Solomon." Everyone including the *Igwe* laughed.

The *Igwe* said, "Are you the Queen of Sheba? If you are, I am not King Solomon because I have only one wife and do not intend to have more than one wife. I differ from my fathers and from Solomon too. I would however like to rule with Solomonic wisdom."

The president of NES, Architect Duru, stood up again, did obeisance and said, "Actually we come in relation to the case of one of us, Mrs. Angelina Ibe of Akpu village. She is an Ngali woman by birth. That woman is a pride to our village and the entire Umuocha community. *Igwe*, I make no empty claims. Angelina is a first class graduate of Agricultural Science from Suka University about twenty years ago. She made the best-recorded result ever at the great Suka Varsity, breaking all the records set before her and setting new ones that have remained unbroken for the last two decades." The *Igwe* shook his head in amazement.

The President continued, "Angelina has a Masters degree in Crop Science and at that level she won a total of fifteen awards during her postgraduate programme. The nearest to hers was five awards incidentally made by Dr. Frank Achike from Akpana village who works with the Food and Agricultural Organization (FAO) in East Africa. Angelina has been a research fellow in different agricultural research institutes in the United States, the United Kingdom, Kenya and Germany.

"The most interesting thing about this woman is her love for this community. Angelina was the toast of several blue *chi*p companies and international agricultural bodies across the developing world. They offered her jobs with mouth-watering offers. She has in her possession over thirty-five letters of appointment without interviews. Her research at the Institute of Root Crops at Mehia led to the genetic hybridisation of several cassava species and she applied that method in this Umuocha before disclosing her results to the Director of the Institute. When asked why she did that, she told the world press that interviewed her that she loved her community and her action was the only way to place Umuocha in a global agricultural science map. That research was published in the International Journal of Root Crops, Volume 215, Number 2 of 1978. The name of our community features prominently anywhere in the world where research in root crops is discussed. It is all because of Mrs. Angelina Ibe. She conducts free annual agricultural clinics for the women of this community and at the state level. She is on the advisory board of different agricultural agencies both locally and internationally.

"Today, Umuocha is the highest producer of improved cassava in the whole country, thanks to Angelina. Angelina has won eighteen national and fifteen international awards, apart from the awards and fellowships of several agricultural bodies in different parts of the globe already mentioned. I have only one national award with no international award. Compare that with hers." There was general laughter, but the *Igwe* was calm, just listening.

Architect Duru went on, "Angelina had every opportunity to live abroad with her family and earn American dollars like some of us are doing, she accepted the position of a visiting professor at Suka University last year after a record count of thirteen offers. *Igwe*, I cannot go on enumerating her achievements for the sake of time. We know you have a meeting in Owerri this afternoon.

"I admire her, not because of these achievements, I admire her because of her humility and deep religious convictions. As a young girl, Angelina received the gospel of Jesus Christ and lived a chaste and virtuous lifestyle, a feat very difficult for most of our girls in this community. She was committed and got married to an Akpu village man, Mr. Polycarp Ibe, who passed on in January this year, leaving her with three children to care for.

"As a religious person willing to set our people free from several bondages, she left her home twenty-one days after the death of Polycarp to preach salvation to her neighbourhood on that fateful morning. After her 'Morning Cry' with her daughter, she was on her way home when she encountered a python on the road. You know how slow some of these pythons can be. It crossed the narrow road, unwilling to move. Angelina, who does not believe in totemic ritual, decided to take out the snake and since then this land has become a hot bed for her and her family. I cannot recount her ordeals and those of her children since then, but such abuses would make a great case at our courts and even the War Crimes Tribunal at The Hague would entertain a hearing on them.

The most annoying part of this abuse is the role played by some of your council members, including the palace secretary here present and the traditional prime minister, Mazi Ikenga, unfortunately Angelina's aunt, Mrs. Nweze, Mgbeke, the leader of *Umuada* Umuocha, and Mazi Titus Ibe, Angelina's brother-in-law, among others. It was learnt that all Angelina's attempts to submit her petitions to you were foiled by the Palace Secretary." As his role in this ordeal was being recounted, the Palace Secretary bent his head in shame and fear of what punishments might be in store for him. The *Igwe* simply gazed at him and continued listening.

Architect Duru went on: "There is connivance between your secretary and Mazi Ikenga to deprive this poor widow. It was learnt that Ikenga persuaded Titus, Angelina's brother-in-law, to institute a land case against her with the knowledge of your secretary. The land in question is the birth right of Polycarp, which according to our customs is transferable to his only son, Obinna. In addition, Ikenga wrote this letter to the principal of our Community Secondary School, asking the staff and students to ostracize Angelina." He tendered the letter to the *Igwe* who read the letter in disbelief especially as the letter was written on the official letterhead of the palace and was sealed with his Majesty's seal. Mr Duru observed *Igwe*'s interest and continued, "Mr. Titus made immoral demands on Angelina; he wanted to sleep with her. Her refusal brought about his resolve to deprive her of the land that is her husband's."

The *Igwe* nodded in agreement.

The president continued, "On an Eke market day last month, Angelina's aunt, Mrs. Nweze, assaulted her in the full view of traders by tearing her dress to shreds and pouring a bucketful of ashes over her. This attracted a huge crowd that almost lynched her. Angelina's 'crimes' include killing a python, leaving her house three weeks after her husband's death, and going to the market where the *Umuada*, *Alutaradi*, etc. have ostracized her.

"*Igwe*, you can see the collusion between the palace secretary, Ikenga, Mgbeke and Mrs. Hilda, the leader of *Alutaradi*. They are the root cause of Angelina's woes. We have therefore come to seek redress for one of us and ask for sweeping changes in the customs and traditions of our people. We no longer live in the dark ages when people behaved wildly and got away with it. We cannot afford to protect the pythons while at the same time persecute a rare gem like Angelina or her children. It is time for unbridled religious freedom for everyone. We have to expose and expel evil conspirators; we have to cleanse our land of the blood of aborted pregnancies. We have preferred to spill the blood of these unborn children and preserved the blood of snakes and other totems. This is unacceptable to the rational mind.

"*Igwe*, here is our communiqué. There is already a call in certain quarters for secession of Ngali from this confederacy. We are not in support of that as long as we are guaranteed an enlightened and egalitarian society where everyone is free and have the right to life and aspiration. Thanks, and may the Almighty God keep the *Igwe* of Umuocha in health and grant him long life."

There was a standing ovation for the president as he walked to the *Igwe*, bowed and handed him a copy of their communiqué, then walked back to his seat. The *Igwe* scanned through the resolutions of NES, and nodded in agreement. Contrary to the NES executive's expectation, the *Igwe* did not give an immediate response. He held the communiqué for a few minutes looking outside through one of the windows of the *ime-obi* like one in a state of deep thought or a confused state of mind.

The assembly was just as quiet. The palace secretary looked dazed by the series of allegations against him. He was sweating profusely as he wiped his face with a brown handkerchief. The suspense was increasing as the NES executive awaited the *Igwe*'s response. The *Igwe*'s son, who also seemed to be embarrassed by his father's silence, motioned to his father to respond to the issues raised by NES. The *Igwe* simply smiled at his son.

He finally stood up, cleared his voice and said, "I thank you my fellow natives of Umuocha for taking the trouble to come here to communicate your grievances to me. Since my coronation I have ran an open administration. I am always attentive to any constructive advice that would move our community forward and make us the envy of our neighbours.

"Let me reserve my detailed comments for tomorrow. However, before you go back to Ngali village, let it be clear to you that I am not aware of the actions of the cabal led by my secretary and Mazi Ikenga. I, the *Igwe* of Umuocha, did not know that the woman in question is such an icon. She should be revered, rather than vilified. You all know my story: I was away from this community for over thirty-five years and have not fully familiarized myself with the people and events since my return. Much of what you said, especially concerning ostracism, was new to me. I was not informed by my secretary that such a thing was happening to the widow.

"Ostracism is a crime against humanity and it is unacceptable in my kingdom. As I said, I do not want to pre-empt what might happen tomorrow. Let me go and sleep over this meeting and let us wait for a few hours from now." He looked at his secretary and said, "Mr. Secretary please postpone indefinitely any other meeting scheduled for today. I have had enough and I do not think I have the desire to attend the meeting in Owerri. Let the *Otimkpu* and all his assistants announce to all the villages that there is an urgent mass meeting of Umuocha sons and daughters at 10 AM tomorrow morning."

He greeted the executives and left the *ime-obi* for his *Ufo* in annoyance without observing any formalities. The secretary, who could not look the way of NES executives, also abandoned the visitors and left. It was the chief security officer of the Inner Gate, who led the visitors out, handing them over to his colleague at the Outer Gate.

When they got to their cars they were highly elated, embracing and congratulating one another for a job well done. They scheduled an executive meeting that evening at the president's residence where they intended to brief Angelina of the developments and to strategize for the next day's mass meeting.

* * *

The next day was an Orie market day, which was not usually a busy day in Umuocha and people were wondering why the emergency meeting had been called. The *Otimkpu* and his group had alerted the community of a very serious issue in the land without elaborating. The announcement created apprehension in the community, and made everyone who heard him or his men want to attend the meeting. Those who had appointments cancelled them in order to be present at the palace.

The secretary instructed Mazi Agodi Ndukwe, the head of the masquerade cult, to set up the ma*chi*nery for security at the palace during this emergency mass meeting. The secretary also informed Agodi that the meeting would likely lead to some serious sanctions against some people in the community, but did not give him further details. As the traditional chief law enforcer in Umuocha, Agodi Ndukwe mobilized over a hundred and seventy of his masquerades. Each of the masquerades had tender palm fronds, which signified calamity and serious sanctions.

The *Igwe* had ordered that there should not be elaborate royal formalities as such a gathering normally attracted. He instructed that there should be fourteen musket shots, fourteen Dane Gun shots, fourteen drumbeats and fourteen trumpet lamentations. In the mythology and legends of Umuocha, the number fourteen signified great danger. Hence, when the fourteen musket shots were fired, the people wailed, left their farms, streams, homes and schools and headed to the palace. Legend has it that in the olden days, the sun turned dark and night fell whenever fourteen muskets and fourteen Dane gunshots were fired in Umuocha.

The assembling of the people from all the villages and neighbouring communities of Kokwa, Rulla, Kpulu and Sikpo was rapid. They came without really knowing what was happening. The suspense and confusion was heightened as the *ime-obi* was calm with no serious activities going on. The suspense created room for rumour mongering. There were speculations that the *Igwe* had lost his beautiful wife - *Lolo*; others said his first son had died and there were many other rumours milling around.

The palace guards hurriedly erected a podium about five feet high and set up the staircase to it. They installed a public address system and extended the loud speakers to various distances as the crowd continued to throng into the palace. The crowd that came surpassed the crowd that had gathered during the trial of Angelina. Someone feared suffocation and another said there might be a stampede if this call turned out to be to inform his people of the death of the *Lolo*.

Meanwhile the NES executives had concluded their meeting and had briefed Angelina, her son and her sisters in-law – Gladys and Nkolika – of their meeting with the *Igwe*. They also told them the *Igwe*'s reactions and the need for them to accompany the NES executives to this all-important mass rally at the palace. Gladys thanked them and narrated all they had done, such as their midnight cry. She remarked that she had faith that profound change was coming to Umuocha. Responding, Angelina said, "I am on your side. We asked for a sweeping change in Umuocha and the Lord is about to answer us." They all nodded and said, "Amen."

More cars were added to their convoy and they set out for the palace at Akpu village. The tension and suspense in everyone's mind made their convoy of cars heading to the palace almost unnoticed. Everyone's attention was focused on the events that might unfold at the palace. However, on their arrival some people noticed the large presence of the members of the Ngali Enlightened Society and also spotted Angelina in their midst. They feared that Ngali indigenes may have come to announce their secession from the Umuocha community, and the presence of Angelina added to the puzzle.

* * *

There had been gloom and despondency in the house of the palace secretary the night before. After the meeting between the NES executives and the *Igwe*, he attempted to talk to the *Igwe*, but the *Igwe* rebuffed him. He refused his wife's dinner, and cried all night, yet did not disclose to any member of his family the reason for his grief. He knew his days in the palace were over, but his fears were about how and when he may be dismissed. The secretary remembered how Ikenga got him to his camp and how reluctant he was initially to follow Ikenga and also how the *Igwe* had once warned him to be wary of clever men like Ikenga.

Ikenga had won over the secretary with occasional bribes and intimidations. Now the two were likely to be punished, but the nature of the punishment remained a mystery to the secretary. He had not seen the full content of the NES communiqué, nor did he know the *Igwe*'s decisions on each point outlined by NES.

* * *

The *Nze-na-ozo* Umuocha, led by Mazi Ikenga, had gathered in their full regalia. Some thought it would be a normal gathering, while others were edgy because of the suddenness of the call. However, they were taken aback when they noticed the very formal attitude of the palace guards who did not give them the fulsome compliments they were used to. The *Igwe* had ordered the guards to withdraw all traditional protocols and privileges for the *Nze-na-ozo*.

When the palace arena was full to the brim and people continued to try to crowd in, they were ordered to stay outside the outer gate. Some climbed trees in order to catch a glimpse of what was happening inside the palace arena. The situation was very tense. The *Otigba* drummed what sounded like a dirge and the people held their hearts in pain, and the *Otimkpu* sounded his lamentation and the people wailed aloud. The two men, *Otigba* and *Otimkpu*, are believed to be inspired by their ancestors and are gifted with discernment of mysteries. This ability to discern the unknown helps them perform in extraordinary manner. The guards fired fourteen Dane gunshots and tears rolled down the cheeks of the lowly and mighty in Umuocha. Calamity had happened but none can tell what it was. Everyone turned their eyes towards the *Opie Igwe* to see when he would come out.

To the surprise of everyone in the arena, *Igwe* Umuocha and his son appeared dressed in their Barrister's robes, and they headed towards the podium with a page boy carrying what looked like a golden crown worn by queens only and another bearing a well-made foreign academic gown in shiny colours.

The mood of the *Igwe* and the accoutrements of his pageboys added more suspense to an already tense environment. Many of those who gathered hushed their questions as the secretary who was supposed to have introduced the *Igwe* was seated with the *Nze-na-ozo*, with his head bowed as if in deep anguish. Even the NES members who gathered at a corner could not understand the significance of the crown and the academic gown. Only the *Igwe* and his son knew the purpose of these instruments.

It was exactly 10 AM and the tropical sunlight was beginning to gather momentum, rising and illuminating different corners of Umuocha. In the olden days in the Umuocha community, such a bright atmosphere solicited sacrifices to *Chukwu nke elu-na-ala*. It was believed that the sun rose to bless Umuocha while it sets on the enemies of *Ala* Umuocha. Legend had it that on one occasion there was no night in the land of Umuocha for two days. As the sun shone continuously for two days over Umuocha, darkness covered Kokwa, the perennial enemy of Umuocha, for the same period. Unfortunately, today, although the sun was rising as a youth with vigour in the land of Umuocha, it was equally setting in the lives of some mighty men and women in Umuocha. These people would soon become the enemies of Umuocha.

The *Igwe* mounted the podium without having his praises sung by the palace secretary as had happened in the past. All ears were tuned to the *Igwe*, and all eyes transfixed on the podium. The silence compared to that of a dreaded cemetery at St. Luke's Anglican Church, two kilometres away. Everyone was sombre, they wanted to hear first hand what the *Igwe* had to say.

The *Igwe* started off, "My dear people of Umuocha. I greet you this day with pain in my heart." The throng was so quiet that on only the whistling of tree branches could be heard. Umuocha had never seen this crowd since the coronation of the *Igwe*.

He went on, "I have not been so grieved since you crowned me with the permission of our ancestors and God almighty, as I am today. Before I continue, may I ask God to bless the good people of Umuocha and may *Ibini-Ukpabi* and *Amadioha* punish in eternal hell all who pervert justice and show wickedness to any person born in Umuocha." "*Iseee*!" the crowd echoed and then fell silent again. The puzzle had not yet been unveiled.

"As we say it Igboland," the *Igwe* said, looking to his right, "a toad does not run in the noontime without a cause. Something terrible must be after its life. I do not want to take much of your time having assembled you here on such short notice. Of course, I want you to go back to your farms and other occupations and live as good citizens of our great community.

"However, before you leave this ground, I want to inform you that I have discovered that some of our *Nze-na-ozo* members are running a parallel government in Umuocha. They are doing what pleases them rather than what pleases the people of Umuocha, their ancestors and their *Igwe*."

There were shouts of "*Tufiakwa*! *tufiakwa*!" Some people spat on the ground as a sign of rejection of an abomination. The pressure was beginning to mount on the *Nze-na-ozo* as they looked at one another with surprise on their faces. Ikenga knew this reference pointed towards him and that his days had shortened to a few hours. He bent down his head in deep anguish. His hand could hardly hold his staff and it fell from his hand. He picked it up and pretended nothing happened.

The *Igwe* continued, "Our fathers said, 'let the wind blow so as to reveal the anus of the hen.' Today, that wind has blown and has revealed the smelly part of our society and the characters that drive it. Men and women of Umuocha, we shall deal with such characters and cleanse our land of their footprints, we have tolerated them for a long time and shall do it no longer. I have found out that some of my trusted staff are neck deep in bribery and other forms of corruption and today their sun has set." The *Igwe* looked up to the sky, pointed his staff at the sun and screamed, "Oh sun of Umuocha, set in the camp of the enemies in our midst!" "*Iseee*! *Iseee*!" the crowd screamed back.

The *Igwe* continued, "May they never see light, may they walk in penury all their lives and become the scorn of their children. May the tormentors of the widows, the orphans and the strangers be like their victims!" The assembly echoed, "*Iseee*!!" The *Igwe* went on, "After today, we shall recognize achievements and no longer exalt the mediocre and opportunists, we shall love humans and not totems, we shall bind the wounded and not increase their afflictions, we shall embrace only the good part of our customs and discard the others.

"My secretary and our traditional prime minister, Mazi Ikenga, concealed a lot of information from me. They used their privileged positions to misdirect me, and thousands of us in this land. They formed alliances to punish a woman who needed help, an icon who has travelled locally and internationally to hoist the flag of Umuocha and has embossed our name on the map of eternity.

"We hold them accountable today and always. They have tolerated those who shed the innocent blood of the unborn children, but they have punished a widow who killed a snake that posed a threat to her life when it crossed the road to her home. We shall not forgive them."

As it became apparent that the *Igwe* was exonerating Angelina from guilt, some traditionalists in the crowd became agitated. Their anger was rooted in the tendency of the *Igwe* to equate the python with other snakes. However, due to the fear of the *Igwe*'s wrath, no one dared to disagree with his position on any customary issue. Their grumbling at the right hand side of the crowd made the *Igwe* pause in his address. As he looked towards the direction of the grumblings, the crowd became as quiet as a graveyard again. He has the final say on these matters and no one could oppose him.

He continued, "They have misled you, saying that I ordered Angelina to be ostracized. I heard about it only yesterday." There were shouts of *Tufiakwa* in the crowd. The *Igwe* went on, "My secretary censored all petitions sent to my palace by this widow and used an official letterhead paper and the royal seal to issue frivolous instructions that he and Mazi Ikenga concocted, purportedly on my behalf. We shall not forgive them.

"I hereby call on these individuals to come out and stand before us and our ancestors." Everyone wanted to know those individuals and there were minor incidents as the crowd surged forward but they were held back by the palace guards and the masquerades who threatened to use whips to stop them from pushing forward.

The *Igwe* ordered the people to exercise patience and listen as he called out their names:

"Mazi Ikenga." There was an uproar from the crowd as the guards held him and brought him out from his exalted seat of the prime minister of Umuocha to stand under the sun that morning.

"Mr. Palace Secretary," as the *Igwe* usually called him.

"Mazi Titus Ibe from Akpu village."

"Mrs. Nweze."

"Mrs. Mgbeke Okafor." As her name was mentioned there was an uproar among the womenfolk. She came out with her hands on her head shouting, "Rita has killed me! Rita has misled me oo!!" The *Igwe* ignored her.

"Mrs. Hilda." She came out with her hands on her head, crying that Mgbeke and Rita had misled her.

"Mrs. Rita." On seeing her, Mgbeke and Hilda pounced on her, but the timely intervention of the palace guards saved her clothes from being torn to shreds.

The *Igwe* looked around and saw Angelina seated in the midst of her compatriots, clut*chi*ng her bible. He said, "May we have our great daughter come out here." Most people did not know whom he meant and there was silence everywhere.

He motioned towards her and said, "Mrs. Angelina Ibe." There was an uproar of surprise, with some shouting *Tufiakwa*! while the Ngali people in the crowd were ecstatic in their thunderous celebrations. Members of the Widows' Association started singing, clapping and dancing to the envy of those around them. The crowd was divided, but no one dared challenge the absolute monarch who had rolled out curses on any recalcitrant member of the community. As the uproar continued, someone murmured,

"What manner of *Igwe* is this? He is destroying our culture." His murmuring was not heard beyond where he was seated.

The members of NES ushered Angelina out and she stood in their midst beaming with smiles and looking graceful. Ikenga covered his face with his handkerchief pretending to wipe off sweat. The *Igwe* motioned to the people and everyone kept silent waiting for another surprise from His Royal Majesty.

The *Igwe* said, "I, the *Igwe* of Umuocha, representing the fathers of our community, hereby confer on you, Mrs. Angelina Ibe, the *Ojimmuta 1* of Umuocha. He directed the palace secretary to dress Angelina with the academic gown. The secretary stepped forward in shame, not wanting to look Angelina's in the face. He decorated her with the gown and then put on her the academic hood provided by the *Igwe*. She smiled and looked up to heaven as if to say, "Thank you, God." The secretary stepped back, clut*chi*ng his hands behind him.

The *Igwe* called Mazi Ikenga and directed him to come forward and put the crown on the head of Angelina. Ikenga had no choice. He dropped his staff on the ground, took the crown and trembled as he moved close to Angelina and whispered to her, "May *Ibini-Ukpabi*, the great deity of Arochukwu strike you down. I will not bow to you, a woman, or to your god." Angelina smiled and told him, "I have forgiven you." The *Igwe* did not hear this exchange.

Angelina bent her head because she was taller than Ikenga. He put the crown on her head grudgingly as he could not have refused the *Igwe*'s command. This time most of those gathered at the palace went wild with rejoicing, and saying, "Now we know the truth from the *Igwe*." Many who had spoken evil against Angelina for fear of Ikenga and his cohorts turned and wished Angelina well and envied her new status.

Igwe said, "By this crown you are now the new *Ugo* Umuocha." The crowd clapped in honour of the new *Ugo* Umuocha. The *Igwe* ordered all of those he called out, including Mazi Titus and Rita, to bow before her and greet her in the traditional way. While most of them showed remorse and asked Angelina for forgiveness, Rita got close to her and said "*I bu anu ofia*". Angelina smiled and told her, "My dear, I have forgiven you." Again, the *Igwe* did not hear this exchange.

The *Igwe* was not done yet. When they had greeted Angelina as ordered by the *Igwe*, he asked the crowd, "Do you want evil rooted out completely?" They shouted, "We want evil rooted out, away with evil!" Some of the people in the crowd gesticulated signs of rejection.

The *Igwe* asked the crowd to take their seats and remain silent. He called Mazi Ikenga. When he came forward, the *Igwe* said to him, "Face the gate and no longer look at my face." He gave the same instruction to Titus, the palace secretary, Mgbeke, Hilda, Nweze and Rita. They complied as directed. He then said to them in a loud voice, "This day I have rejected you all and so have our ancestors rejected you for deceiving their children. You are to trek to the evil forest at the boundary of our community with Kokwa community. Forty of our most dreaded masquerades will accompany you. There, they will hand you over to the gods of the land and the spirits that dwell in the Evil Forest.

"Ikenga is exiled for ten years, and if he dies within this period, the land of Umuocha will not receive his body. Mr. Palace Secretary is exiled for eight years and if he dies within this period this land will not receive his corpse. Titus is exiled for three years and if he dies within this period, the land of Umuocha will not receive his corpse. The same sentence is passed on Rita and Nweze. If they die within this period, our community will not receive their corpses. Mgbeke is exiled for one year and if she dies within this period, the land of Umuocha will not receive her corpse. The same sentence is passed on Hilda. If she dies within this period, the land of Umuocha will not receive her corpse." After *Igwe*'s pronouncements, forty *Achikwu* and ten *Oku ekwe* masquerades in the arena formed a cordon between the convicts and the people and led them to the boundary of Kokwa and Umuocha where the Evil Forest is located.

Turning to Angelina, the *Igwe* said, "I hereby free you, *Ugo* Umuocha and our *Ojimmuta* 1." There was rejoicing everywhere. The *Igwe* said, "There is a curse hanging on anyone that threatens your life from this day till the time you return to your maker." Angelina said, "Amen."

The *Igwe* turned to the people and said "From this day, abortion among our girls in this community is ba*nne*d and anyone caught committing it will be prosecuted together with their accomplices. The executive committees of *Umuada* and *Alutaradi* organizations are hereby dissolved and elections will be held in a fortnight. No animal is henceforth an object of religious idolatry in Umuocha; but let me warn you that the abuse of any animal will not be tolerated in this community. Abuse is a blatant violation of God's created order, and our ancestors will punish violators. Thank you, may God and our ancestors be with you all." There were shouts of "*Igweee* live for ever".

He called on Angelina to respond. Angelina climbed the podium amid cheers from the thousands that had gathered. She looked round, waved her hands and held out the hood, touched the crown and her gown and tears of joy rolled from her eyes. She was a strong woman but she could not hold back her emotions.

"Thank you, Jesus," she said, her voice cracking. She continued, "Oh my eyes have seen a rebirth of the land of my birth; the land I have lived in and dreamt of her goodness and glory. I thank you, Lord, that this day you have proved that you alone promote and debase, that power and authority belong to you alone."

As the exiled men and women were being led out of the Arena by *Achikwu* and *Oku ekwe* masquerades, she turned to the *Igwe* and said, "My lord, how I wish these ones could be forgiven and granted general amnesty for my sake." The *Igwe* indicated his rejection of her wish and asked her to continue her speech. She said to them in a shaky voice, "I have forgiven you all!" She mentioned each by name as the exiled men and women broke down and wept aloud. They could not look back because of the curses that the *Igwe* heaped on them. It was believed that if anyone looked back, he or she would become blind, be killed by lightening or suffer some terrible mental disorder.

A mild drama occurred when Angelina mentioned Ikenga's name. He stopped his march toward the outer gate of the palace, knelt down, raised his hands, and wailed in anguish: "The face of Umuocha has been smeared and veiled with the linen of the White man's religion, and our glory has departed! We have become hypnotised by the allures of their bet, and the *Igwe* has fallen to the fantasies of the White man. He has betrayed the royal mandate of the warriors who begat him, and broken the mantle of his forebears!"

"Oh, I see these warriors turn and weep in their graves. Their seed has forgotten their path and betrayed their cause. The sharp arrows have become blunt and the shooters are cowered by the lies of colonialists and their religionists. I weep for you, *Igwe*. I weep for you, oh beautiful land of my fathers. Your honour is broken, and your peace arrested. Angelina has won, but our light has dimmed. The face of Umuocha is no more, and her pride is thwarted. They have taken our potency away. They have raped us, and we are rejected. Our gods are assailed and shut down. Our enemies have triumphed, our horns are broken. I weep for you, oh beautiful land of my fathers."

As much as Ikenga tried to make himself heard, his voice was drowned by the elation of the crowd over what they saw as a new dawn in their community. When he noticed that the throng did not hear his voice, he yelled: "May the sun, the stars and the moon be my witnesses against you this day. Your children will hear how you abandoned the ancient landmarks of your ancestors." The masquerades who gathered around him while he spoke, lifted him and ordered him to continue his walk. Ikenga no longer uttered a word.

As the convicts left, some of the seminarians working with Ezekwunna took very long brooms and swept away their footprints as a symbolic mark of cleansing.

Once the convicts had left the palace precincts, Angelina then turned to the crowd and said, "On the last day, my Lord will come back in glory, so shall He reward the faithful ones who have believed in Him; but the evil doers, He shall commit to eternal punishment." She thanked the *Igwe* and the NES members. In conclusion, she said, "my hands have been strengthened, I will not quit the fight and Umuocha will win at last." There was a standing ovation as she stepped out of the podium to the embrace of NES members.

As the *Igwe* descended from the podium with his son to return to the *Ufo*, he said, "I see a new Umuocha where righteousness and truth will reign supreme over fear and deceit. I see a new Umuocha where men and women are treated equally, where life is respected and truth and righteousness reign. God bless Umuocha, go in peace, the sun has set on our enemies."

As Angelina arrived home in the company of Gladys, Nkolika, Obinna and some of her church members, they sang songs of praise and danced and worshipped God for over an hour. The joy was so great that neighbours who had despised her and her children rejoiced with her. Over eighty men, women and children gathered to celebrate with her in her courtyard. Angelina was so elated that she broke down, crying and saying these lines:

My soul magnifies the Lord
Who has lifted The Widow's Cross
He has wiped away my tears
And filled my heart with rejoicing
He took me up from the land of the dead
Oiled me, crowned me and set me above my enemies.

Glossary of Igbo terms and Phrases

Igbo Terms	**Meanings**
Achikwu	Often referred to as "visible spirits." This class of masquerade is the most dreaded
Ada	Daughter
Ada Bekee	Literally, daughter of a White man (used to symbolise a very beautiful girl or woman).
Adannaya	Pet name, meaning, "her father's daughter"
Ada ukwu	Great Daughter (often used for the first daughter in a family
Ada nta	Last daughter (or literally, small daughter). It also implies the younger daughter
Afo	An Igbo market day
Agbala	Name of a deity
Akamu	Corn pap
Akara	Fried bean cake
Ala Umuocha oo!	The land of Umuocha oo!
Alutaradi	Association of women from other communities married to Umuocha men, it is not as powerful as the *Umuada*. They do not have much say in the way their matrimonial community is governed. The interesting thing is that the *alutaradi* in one community belongs to an *umuada* in her natal community.
Amadioha	Name of a deity
Anuofia	Wild or bush animals
Aru	Abomination, evil
Chaplet	Catholic prayer bead
Chi	Personal god
Chukwu nke elu-na-ala	God of heaven and earth, or the Almighty God

Dane gun	The Dane gun is a type of long-barreled musket gun introduced into West Africa by Danish traders. It uses gunpowder, hence, among the Igbo, it is called, *Egbe ntu. Ntu* is powder. It was already in use prior to formal colonization of West Africa in the 19th Century and was used by different communities to fight against European colonization. The gun is still popular in different parts of West Africa.
Dike-na-dimkpa	A warrior and a strong man
Ekwueme	He who does what he says
Eke	An Igbo market day
George wrapper	A special wrapper made from raw silk. It is popular with Igbo women and used for special occasions
Ibini-Ukpabi	Name of a deity
I bu Anu ofia	You are a bush animal (a very spiteful insult in Igbo land).
Igba	African talking drum.
Igwe	The absolute monarch of Umuocha community
Ime-obi	Inner chamber of the palace
Imo state	One of the states in Nigeria. Umuocha is a community in Imo state
Iroko	The tallest and strongest tree in Igbo land. Often personified to signify an important personality
Isi-ada	First daughter
Iseee!	An agreement like the Christian "Amen".
Iyioma	Name of a stream
Iyololo	A traditional dance of joy
Jigida	Beads woven with threads and worn by women
Lolo	Queen. *Igwe*'s wife
Kamalu	Name of a deity
Mazi	Mr.

Mgbadi	A very large wooden drum used occasionally to announce calamities
Mgbadike	Youthful and action-packed class of masquerades
Mkpo n'ala	This is a large musket stuffed with gunpowder and sand. Once it is ignited with naked flame, it produces deafening sound. It is fired during festivities and burial ceremonies.
Mmiri Cult	The dreaded mermaid cult
Mmiri na anwu maaram ebe m na eso Jesu, anwu maaram ebe m na eso Jesu	I was drenched by rain and beaten by the sun in my pilgrimage with Jesus
Morning Cry	A name given to sermons that individual Christians preach in their neighbourhoods early in the morning
Ndi Otimkpu	Heralders and announcers
Ndi uka akwa	Members of the Weeping Church
Nkwo	An Igbo market day
Nna anyi	Our father
Nna anyi, Ezekwunna	Our father Ezekwunna
Nne anyi	Our mother
Nnem, Nnem oo	A sorrowful cry. My mother, my mother oo
Nnem oo! nnam oo!	My mother oo! My father oo!
Nwannaya	His father's true son depicting honour
Nze-na-Ozo	Council of red-capped chiefs; *Igwe*'s assistants
Obataosu	Action man
Obi	*Igwe*'s court
Obu aru	This is an abomination
Ogaa	A female game that involves clapping and dancing on a mapped lawn
Ogwugwu	Name of a deity
Ohia Udonshi	Evil forest

Oja	Local flute
Ojimmuta 1 of Umuocha	The custodian of learning in Umuocha, the highest academic recognition in Umuocha.
Oka	Name of a stream
Okara mmadu, okara mmuo!	Half human, half spirit!
Oku Ekwe	Gentle class of masquerades, but can also be very diabolical
Omu	Tender palm fronds, used to symbolize mishaps
Onu ndi mmuo	The mouthpiece of the spirits
Onugo	An insane woman who walks around the market half-naked
Onye nche eze	Chief security officer
Opie ***Igwe***	*Igwe*'s private door
Orie	An Igbo market day
Osu	A caste of outcasts
Otigba	Palace drummer. He occupies a significant position in religious rituals. It is believed that he communicates with the ancestors through his drumming.
Otimkpu	Announcer or town crier
Otu Umuagbogho	Group of single girls
Tufiakwa	Exclamation of rejection and abhorrence
Tufiakwa, nkea bu *aru*	I reject it, this is abomination
Udara	A tree that produces edible fruit-latex, widely eaten by both children and adults.
Ufo	The *Igwe*'s personal residence in the palace
Ugo ***Umuocha***	The Eagle of Umuocha
Ugwu Umuocha	Pride of Umuocha
Ukpakanyi	Reserved farming area of Umuocha. Families and individuals own portions of land in this area
Ukwu-Orji	Under the Iroko tree

Ukwu-Udara	Under the *Udara* tree
Umuada	Association of Daughters of the community, a very powerful group of married daughters of Umuocha. The *umuada* association exercises some traditional roles in the governance of their natal community
Umuada Ibe	Ibe's daughters
Urashi	A river deity

Some Igbo proverbs used in this book and their relative meaning

1. The forest where thorns pricked the sole of a fowl will never be entered by a human being. [*A weakling cannot succeed where tough people fail*]
2. Whatever the fowl chases under the rain and under the sun must be very important to it. [*We put high priority to issues that are of high importance to us no matter the cost*]
3. The toad does not run in vain at noontime; there must be something pursuing it. [*Something does not just happen, there is always a cause for every phenomenon; or there is no smoke without fire*]
4. The snake that bites the tortoise is injuring its teeth. [*Do not waste your energy on impossible venture*]
5. He, who the train kills must be deaf. [*He, who ignores many warnings has chosen to perish*]
6. The rat should not dare eat up the native doctor's bag; the native doctor should not dare beat up the rat. [*Mutual respect should be maintained between the high and the lowly*]
7. When a vulture absents itself from sacrifice, then there must be a great incident in the land of the spirits. [*It is only a great tragedy that can prevent a person who regularly attends an occasion*]
8. If the dog enters the bush with a bag in anger, then all the faeces in the bush will eaten. [*When someone approaches an issue with a fit of rage, he causes much damage*]
9. It is the animal that climbs trees with its teeth can tell a bitter tree. [*It is only the wearer knows where the shoe pinches*]
10. Any message you send through the smoke has reached heaven [*It is important to identify a proxy and work with him*]
11. The goat that derives its pasture from the base of Breadfruit tree should be wary, because, the breadfruit can fall on it and kill it. [*Whoever threads on a dangerous ground should be wary of dangers lurking in the corner*]
12. He who accompanies a lion eats what the lion eats, and that is meat; but he who accompanies a goat also eats what a goat eats, and that is grass.

[Build relationship with the powerful and you will become powerful; or build relationship with the weak and you will become a weakling]

13. When an old woman falls a second time, let her count what is in her basket. [*Whoever makes mistakes consistently must do a soul*-searching]
14. The Doctor treats a disease, yet a disease kills a doctor. [*Death is inevitable, no matter who you are*]
15. You do not advice a wise person to come out from the sun. [*The situations we find ourselves in life informs the decisions we take*]
16. It is only a foolish son that buys yam seedlings from his father's farm. [*A foolish* child *does not know that his father's possessions belong to him*]
17. The foolish person does not know when an important decision is reached even though he is part of the meeting. [*It is important to be focused and alert when critical issues are discussed, lest a decision is taken on your behalf which you did not approve*]
18. When the head disturbs the wasp, it suffers sting. [*Whoever lives carelessly, he suffers the consequences*]
19. The drum sounds twice for the warrior, either in life, or in death. [*There are two inevitable things that you cannot rule out in everyone's life – life and death*]
20. A foolish man hunts the vulture. [*Do not waste your time on something you cannot use or eat; or do not waste your time on frivolities*]
21. When a lion's leg is broken, antelopes leisure around it. [*When someone is sick or weak, he is unable to take care of his needs, or unable to do the things he used to do*]
22. A visitor should not weary his host so that when he is going, he will not develop hunch back. [*Do not pose a problem when you visit someone, so that you do not leave his house with curses*]
23. When a child is separated in a fight, he hungers for more fights not knowing that fights can lead to his death. [*Someone who was assisted to accomplish a task, does not realise how difficult that task was in the first place*]
24. It is with patience that the earthworm burrows the ground. [*You can accomplish any seemingly difficult with patience*]
25. All heads are equal is only in words. [*We are not all equals, we merely assume*

we are. This is a recognition there are classes in Igbo society]

26. The sparrow said, "Since children learnt how to shoot without missing; he has learnt how to fly without perching". [*Utmost care is required in every situation we face, especially in very trying times*] (Widows advice to Angelina after her attack in the market)
27. You do not know a cripple in a car, until the car discharges its passengers. [*Do not judge someone's ability until he demonstrates it*]
28. He, who excludes himself from entering a car, should not say he was denied a seat in the car. [*Do not alienate yourself from a good project, and do not turn around to accuse others of denying you the enjoyment from that project*)
29. He, whose house is on fire, does not pursue rats [*The time to be serious over an important issue should not be used for frivolities*].
30. A greenhorn should not challenge a deft warrior for the sake of his life. [*An amateur should recognise his limitations or he will make a fatal mistake*]
31. When Truth is guilty, look round, you will find Bribery lurking in the corner. [*There is obvious corruption when a glaring fact is denied*]
32. An old man who does not know how to dig a hole is just a pretender. [*Feigning ignorance is same as falsehood*]
33. A king's wealth and might are expressed in the multitude that follows him. [*Royalty is defined by wealth and loyalty*]
34. He who competes with his father in proverbs should endeavour to pay his father's debt. [*Do not pretend to know what your father knows because you will never achieve what your father achieved. This is not a literal achievement. It was believed that a* child *would never achieve his father 'feat.' That feat is fathering himself. Of course, no one fathers himself*]
35. You do not tell the deaf that war has started. [*Action speaks louder than voice. The deaf does not hear voices, but he sees actions*]
36. It is the relation of the mad man who is ashamed, not the mad man. [*We are the same with our family members and whatever touches them concerns us. This is meant to protect family honour*]
37. It is the home fly that informed the bush fly there is fish in the kitchen. [*It is someone who knows your deepest secret who could betray you*]
38. When it is the time for a dog to die, it does not perceive the odour of faeces.

[*Whoever gets fixated on attractive things and ignores dangers risks his life. It is believed that most local dogs in Nigeria eat human faeces*]

39. The dog told its owner, throw the bone at me and leave the fight with the spirits, for me. [*Believe in my ability to stand alone*]
40. The pride and prestige of the king is in his entourage. [*Followership is an important factor that defines leadership*]
41. He, who respects the king, becomes king one day. [*You will reap what you sow*]
42. The fool did not know when judgment was passed even though he was a part of the panel. [*It is important to be focused and alert when critical issues are discussed, lest a decision is taken on your behalf which you did not approve*]
43. The gods answered a fool's prayer, but he thought a problem was created for him. [*Some people do not realise the solution to a problem they long yearned had come; they continue to live as though they still had the old problem – a sort of déjà vu*].
44. When a man behaves like a rat, pussycat pursues him. [*People who are lower than you in the society can insult when you lose your integrity*]
45. Let the wind blow so as to reveal the anus of the hen. [*Let the inevitable happen so that what is hidden is revealed.*]

ABOUT THE AUTHOR

Ikechukwu Umejesi (Ike) holds a PhD in environmental sociology and currently teaches sociology at the University of Fort Hare, East London campus, South Africa. He has published in international journals and contributed book chapters on various themes including African history, the environment, mining, risk and vulnerability, and gender issues in Africa. Ike is the author of ***From Pilgrim To Pilgrims: A Poetic Interaction*** (2005). *The Widow's Cross* is his début novel.

Printed in the United States
By Bookmasters